"*The Ash Garden* is a haunting work, written with power and eloquence. Intellectually provocative and emotionally moving, it's a fine novel by any standard."

– *The Record* (Kitchener)

"Harrowing . . . mysterious and compelling . . . An elegant, unnerving novel that illuminates the personal consequences of war, transforming characters who might easily have been mere symbols or representative types into keenly observed individuals: people indelibly shaped, in anomalous ways, by their losses and their grief . . ."

– Michiko Kakutani, *New York Times*

"Bock's deft touch isn't limited to weaving cinematic scenes. His characters have complex interior lives, lives that play out in a historically authentic plot-driven story."

– *Winnipeg Free Press*

"With *The Ash Garden*, Bock cements his reputation. Through an ingenious, ambitious selection of narrators, Bock personalizes the bombing of Hiroshima."

– *Georgia Straight*

". . . a remarkably mature first novel."

– *The Gazette* (Montreal)

"Vividly realized . . . Each panel of Bock's triptych is created with exquisite care, and the three portraits that emerge together illustrate an eloquent truth about the aftermath of war."

– *Washington Post Book World*

"Fluent, insightful, transiting smoothly from one scene, one set of characters, one part of the world to another, plainly written in sentences that often demand two readings or more to savour their prose."

– *The Citizen's Weekly*

"Dennis Bock's searching, ambitious first novel . . . quickly hardens into a crystalline meditation on the defining event of the 20th century and its aftermath . . . Inventive [and] consistently challenging."

– LA Times Book Review

"The author's restraint about his characters is only one of *The Ash Garden*'s strengths. Bock is a superb stylist . . ."

– Maclean's

". . . *The Ash Garden* comes close to being indispensable . . . Bock has shined an illuminating searchlight on the terra incognita where the personal and the political intersect."

– Newsday

"*The Ash Garden* is certainly a refreshing and thoughtful work. It's neither mournful nor too overcome with lament. In fact, it carries a number of positive messages, not the least being the discovery of Dennis Bock as a bright, new force on the Canadian literary scene."

– The Edmonton Journal

". . . there's much to admire in *The Ash Garden* . . . Perhaps most compelling is the way that *The Ash Garden* forces us to re-examine our own views on the bombing of Hiroshima."

– Books in Canada

". . . [*The Ash Garden*] is absorbing, beautifully written and full of the aftershocks of sorrow its narrative demands. A debut novel, it surpasses expectations set by *Olympia*, Bock's widely praised collection of linked short stories, published in 1998, and takes its place among this year's most remarkable fiction."

– The London Free Press

ALSO BY DENNIS BOCK

Olympia

The Ash Garden

A NOVEL

Dennis Bock

HARPER **PERENNIAL**

A Phyllis Bruce Book

The Ash Garden
© 2001 by Dennis Bock.
P.S. section © HarperCollins Publishers Ltd 2005.
All rights reserved.

A Phyllis Bruce Book, published by Harper*Perennial*,
an imprint of HarperCollins Publishers Ltd

First published in hardcover by Phyllis Bruce
Books, an imprint of HarperCollins Publishers
Ltd, 2001. First Harper*Perennial*Canada edition:
2002. This Harper*Perennial* edition: 2005.

HarperCollins books may be purchased for
educational, business, or sales promotional use
through our Special Markets Department.

HarperCollins Publishers Ltd
2 Bloor Street East, 20th Floor
Toronto, Ontario, Canada
M4W 1A8

www.harpercollins.ca

National Library of Canada Cataloguing in
Publication

Bock, Dennis
The ash garden / Dennis Bock.

"A Phyllis Bruce Book".
ISBN-13: 978-0-00-648545-2
ISBN-10: 0-00-648545-6

I. Title.

PS8553.042A74 2002   C813'.54   C2002-902410-2
PR9199.3.B559A9 2002

RRD 11 10 9 8 7 6 5

Printed and bound in the United States
Set in Minion

for my mother and father

What is the path? There is no path. On Into the unknown.

GOETHE, *FAUST*

Prologue

The whole passage

One morning toward the end of the summer they burned away my face, my little brother and I were playing on the bank of the river that flowed past the eastern edge of our old neighbourhood, on the grassy floodplain that had been my people's home and misery for centuries. It was there I used to draw mud pictures on Mitsuo's back with a wide-edged cherry switch, which I hid in a nearby hickory bush when it was time to go home. I liked its shape and how it felt in my hand, like a fine pen or paintbrush. I scooped up mud from the bank and shaped it into pictures of all sorts: trees, fishes, animals. The day my parents were killed I'd decided to paint my grandfather's face. I had turned six just a few weeks earlier. Mitsuo, my little brother, was only four years old and three months.

I enjoyed the way the black mud quivered like a fat pudding and glistened in the clear morning sunshine as I held it up to my face. When I fingered the first dab to apply to the cotton of his white shirt, I

3

felt a child's pleasure in making such a mess, which we were always punished for; but I was also excited to be able to create something almost beautiful from this thick smelly puddle. Whenever my brother squirmed I threatened to call off our game and march him home. I knew he liked getting dirty, and enjoyed the tickle of my stick on his back. Sometimes he tried to guess what I was drawing there between his shoulder blades. I knew this because his fidgeting stopped and he was silent, concentrating with all his energy on the image I held in my imagination. It was as if he were looking with my own eyes at the drawing emerging before me. But today he was impatient. At first he was unable to follow in his mind's eye the lines of the cherry switch. Something had made him anxious, I thought. After a few minutes, though, I settled him down and my grandfather's old wrinkled face began to take shape in earnest.

I did not choose to draw my grandfather for any particular reason. Of course I had seen him earlier that morning, as I did every day. His face was fresh in my mind, I suppose. And so, with a dab and a blob here and there and a simple sweeping circle, accurately placed, the old round mouth slowly appeared. Next I added his crooked teeth. I drew the eyes closed and tufts of hair sprouting from the top of his head. At the sides, below the small pits of my brother's underarms, I placed the floppy, exaggerated version of the ears we often teased our grandfather about.

As a whole the portrait bore at best a crude resemblance, perhaps recognizable to those who knew him, perhaps not. But it did look like a face, and that was good enough for me. I continued to bend and scoop mud from the bank and apply it, with increasing delicacy and accuracy, to my brother's back. To capture the shading under the eyes and his light mustache, I employed a thinner paste, which I made by letting less water drain from between my fingers before touching it to the cotton shirt. During this lighter dabbing, Mitsuo began to giggle and shift again. I stopped and told him in a stern voice to hold still.

He knew he had to listen, because I was his older sister. When we were away from our parents I made the rules.

That's when we heard the plane. We both looked up at the same time. It was still very high in the air and a good distance away, trailing a white plume of smoke in its wake. I knew that this was a B-chan and that we should run home, as we had been told often enough. But it was farther off than the other planes that regularly flew high above our city on their way to and from the war. We waited for some time, watching in a sort of excited trance. Water swirled about my ankles. I marvelled as a dark round object, like a bloated body with dark skin, was released from the plane's belly.

Mud slid from the cup of my hand and plopped at my ankle into the river and was carried away by the rushing water. The falling man seemed in no great rush to join us down here, as if enjoying, while he could, a beautiful and rare glimpse of the world below. I saw a second plane then, and a third, both farther away than the first and headed in the opposite direction. I turned back to the falling body and imagined it landing with a thud. I imagined people gathering around, reaching out to feel the foreign skin, the broad nose so unlike the small nose on my own face. I imagined how the circle would part when the authorities arrived to take him away. I hoped that he was a spy and that he would be caught and punished for the bad things I had seen happen since the war began, what it had turned my father into.

I stepped deeper into the river, almost to the knees, and began to rinse the mud from my arms and legs. "Mitsuo," I called, "come into the water. It's time to leave."

It was my responsibility to get my brother home whenever we saw planes that were not ours. But Mitsuo ignored me. His back was turned. That recently painted face glared back at me. I knew what my brother was thinking. Sometimes we played a game when we saw our own planes above us. We imagined that they flew over Hiroshima in order to drop sweets and toys and puzzles, and when they passed beyond the horizon our job was to set to finding them, often believing that if we wished hard enough the falling parcels might drift in our direction. That's what he was doing now, I thought, hoping for this strange dark package to drop somewhere in our neighbourhood.

"Come here now," I ordered. I had just about finished washing the mud off my hands and arms. "That's just a game, you know. There are no toys up there. That's the wrong sort of plane." But he seemed content to ignore me, despite the fact he must do as his older sister said. He licked his lips, still watching the strange object fall. I saw his eyes—then his whole body—turn away from the scene that had interrupted our morning game. The glint of a smooth stone had stolen away his attention. It glistened at his knees in the brilliant morning sun, and suddenly it began to glow and the stone rose up from its mud pocket, which in an instant turned hard-baked and grey, and then I could not breathe and my mouth became a desert and the air jumped alive with objects that never had flown before.

1

Anton Böll especially liked the smell of the place. The lecture hall was finished with dark wood and the sweating bodies of the assembled there that day coaxed a sweetness from the worn oak panelling and bookshelves. Through the window overlooking Amsterdam Avenue the mid-afternoon sun entered the room and warmed the left side of his slight, wilting frame. He lifted his eyes from the small typed script laid before him on the deeply grained surface of the lectern, then glanced up at the ceiling fan thumping slowly above his audience, and as he began to speak Anton Böll observed the many particles swirling in the disturbed air and the light slanting through the tall, church-like windows.

At the back of the hall a late arrival pushed open the door. Anton waited, adjusting his glasses. The woman took the first seat in the last row. A chair leg scraped against the floor.

Silence. Then he began:

"Fifty years ago, my colleagues and I gathered around a radio in Robert Oppenheimer's office, in Los Alamos, New Mexico, waiting for official confirmation of what, for all of us there, had been a life-long dream." The authority carried in his words was heightened by his thick accent.

He straightened his back, paused a moment and conceded, "And as we all know, dreams sometimes become nightmares."

Anton Böll, Professor Emeritus, knew how to capture his audience's attention. After years of public speaking he had found that a slight hint of contrition at the beginning of such an address helped to prepare the point about to be made. He'd been a pillar at the Niels Bohr Memorial Lecture Series, most often held at Columbia and the New School, but also, for a number of years, at NYU, since participating in the Pugwash Conference in Nova Scotia thirty-eight years earlier. He was an old hand, a polished performer. At seventy-seven, he was practically as old as the various lecture halls he brought his message to; and even to those who knew neither him nor his work and reputation, it was easy enough to see, listening to one of his talks, that he was a man with a particular and unforgiving point, which was that the nightmare, terrible as it had been, would always be overshadowed by the majesty of the dream.

"The pivotal event of the twentieth century continues to resonate today," he said, "regardless of race and nationality, age and ideology. We have one and all been touched by this nightmare. Permit me now, however, to comment on the nature and necessity of the dream in relation to its darker brother."

Come August he liked to keep his eye on things down here in New York. In private conversations he said he wanted to ensure that the truth was being told, and considered his participation part of his duty to those who could not defend themselves, or the time they had spent in the world, doing the things which had won them such distinction. These people generally did not have names. Some were dead colleagues, whom he never mentioned directly in any of his talks or lectures or conversations. They were not specific people, really, nor were people the point. The focus, more accurately, was on the ideas these people had represented and fought for in their living years, which he still held dearly and even desperately to his heart. So every August he guaranteed himself a room at the Gramercy Park Hotel and mounted from there his defence against those whose peculiar and highly personalized sense of the world would rewrite the history he had seen, lived through, and helped shape.

He saw the faithful relating of this pivotal event and the circumstances that led to it as his last responsibility to those men, to those ideas, to himself. We must not forget the context of a world at war with itself, he often said. We must remember what we were up against. He almost always kept his tone civil and, he thought, balanced. His was generally meant to be a formal presentation. Let the young ones rant and rave. On those occasions in the sober, well-lit halls of NYU and Columbia and the New School he spoke convincingly to the gatherings of academics, many of them his contemporaries. He wore a suit and tie, correct shoes, even a flower in his lapel. Uniformly reverent, he never failed to mention the victims. Most important on such an occasion, he would say. He would not tolerate the suggestion that those involved had worked in isolation from the ethical concerns surrounding this new science. These were hard decisions, made by studious and good men mindful of their responsibilities to mankind. Yes, in a perfect world it could have been otherwise, only in a perfect world. . . .

When Emiko Amai approached after the conclusion of his address at Columbia that afternoon, he felt, if only for a moment, the wavering of life-long convictions. He did not have to look twice to know who she was. He knew her scar as if it were his own. He knew also that convincing her of anything would be difficult, and that his opportunities were no longer so numerous. At fifty-six, she was old now herself. He saw it in her face. He felt it in the weakening in his heart.

He might choose to listen politely to her criticism, more likely her damnation, which he knew was her right to cast, for it was clear she was not a woman who had come in support of his ideas. He knew her by reputation and by the sign that marked her, that unusual and other-worldly sheen on the left side of her face, which he well knew suggested skin grafting. He knew its shape, imprinted there between her eye and jaw like a map of some rugged, dreadful country. He had seen it many times before, always from afar. But now, from this close vantage point, he saw the wreckage that had once been there, and the skilled touch of the surgeons' hands.

He was no stranger to this sort of ambush, which was not uncommon during these hot and emotional summer days. He'd been sought out often enough to know he had to prepare in advance for whatever words came: *war criminal, butcher, mass murderer.* He had learned to hold his tongue. To offer the silent respect each of his accusers deserved, without, of course, ceding a single point. Sympathy and understanding was one thing; emotional blackmail and sensational tirades was quite another. He would not budge. His testimony did not deny the pain that had been caused. He had no intention of minimizing or forgetting the brutality of that single blinding Monday morning. He was not an animal. Yet cold hard fact must remain just that: cold, hard, scientific.

Now he braced himself to hear this very accusation, and from this woman.

He had seen many such children—adults now—over the course of his New York memorial visits. Many dozens of men and women arrived from Japan every summer, sickly and scarred and often close to death, their numbers diminishing with each consecutive August, to gather in front of the United Nations and make their presence known. But he did not confuse this woman with the other Japanese he had seen earlier that day. She was well dressed, in a style clearly more Western than Oriental. She moved differently, too, more fluid, easier in her body. Hers were not the stiff, deferential limbs and abrupt kinetic statements of the type of victim he had come to know in his many years among these people. She was easily his height, if not an inch taller, and thin. Her hair, cut to the shoulders, showed streaks of grey.

Emiko Amai offered a hand. Anton Böll took it.

The lecture hall was emptying.

"I'm interested in hearing more of what you said up there tonight," she said. Her English was better than his own, wholly unaccented, which pleased him.

"Yes?" Having seen her work, he knew she would be unwilling to listen for very long to his ideas of necessary evil and historical context. But at the same time, wasn't she his perfect audience?

"I'm sure my father would have said the same thing. That such a decision, any decision, is justified in the heat of war. What befalls the aggressor, and so on. He thought like that, too. Of course, his was an older generation. But we've evolved since then, I think."

He waited for the assault to begin—*war criminal, crime against humanity*—as he studied her face. "We must remember," he said, with rote precision, "that for many it's next to impossible to view such a necessity in its proper context."

She nodded. "I understand. Yes, that's why I wanted to talk to you." She pulled a card from a pocket.

He accepted it and reached for his glasses, angling the card to catch the light from the window. Yellow Crane Films. "I see," he said. "You would like to film part of the Bohr Lecture Series?"

"No. I'd like to talk to you about your role in the making of the bomb. I'm preparing a documentary. In the documentary the interviews will be less formal, less rehearsed."

"You might need a Ouija board," he said. "Most of us are dead."

She smiled. "Of course. I know that."

"Nuclear madness, I imagine? Is that the point?"

"No. I don't begin with themes. I begin with time and place and event. Themes reveal themselves later, if at all."

He nodded his head, then removed his glasses and placed them in his breast pocket. "I see. Nothing but the truth."

"That's right," she said.

He took her elbow and led her towards the hallway, like a gentleman scholar proceeding to his next lecture. Their footsteps echoed.

"I've talked to dozens of people," she said, "all somehow involved, in their own way."

"And you come to me." He smiled. "I should be flattered."

He examined the card when he got back to the hotel. He had not stopped thinking about the meeting this Japanese woman had proposed. Now he considered if he wanted to talk to her as badly as that. She'd solicited his point of view; that, in itself, was surprising. But once you give your words to people like this, you don't know what might happen. Your words can be brutalized. Ironically laid over tortured images of burnt babies and vacant eyes. Something short of historical accuracy, although highly sensational. This was nothing like the cold, hard facts he required. Yet she had offered him a point of entry—and time was running out. At least he would have her ear for the time it took to complete what she had in mind. He knew she might manipulate what was said in the hope of somehow offering to the world a portrait of the man she thought he was, but the truth of his words would stay with her.

He studied the Brooklyn address and phone number at the bottom of the card. Though he had lived here for more than thirty years, before moving with his wife to Canada, he did not recognize the street. He picked up the phone and instead placed a call to Port

Elizabeth. Sophie got it in seven rings, which, he imagined, put her somewhere out in the garden, clipping in the light of the flood-lamps at the edge of the stone patio.

She told him that she had rested well that day and the day before, and that her fatigue was not as bad as before he'd left. With the exception of the down-time required for dialysis, to which she subjected herself three days a week, there had been no discomfort.

"I'm fine here by myself," she added.

He told her about his talk. Near the end of their conversation he mentioned the woman who wanted to include him in her documentary.

"Well, that's wonderful."

"Is it?" he said.

"Why wouldn't it be? Who is she?"

"I have her card," he said. "I think I've seen something by her. I think she's quite famous. In a small way."

He dialled the Brooklyn number afterwards, watching the black phone itself, head resting in his left hand, as if expecting something of it, as he waited for a voice to issue from the other end. There was no answer, and though he normally did not take such absences to mean more than they did, he chose to believe this was a sign that he should forget about trying her a second time.

He occupied himself with getting ready for bed. He brushed his teeth and washed his face. Already it was past ten. He'd risen at six, his usual hour of waking. A long day was just now coming to a close, and tomorrow, with more talks and meetings scheduled and only a short break mid-afternoon during which he planned to come back to his room to rest, would be equally draining. He did not begrudge this. After all, it was why he'd come. Once back home he would have as much time as he needed to catch up on sleep. When he was finished he left the light on above the mirror and the door ajar.

Anton sat at the edge of the bed and slid his feet out of the slippers he'd brought with him. He breathed deeply, eyes closed, and tried to clear his head. He tucked himself in and lay motionless. He stared up at the ceiling and listened to the foreign hotel sounds through the walls and the muted traffic and voices of pedestrians down on Lexington. He turned on his side. He put the second pillow over his head. After fifteen minutes he switched the bedside lamp on again and redialled the phone number.

This time she answered.

"Is it too late?" he asked after introducing himself, now sitting upright. "I'm sorry to phone so late. I was just thinking."

"About the interview? You're interested? Good."

"Yes."

"The offer's still there. If you're comfortable with what I've told you."

"I was wondering, though, if I might see something first. To see what I'm getting into, you understand."

2

Eight days later, home now, Anton drove up the Burnt River a mile or so and parked along a dirt side road not far south of where the Port Elizabeth Cemetery sat up on a hill. The town of Port Elizabeth, on the north shore of Lake Ontario, was situated some forty-three kilometres east of Toronto, near the generating station where Anton had worked for many years after leaving New York, and before that Munich and Leipzig, and the small city of his birth, Tübingen, in south-western Germany. Port Elizabeth was isolated enough that it hadn't become another de-facto Toronto bedroom community, stripped of its core and identity and the quiet summer and winter streets over which couples and children strolled without fear. The large, comfortable homes down by the lakeshore, one of which Anton and Sophie had bought in the fall of 1980, mostly were turn-of-the-century, though a few were older. Only a handful of these had been bought up by the executives and corporate lawyers who later claimed for themselves the small-town charms and generous bright backyards and bay-windowed views to the lake. By and large, these were still owned by families who had been here for decades, if not generations, many of them old now, the kids having moved off to build their own lives.

He slipped on his boots, vest and hat and walked brusquely into the bush and down a steep incline, undaunted by the precipitous turns and falls of the trail, dangerous for a man of his years. The air was already warm, at seven in the morning. He felt the sun slip through the leaves over his head and touch the backs of his hands and warm his shoulders as he marched ahead, listening for the water. His hip waders, sagging loosely outwards at the pelvis, made walking awkward. The path was strewn with large stones and fallen branches. No one had made an effort to clear it for some time. He hoped no one would be fishing this section of river.

The sound came up gradually, a small, light texture on the air, like the chiming of distant bells, faint but densely filling the space he walked through. It grew louder as he continued, and soon a brown opening appeared through the trees and suddenly the bush ended. He stepped onto a rock and smelt the rushing water with satisfaction, looking up and down its length. Where he stood the river was twenty feet across and ran upstream for perhaps fifty feet before bending away out of sight; downstream, in half that distance, it jagged westerly into a stand of maples. Cedar and tamarack leaned lazily over the surface, and their inverted images floated where water collected in pools and he knew this was where the big fish would be resting, close to the bottom.

He watched for insects and matched what he saw in the air to a blue-winged olive he carried in his fly box, tied it to his tippet and stepped carefully into the river. The rubber of the hip waders gripped his legs. The water temperature was at season's peak, and he knew the fish would be sluggish and indifferent. He walked slowly through the riffles, where it would be easier to catch the smaller browns, stopping well short of the drop-off that began mid-river. Facing the opposite bank, he began to fish across and down. He pulled line from his reel and began casting as he slowly worked his way south towards the lake, paying special attention to the deep water beneath the cedars. He chose to ignore certain pools because of excessive overhang—there was no hope of placing a fly well without getting tangled. Where it was possible he cast above the pool and let the current float the fly under the branches, though the drag from the central current often bowed his line downstream too quickly and pulled the blue-winged olive across the pool with unnatural speed. He tried correcting the drag by flicking his wrist upstream as he cast, so as to give the fly extra time in the slow-moving water, but this was a trick he had never mastered.

He heard voices carry through a high stand of cattails behind him. Other fishermen, he thought. He did not feel like talking to other fishermen. As he worked the rod above his head, lifting the line from the water and replacing it farther and farther downstream, he saw it wasn't fishermen he'd heard.

He nodded to the children, who seemed only to be meandering along the bank, looking for something to capture their interest, carrying their sneakers in their hands.

As he studied one of them, her name came to him. It was the girl from the tobogganing hill, not far from the house. The one who'd hurt herself last winter.

He didn't wish to seem nosy, though suddenly he felt the urge to introduce himself. Would she remember his helping her? He continued casting, refocussed on the river, not wanting to disturb their summer games as they searched out diversion. He wondered if they hadn't spooked the fish downstream.

The girl, Marlie, approached.

"My leg's better," she said.

He smiled at her. "I'm glad about that."

The two other children, one boy and another girl, roughly the same age, stayed back. They did not recognize him.

"I told my mother that a doctor helped me on the hill. You helped me. She wanted to send you a card or something, but I didn't know where you live."

"That's all right," he said. "I am glad your leg's better."

She smiled then, and the three of them continued upriver.

That had been a simple affair, he thought, remembering the night almost nostalgically, though it was only seven months ago. A child in need, an adult taking control.

Back at the house, he went upstairs to check on Sophie. He'd been gone longer than he'd anticipated. He checked the machine for her. When she asked if he'd caught anything, he shook his head. "Not a good day," she said, breathing deeply, "for either of us."

"Do you need anything from downstairs?"

She told him no, and closed her eyes.

Sophie had been confined to her bed most afternoons since the latest flare-up, five days before. Usually during times like this, she made lists for Anton, in which she prioritized the plants and flowers that needed tending to. She produced small, shaky sketches he could refer to as he dug and clipped, soil-smudged and sweat-soaked, to keep her garden intact for her return to health.

"The boxwood, that salmon boxwood," she'd say, "it's time you engraved the gills. I'm sorry I can't, but you—cut them into the body. Like so." She'd motion with her hand at the side of her head.

"And the yarpon holly. You know that one? Half a century with a gardener and you still don't know your flowers and plants."

The lists she'd compiled for him through the months of May and June had detailed watering schedules, fertilizers, which shears for which tasks. By mid-day, every day, he'd find a new piece of paper waiting for him beside the bed before he was finished with the old list. Often he found it difficult to decipher her handwriting, which had become scratchy and unsure due to the cramping and poor circulation. She generally went over it with him, explaining the tasks, except on the worst days, when she explained nothing and said nothing.

Today she had not made such a list.

"Tomorrow will be better," he said. He took her hand in his and lowered his mouth close to her face. "Tomorrow will be a better day."

He walked down the stairs, hand sliding along the length of the smooth oak bannister, and entered his study. The window here gave onto a view of the garden and, beyond it, the lake. His desk was a cluttered mess of papers and books. The card, Yellow Crane Films, was propped up between the keys of his old manual typewriter. He knew he'd lost an opportunity that would not come again without his intervention. He picked up the phone and dialled the number.

Emiko Amai's voice answered.

"Hello," he said, and reintroduced himself.

"Yes?"

"There is something here," he told her, "that might be of interest to you." His voice was contrite, strained. "I know I should have told you while I was there. It would've saved time."

"What is it?"

"You will find it interesting to know what I have here for you. I have something here for you."

"Yes?"

He paused. "I would be more comfortable talking about this in person. Not over the phone. It's better we meet. Can you come here?"

"What do you have?"

"Films," he said. "Old films."

Emiko

We had very little in the days when the war was still far away, in the remote place I imagined all wars lived when I was a girl. When it finally came to our city in August 1945 it consumed what little we had left, and years later, when there was nothing left at all, I was forced to journey to America to begin my surgeries. Of course, when I was a child it had seemed to me that what we'd had in those early days was sufficient. All but the barest necessities had been taken from us, but we didn't know any better. I often thought of the war as some great famished beast that ate away at the heart of my people. But my family was no different from any other family in the Asaminami district, the area of the city we lived in, and my brother and I never missed what we'd never had. I do not know if our parents and grandfather felt the same way.

In what might seem a rare gift in the legacy of my family's suffering, my mother and father were lucky enough to die at the same instant, which, for me, is a slight but not insignificant consolation. Neither had to endure the other's death, or the death of my little brother, who followed them not long after. I was left with only my grandfather to take care of me, a scarred and disfigured girl of six with only half a face; and my grandfather had only me to take care of him. Ten years later, when Grandfather fell ill with tuberculosis and finally joined the rest of my departed family, I was in the process of getting a version of my face back, at Mount Sinai Hospital, in New York City. Before I left for America he had made me promise I would not, no matter the circumstance, return to him before the surgeons had completed their work and I was again his beautiful granddaughter. I kept that last promise, and as a consequence he died alone. But slowly my face—or at least a version of it—was restored to me, just as he had always said it would be.

As I have said, my brother and I did not feel the sacrifice as my parents or grandfather might have. We knew nothing different from what we were living through then. It had been like that all our lives, it seemed. The drone of high-flying airplanes, the piercing song the sirens played when a fire- or bombing-drill was staged, the general absence of men in civilian dress, blackout paper covering every window, nothing to eat but rice and bean-paste soup and cabbage. These things did not occur to me as anything special. We knew nothing but war. Planes trolled the skies above our heads. Sirens woke us most mornings. The trenches we'd constructed to contain the spread of fire split neighbourhoods into sections. That men must wear uniforms seemed so normal that a young man seen wearing slacks and jacket and fedora looked wildly eccentric to my eyes. Similarly, my father stood out conspicuously. He had not been allowed to join the army. He had been forced to stay home.

The fear I heard in my mother's voice, too, was unexceptional, as were the attempts she made to mask it with reassuring pronouncements and stern, even confident instructions. Outside the home she obeyed my father, as tradition dictated. But inside, where it counted most, I learned, it was the other way around. When action was to be taken, or caution to be exercised, it was my mother who decided which action or cautionary measure. It was she who protected me and my brother, and cared for our grandfather when his breathing became weak or his rheumatism became unbearable, and it was she who tended to my father when he came home disoriented late at night (I didn't know what drunkenness was then), which he did more frequently as the war drew on.

One night I heard my father admit to my mother that he had brought shame to his family and to himself by failing to gain entry to the war. After hearing a loud noise, I'd risen from the mattress I shared with Mitsuo and watched my father cry into my mother's arms, as I stood there at the top of the stairs, hidden in shadow. He insisted that he had been condemned to live out his days branded a coward and a pacifist, a word which was new to me. Pitiful tears streamed down his face. My mother cradled his head and smoothed his cheeks as he pinched the bridge of his nose with his fingers, as if trying to stanch the flow of tears. I wondered if I would be capable of this same tenderness my mother showed. I had never seen my father in this state. But I saw from how she held him in her arms that it was not unknown to her, and that this was something the grown-up world had suddenly, just then, thrust upon me.

My mother listened patiently. She let my father finish talking-crying, then got him in a chair and washed his face with a kitchen cloth. He was mumbling, looking down at his hands. I was afraid for him, and of him. He said the word *children* under his breath, and my little brother's name, but as far as I could tell he did not speak of me.

My father did not go to work the following morning. He stayed in his bed while we assembled downstairs and ate our gruel and rice-bran dumplings. After breakfast, my mother sent Grandfather to the bank, despite his sore legs, to tell the people there that Father was ill. I accompanied him through the streets to deliver our message.

Though we had all been affected by the war, and the network of trenches and water-filled ditches constructed in the event of an enemy firestorm now marked the city into grids, none of the buildings we passed had been destroyed. As we walked, my grand-father told me that even the enemy respected the beauty of some of our most ancient cities. Not even barbarians would consider destroying our lovely town. Trying to put me at ease, he told me that people of Japanese ancestry were living among the enemy, in distant America, where they had worked to convince their govern-ment to spare us. Naturally this knowledge did calm my anxiety,

but I was agitated for another reason. What I had seen the previous
night was with me still. I wondered if my grandfather knew about
my father, and the real reason he was unable to represent us in the
world that day.

The streets were already busy that morning. I watched the
Miyajima streetcar make its slow crawl up from the harbour,
where it always began its run, carrying the older men to their
places of work, or housewives to their shopping. Work gangs from
outlying communities assembled on street corners, waiting for
their morning assignment. There was always more to be done in
preparing our city for what might come, and not a morning went
by when these work gangs did not collect on street corners in every
district, focussing their attention on the tasks ahead. That day
there were many soldiers in the streets and on the tram, and their
presence further eased my nervousness. We knew they were our
protectors, and I secretly understood my father's shame at not
being permitted to be one of them on account of his leg, the consequence of a childhood affliction. It would have been a great honour for us. The fathers of many of the children in our
neighbourhood were away at the war, and at school these children
were awarded a special status that I envied. The teachers told us
that we were all able to contribute equally, whether at home or
away at the war, but the daughters of soldiers were emboldened by
the absence of their fathers.

On our route to my father's place of employment to deliver our
deceitful message, an odd sensation crept over me. He might
indeed be ill, I considered, but he suffered from a different sort of
illness from the one we meant to suggest. I was not supposed to
know this, of course. My mother was not aware I had heard what
had passed between them the night before. But telling a lie—and
to the bank! This seemed dangerous and exciting, and opened up
for me a new world of unknown possibilities.

We turned left, then right onto the business street, where my father's bank was located. Many of these buildings had been here longer than my grandfather, which seemed an impossibly long time to me. Sometimes I liked to walk along this street—and others, in different neighbourhoods—and imagine Grandfather here, as he might have appeared at my young age of six. He had spent the whole of his youth in Hiroshima and, in my mind, it was not difficult for me to create a picture of him as a boy. I used my little brother's small frame as a stand-in when I thought back to what it must have been like, in another century. My imagination simply drew his clear, youthful face and body over my grandfather's old, wrinkled one. I painted his portrait in my head, and a streetscape of what Hiroshima had looked like back then, without soldiers carrying rifles on every corner and blackout paper pasted over every pane of glass. I painted men who wore their dark robes like lords, and wealthy landowners and women costumed in traditional flame-coloured kimonos, which had been replaced during the war years by the durable *monpe* pantaloons all women had taken to wearing.

When we entered the bank, my grandfather asked for Mr. Hatano, the manager. We waited silently at one end of a large room for him to meet with us. Finally his office door opened and he emerged. He crossed the hardwood floor, a stack of papers clutched under his right arm, and bowed respectfully to my grandfather. His shoes creaked. He smelled of soap and hair grease.

"I have been sent by my daughter," my grandfather began, after returning an equally deep bow, "Mrs. Yokuo Amai, to tell you that my son-in-law, Haruki Amai, a diligent employee of this institution, is ill today and is unable to honour his responsibilities. I am to tell you that he will be well tomorrow and that he is deeply regretful he cannot take his post today."

This was my grandfather's particular way of speaking, but it was a manner appreciated by those of his generation, a part of which the man he was addressing seemed to be.

We walked home hand in hand, slowly because of Grandfather's bad legs. I did not ask if he knew he'd been entrusted with
a lie. It occurred to me that I might be the only one, besides my
mother, to know the true cause of my father's malaise. My child's
mind wrestled with this, and finally I decided that my mother
must have good reason to do what she had done, though I still had
no idea what that could be. Her decision was based on an adult
interpretation of the world that was beyond my experience.

She was sitting by my father's bed, talking quietly, when we
returned. I heard her voice through the wall and waited patiently
for her to come downstairs before I asked her permission to take
Mitsuo to the river, a five-minute walk from the house, where we
liked to play under the Bantai Bridge.

2

For months, after waking up in the Red Cross Hospital, I was
forced to lie on my stomach in order to let the wounds on my back
breathe and heal. My left eye had sealed over with scar tissue and
pus since I was shipped here from the Oshiba Aid Station, where
we had been taken after being found near the river by a group of
soldiers. Mitsuo's cot sat to the left of mine. When the doctors con-
ferred over him I was able to see only their legs and shoes, because
I could not lift my head. But my ears were among the few things
that had not been damaged. I listened to their voices, and soon
began to hate how they spoke when they discussed my brother.
They said he was a lost case and soon would die. They wondered
aloud what kept him alive. Every morning they seemed surprised
that he had survived the night. There was no hope for him, they
said.

Nor did I like how they discussed my own condition, gathering around my bed like old men talking politics at a newsstand, bending my arms, poking at my burns. We seemed to them interesting experiments, as you might find the extended and exceptional life of a gnat or beetle interesting. They would stop briefly between our beds, add or subtract some observations from each of our charts and move on again to the next bandaged patient.

The ward was thirty-eight footsteps in length. I knew this because I had counted the paces of a nurse as she moved from end to end, tending to her helpless patients. It was a narrow room, wide enough only to accommodate the length of a cot on either side, with a space running up the centre along which new patients could be rolled in or the dead removed on a squeaking gurney. The walls of unpainted plaster, a dull white-grey, had been fashioned roughly. In certain sections I was able to make out the horsehair and straw mixed into the plaster, material that rose to the surface of the wall at the head of my bed like roots pushing up through a sidewalk. Four lamps hung from the wooden ceiling on long black wires. Sometimes the lamps moved slightly when a breeze entered the ward through the windows, which were opened most mornings in order to release the fetid night stink that grew under our bedsheets while we slept. There was one picture in the centre of the ward, on the far wall, preserved under a sheet of glass which one of the nurses dusted each morning. This was a portrait of Emperor Hirohito, at whom I could not look directly. This was not due to my awkward position in the bed but because he was more god than man to us then and such unabashed glaring would have shown grave disrespect.

Many nights I could not sleep for the pain that occupied my body like a razing army, and for the news my grandfather had brought soon after he found us here, almost three weeks after the bomb. He told me that our parents had been killed. He told me he had found Mother lying in the street, and Father still in bed. There can be no mistake, he said. You must be strong. After he left that day I tried to destroy the image of their deaths that I held in my head. I did all I could to forget the feeling that came over me the instant the mud around us had turned to stone. But I could not dispel the burning heat in my lungs, and the pain I felt on my skin as it split when the flash of light burned across our path and seared our grandfather's resemblance into Mitsuo's flesh.

It was after Grandfather found us that I started telling Mitsuo stories, which helped me pass those dark nights while everyone else was asleep. They forced the image of my dead parents from my imagination, if only temporarily, and the presence of the groaning mummies that lined the walls on either side of us. After the lights went down I would turn my head left to face Mitsuo and begin one of the tales I knew from our grandfather, who often had told us bedtime stories. At first I was not sure Mitsuo could hear me. He had not awakened since being brought here from the aid station, a few days after I had arrived. Every day the Japanese doctors saw us. Sometimes American doctors came, occasionally accompanied by men with cameras, who took pictures of us lying in our beds like drugged beasts.

When these people appeared, a wave of apprehension rolled from one end of the ward to the other. I knew only what we had been taught in school. That they were the people we had built the fire pits to protect the city against. That they were a soulless, mad and destructive race always to be feared and never to be trusted. Now they came to our bedsides with notepads and cameras, even sketchbooks, to record what they had done to us. When they touched my burns I was unable to maintain my silence, despite myself.

One morning an American leaned over my back and began to inspect my burns. I was an object of fascination. He spoke to the man beside him, another American. I could not understand their language. The first man touched my shoulder. I turned my head away. He lifted the light gauze that covered my wounds. That simple lifting motion sent violent spasms of pain racing through my body. I bit my lip until it bled—first because of the pain, then in anger—yet his hands continued. He spoke to his colleague with great calm. He did not stop what he was doing to me. Another man approached and began to make photographs.

Every night I promised myself not to cry again in their presence. Silence, apart from those shared stories, became my only escape. If I was hidden within it, they could not know me. Already I knew I would never acknowledge the pain I endured. I would feel it. Yes. It would forever hold me in its grip. But I would never submit willingly to these men. They were the people who had done this to me and my brother, the men who had killed my parents. Revealing my pain to them increased my humiliation, serving to tell them I had been defeated, just as they'd hoped I would be.

If the regular doctors ever told my grandfather of Mitsuo's prognosis he did not let on to me during his morning and afternoon visits. He would sit on my brother's bed, facing me, and we would speak, holding hands, until the nurses came and told him it was time for my morphine. Often he was allowed to stay for hours. He said Mitsuo was in a deep sleep, but surely would awake one day soon to join our bedside conversations. Although my brother was never able to open his eyes or speak, my grandfather told me that he understood what we were saying to him, and depended on us, and on me especially, because I was with him twenty-four hours a day and it might be lonely there inside his head.

One day I told him that I thought Mitsuo was getting better. "Grandfather," I said. "I know my little brother is healing."

He said he thought so, too.

"But it's true," I insisted. "I felt it in his hand. His hand moves for me. He understands things when I touch him."

"Yes," he said. "I know he does."

My grandfather took Mitsuo's right hand in his. He waited and closed his eyes, as if concentrating. "Ah, yes," he said. "I feel it now. He is telling us he loves us. We should both be strong."

I knew he did not believe me. But I knew it was true.

At the end of each visit Grandfather would lean over Mitsuo and gently kiss an unburned portion of his face goodbye. As he struggled to his feet I would ask him how his knees were without me at home to massage them like I used to. He would shake his head and say I should not be such a silly girl, I should worry instead about myself and Mitsuo. He would then bend down and kiss me, too.

After dark, when the ward was quiet, I could concentrate on my brother's sleeping fingers. We communicated by touch. That's why I held his hand between our beds. I sometimes felt him stir when I played with his fingers. No one ever knew that we stayed awake at night. Me in my way, Mitsuo in his. Because it was against the rules, I told no one but our grandfather. When the lights went out it was time to sleep, even if you weren't able to. We were not allowed to talk, and to my knowledge no one else did, though I was sure that many people in the ward were in the same sleepless condition. But it was always silent at night in that hospital, excepting the troubled moans that escaped someone's lips every so often. I never told any of the doctors or nurses that I whispered stories at night because I feared they would separate us if they knew I kept the both of us up. That was also why I never told them when his hand began to squeeze back.

The hand was one of the small areas on Mitsuo that had remained intact. It was warm, as a hand should be, and without the memory of that day burned into it, as had happened over the rest of his body. I spoke to him through that hand—his right, my left—and somehow I knew he listened through it. I could feel him listening. Sometimes, as I retold our grandfather's bedtime stories, his thumb pressed against mine. This simple act was for me as miraculous as if he'd opened his eyes and winked across the space between us. The joy it gave me was immeasurable. It was his sign, this small movement of his thumb, that he was here still and I was not alone. I believed he could answer me in this same way when I asked if I should tell him such-and-such story—for instance, did he like that one about the Mouse and the Rabbit? A faint pressure was all I needed to understand. A yes or a no. The hand had become his voice, as the stories had become our conversation. It was unburned and perfect, and I caressed it so he would not forget I was there in the sleepless hours before the sun came to the window.

In our ward the beds faced south, but because of the position I was forced to take I could not look across my bed and out the opposite window, only to my right or left. By turning my chin into my collarbone I was able to see one of the windows farther down on the opposite wall. In any case, our beds were very low to the wooden planks that constituted the floor, and the windows were placed very high on the wall facing us. As a result I could see only the sky, and not the broken ground that I knew moved off in every direction. Sometimes I waited for hours with my chin pushing into my collarbone, watching for a bird to fly past or a cloud to drift by. No airplanes passed through that small framed area. But when something moved across the sky I watched it eagerly. Clouds were frequent, and darkened as the autumn wore on, and in their plumes my mind found shapes and possibilities that delivered me far from thoughts of my dead mother and father, my crippled body and the stink and moaning of the place we were trapped in.

When there was nothing to be seen outside my window, I observed the simple and beautiful qualities of the light shining there. I studied its texture and brilliance—my head turned awkwardly, often painfully—with an intensity that surprised me. What I saw outside that window was mostly the light-blue sky of early fall. During those long days spent watching, I thought about our terrible circumstances and prayed we would all be well again. When the doctors or nurses attended to us I feigned greater interest in this view, or pretended that I was asleep, as I did not like looking at them.

I had seen many proud photographs of Grandfather, as a young man, at Tokyo Imperial University. In some of these he wore a lab coat not unlike the ones they wore at the hospital where my brother and I stayed. He had always told us of how he had devoted his life to saving people, though we did not know what he was saving them from when he told us his stories. What he told us was as unreal as the fairy tales he delivered after our mother tucked us into bed. What I saw around me was not like any of the stories we were familiar with. No healed bodies ever left this place. The dead were wheeled away at all hours of the day on that endlessly squeaking gurney. There was no use in trying to obscure their presence from the many children whose home this place had become. Death was now more common than life, and soon those lifeless forms wheeled along the single corridor splitting the ward in half did not matter to me either way. At least they were dead, I thought. My own unceasing pain erased any concern for those people. I did not care. There are things you get used to. There are things you learn not to see. I came to a point where I would not have cared if they all had died, and might not even have noticed them if somehow I'd been given the promise that my brother and I would leave this place together and alive. I am not proud of this. I would not know the truth of such a terrible confession had I not lived through that time. But early in my childhood I was forced to understand that there is no terror or pain greater than your own.

I soon learned to stop expecting the recoveries so reverently told in Grandfather's doctoring stories. But I did not give up hope entirely. There was still the possibility represented by my brother's tender thumb, and of our grandfather's fairy tales, though I did not relate these to Mitsuo for the same reason my grandfather told them to us. I was not interested in the wisdom they were meant to impart. On some level, I may have been aware of their good intentions, but I whispered those tales in my brother's ear because they helped us leave behind the world we were living in. It was only that.

Most often I became a beautiful shining light in the sky. I was the Moon Princess. I would begin my story at the point where the humble old farmer named Kazuo was hard at work, cutting bamboo in his grove. On that particular day he looked up and noticed a certain shoot from which glowed a bright light. It was like nothing he had ever seen before. When he cut the shoot with his sharp knife he was astonished to find a baby girl inside, a child of such beauty that tears sprang to his eyes. He took the girl home and showed his old wife what he had found, and the ancient, childless couple decided to keep the baby and name her Princess Moonlight because her face shone as brightly as the real moon in the night sky.

On subsequent trips to the bamboo grove the farmer discovered that his farm had become enchanted, for from every shoot he cut issued forth a wealth of pearls and gold coins. Soon the old couple was very rich. But in their humility they understood this new wealth must be spent on the Moon Princess. They brought to her the best teachers of ancient Japan. She learned to write beautiful haiku, to paint upon silk and to play all musical instruments. She learned every language of the world. Whatever the teachers presented her with, she mastered it with grace and speed. All the while she was as loving and committed a daughter as any parents could ever dream of.

As she grew into a young woman her beauty only increased. The dazzling light that emanated from her round face never dimmed, but on nights of a full moon she sat in her old father's bamboo garden and sighed as if homesick. Young men began to call at her door, each one rich and handsome, but she refused them all. Finally even the Emperor of Japan heard of the Moon

Princess's extreme beauty and sent for her. But she refused to leave her mother and father, so the Emperor himself travelled to the bamboo garden to meet the young woman, angry that she had not heeded his demand. Yet once he saw her loveliness all his anger dissipated and he fell instantly in love and asked her to be his Queen.

"I cannot marry," she said, "not even you, Emperor, because I am not long for this world. Soon my true father will send for me and I will be gone!"

Naturally, the Emperor did not believe what the girl said, and when called away on affairs of state he had his soldiers surround the bamboo garden so no one might steal her away while he was gone. Nonetheless, not even five hundred of his Elite Guard could prevent what soon happened. On the night of the next full moon she wrote the Emperor a letter on a silk scarf: "My dear Emperor, I leave tonight. My true father has let me know that I will be quitting this place. I shall not see you again. Farewell."

Immediately the Emperor set out to stop her, but he did not arrive at the bamboo garden until late the following morning, for it was many leagues away. And even before he received the Princess's letter, a cloud that had obscured the moon settled in her bamboo garden and revealed itself to be a chariot of light driven by a man with luminous skin and dressed in shining robes.

"I have come," he said, "for the Princess Moonlight."

"You cannot take our beloved daughter away from us," her old father cried. "Please leave her. She is all we have. She is my heart and soul!"

When the old woman and man began to weep the Moon Princess cradled them each in her gentle arms, to comfort those who had been so kind all her life.

"It is not because I do not love you that I leave. I must return to my real father and assume my responsibilities as the Empress of the Moon. For many years he has protected you during the dark hours of the night, and when I leave I will always protect you just as he has done."

She kissed the old couple goodbye and climbed aboard the shining chariot, where she produced a jade bottle from the sleeve of her kimono and handed it to the old man, asking him to give this bottle to the Emperor, and to tell him he must drink of the potion so he might cease to grieve for her. Once she passed the bottle to him the chariot began to rise into the sky, growing brighter and brighter until a blinding flash erupted from the night and she was gone.

In the morning, the Emperor was heartbroken to find he had missed his beloved Moon Princess. When the old man offered him the message and the potion, the Emperor said, "I would rather grieve forever than forget the truest love of my life," and every night afterward, the heartsick Emperor would stare up into the sky at the full, round moon and see the beautiful face staring down at him through the darkness, present yet unattainable, guarding him and all in the bamboo garden just as she said she would.

3

I was usually able to sleep the few minutes between dawn and the nurse's first morning visit, and often was awakened by the sound of feet padding up the same aisle down which that laden gurney was pushed. Those of us who could take food were brought weak tea and a small portion of rice. I knew the nurse by her smell, which I remembered from life before—the smell of healthy skin, not charred like mine was now—and which never failed to remind me of what I had lost. She seemed somehow to have escaped what had befallen us. To occupy myself I sometimes imagined her at her home, unscathed, pitying us; but also grateful that this had not touched her family, happy that she had not had to make this particular sacrifice for her country. I grew to resent her, as I grew to resent all those who had not been touched by the same fire. She was clean and efficient, as fresh as lilacs growing in a pot of moist soil, and I resented her for the life that had not been taken away from her.

She was one of many who came and went. Their stern faces made me dream of healthy skin and naked peaches and warm rice while they swabbed my open wounds. They told me to hold still, to be strong. My mother had often demanded the same of me. I had understood this to mean, *Be silent, put your thoughts elsewhere until this goes away. There will be better times. One day the pain will be gone.* I tried to remember the pleasures we had enjoyed, but always those memories included my mother, and this made me sadder still.

Dreams floated through my mind like the clouds I watched drift past in the distance outside that window. I wondered where those dreams came from. When they were bad I knew the answer to that question well enough. They had come from here, from all around me. Yet dreams in which I could fly, or was unable to feel pain, in which only pleasant thoughts and sensations visited me— these dreams, strangely enough, unsettled me just as much as the others. I was anxious to discover their origins, so as to tap into some hidden well from which I might draw strength. And though I searched whatever memories were available to me—stories I'd heard from teachers at school, and popular stories and fables—I was unable to find their source and feared they might come only at their convenience and not when I needed them most.

The nurse would feed me and change the IV that dripped into Mitsuo's arm and take away the bedpans that we filled during the night. I watched the sores spread like mushrooms over my body, so quickly did they grow. I could hear the doctors' puzzlement. This type of burn was vastly different from the incendiary burns our doctors had been treating throughout the war. The left side of my face ballooned prodigiously. The Americans harvested live samples of the burgeoning secret life that populated our bodies like pink toadstools, then rushed them back, I imagined, to their laboratories for further study. One day one of them removed a small flap of skin from my shoulder and placed it in a glass dish. I did not feel its removal but watched with intense fear as the shining tongs pulled back the skin, peeling it away like a translucent layer of onion, tinged with a barely noticeable cloud of pink and yellow. It was dead, already no longer part of my body.

That these people were not in possession of the cure for what they had done to us never occurred to me. I had been taught that the slap should always be followed by the caress, the question always by the answer. But I soon learned that these men were as mystified by the sores on my body as our own doctors were. They hovered over us with the same sense of confusion and hesitancy, the same helpless embarrassment and pity and creeping disgust.

I woke up one morning and found Mitsuo's bed empty.

"Your brother died in the night," the lilac-smelling nurse told me. "I am sorry. Many people have died. You must remain strong."

I closed my eyes and attempted not to cry.

"Take your tea. You must keep your strength."

I did not know when or how he died. I had whispered to him all that previous night, because the pain had been too fierce for sleep, and I had not been able to push from my imagination the picture of my mother lying dead in the street, her beautiful legs twisted and burned. I decided my voice could soothe him. This was the only good I could bring into the world. Comforting my brother. His hand had sometimes failed to respond to my voice, but that was not unusual. Maybe I had fallen asleep for brief periods, I thought, and dropped my hand away from his. I did not remember his hand growing cold. I did not remember anything like this. This could not be true, I decided. He had simply been transferred to a new hospital. That happened often enough.

Of course I knew the nurse would not have made such a mistake. There could be no error. My brother had died and I was alone here now. Behind my closed eyes the river's current rose at my knees. That day returned to me, the image of that dark object emerging from the belly of the distant aircraft, as if some flying bird-monster was giving birth to its dumb offspring, a wingless fledgling bird that would fall stupidly to the ground below and explode its body over the land.

I had never required the existence of a guilty party to understand the deaths my parents suffered that terrible day, never considered their passing as anything more than pointless and random. I sought no villain, needed no culprit. This was our lot, as it had been the lot of my ancestors. We had been taught to accept death as an inevitable consequence of life, and of the war our Emperor had declared just and right. Like so many lives of that time, ours had been shaped by a faceless violence; I understood that, and did not feel, beyond a slow-burning hatred for the American doctors and photographers who tormented us, any desire to cast blame.

Even by that age I believed I comprehended the true meaning of war. Imagine! Experience had taught us to expect hardship and pain. I mourned the loss of my parents, yes. But their deaths fell within a knowledge that had been drummed into my bones from birth. My grandfather, and the history of my people, helped me understand their fates.

My brother's death was different, though, because he had had no life to speak of. Like me, he had survived the day of the bomb, yet it was the bomb, or its lingering effects, that killed him; it was the secret poison that had claimed his life. But why had it not claimed mine? This was the question I was forced to contend with. This was why, from that day on, I dreamed his death over and over again. My child's imagination gave the sickness that had invaded his body a human form, because in no other way could I understand what had taken his life. The poison was too mysterious to me, this new sickness that grew lumps on his body, and thinned his blood to water. I gave it a masked face and dark gloves and heavy boots as it approached that night it came for him. My memories insisted I was awake for his death and watched his agony breathlessly. In my imagination I witnessed a thousand times the terrible violence it brought down upon his wasted body. A thousand times I heard his small lungs struggling to call out through his last breaths. "Sister," he cried, "why don't you help me?"

But I did not help him. Frozen by fear, I could not help him. I believed its grip would catch me, too. I feared the unknown poison in his veins might choke from my body what little life remained inside me.

"Please," he said. I heard his heavy breaths. The sheet that had covered him fell to the floor.

Then he began to whimper, and his cries trailed off, and I was alone. Those boots I had created in my mind moved down the centre of the floor toward the exit—hollow, wooden steps that sounded in my head for years after. I did not reach across the aisle to check for Mitsuo's hand as I usually did. Instead I lay still and listened in the dark.

A Bowl of Light, 1945–46

The road in from Santa Fe was thirty-six miles of sharp dry scrub and packed stone, and the shimmering heat moved the reds and browns and yellows on the landscape like water vapours rising from a steaming pan. The blue snow-capped mountains, far off to the north, glistened and danced through the windshield. Anton watched the back of the white helmet of the military man as he negotiated the jeep over the dirt road with stomach-turning indifference. In the distance a small rock became an abandoned building. One room, half a roof, red clay shingles. This was deep in the heart of New Mexico.

Anton leaned forward and spoke to the driver, who then stopped in the middle of the road. There had been no cars since Santa Fe, more than an hour now. Anton pushed open his door and walked over the broken stone and relieved himself against the side of the building. A lizard as small as his baby finger sat horizontal in a groove of the worn stone wall; enlivened by the curious scent of urine, it licked its tongue at the air.

He put himself back into his trousers and walked back to the car.

Driving on, they soon passed through a double line of barbed wire. It was very hot. He stepped from the car, sweating and dry-mouthed and dust-covered. The door of the building before them opened and a tall man appeared. The T-shirt he wore swirled up in a gust as he walked across the dirt compound to offer his hand. This was the welcoming party. The man's face and arms were peeling with sun. Anton Böll knew him from his photographs. He was a thin man, tired-looking.

The driver unloaded Anton's three bags from the trunk and set them on the ground. Then he pulled the car out the way they'd come, through barbed wire and miles of desert.

Oppenheimer escorted Böll to his new home. A one-room wood-panelled box-trailer propped up on two half-inflated tires and eight upended cinder blocks. It was one of fifteen identical trailers provided for the team of scientists who'd joined the project in its later stages. Housing was scarce, at the beginning of the project and also near the end, when the number of participants was at its greatest.

Oppenheimer tapped out a cigarette and rolled it in his fingers, then offered one to Anton. "Tell me about U-235," he said, then lit each cigarette with a wooden match.

"They've given up on it. They think the answer will be found in Norsk."

"The plant there?"

"Yes, heavy water."

Oppenheimer coughed into his hand.

"Uranium hexafluoride," Anton continued. "That was where they stopped. They couldn't get around it."

"And you think you can?"

"I know it," Anton said.

"You consider it an honour to be here?"

"I am not interested in honours. We will win the war from here, Professor. That is the only concern for me. It needs to be won."

Oppenheimer nodded. "Wait," he said. "I'll show you inside later." He carried Anton's bags into the trailer and came out again with a cowboy hat and a glass of water. He handed him the water, then the white hat.

"It doesn't look like much, your new home. But it has running water."

"You treat your scientists well," Anton said.

"Put this on. You're with the good guys now. Now tell me about Dahlem."

• • •

He rode to the lab every morning on the bicycle they'd provided. It was eight minutes of potholes and gravel. At a fork in the road was a billboard that always managed to slow him down. Sometimes he'd stop, crunching his foot on the packed stone, and admire it. It showed an American soldier lying on the broken ground, bleeding from the stomach. A pitched battle continued around him. Anton saw it every morning. Standing there, he'd stare up at it, as if it were a great monument, though the drawing itself was more cartoonlike. Underneath the illustration, a caption: *Whose son will die in the last minute of the war?*

He mouthed the words.

Minutes count!

He'd stand on the pedals again and continue on to work. You couldn't argue the truth of the matter.

Early one morning, the sweet coconut taste of the flavoured oil he'd massaged into his skin invaded his mouth and crept up the length of his tongue as he watched the sky through the bunker's observation window. The dark mountain shapes on the horizon went unseen as he lay flat on his back, feet facing zero by order of the Health Physics Department. This protective position was imperative, they said, but no one paid attention. Why bother down here in the bunker? So, like the rest of them, he got up before the countdown was finished. He leaned forward against a concrete wall, rubbing more of the oil onto the backs of his hands and on the front of his neck. The pair of welder's goggles hung loosely against his chest, rode the anxious beat of his heart. He dragged his sleeve over his mouth and smeared another dab onto his left cheek. Such an odd day for suntan lotion, he thought.

Nineteen men waited for the clock to tick down to zero. When the flash spread suddenly, beautifully, over the desert floor, turning the dark basin of sand and rock into a bowl of yellow light, the cloud began to shape in the distance, and the perfect silence, yet unbroken in the bunker, hung in the air.

"Fucking marvellous," said the man beside him. Somewhere down the line there was a nervous laugh. But still no sound of the explosion.

Then the understanding. A man to his right said quietly, "I guess we're all sons of bitches now." Forty seconds after zero, the roll of thunder and heat washed over them with a fury that filled the bunker, whipping up the hair on his head and throwing to the concrete floor the goggles someone had left untended on a table. The doors of a giant coal furnace seemed to open before them, and the nineteen men stood without speaking and watched the dusty rainbow light the pre-dawn sky.

Three weeks later, he was still thinking about it, repeating it over and over in his mind. It *had* been marvellous. Now he sat at the small table, waiting for news. He watched the moon over the American desert. Finally the knock against the door frame sounded. The floor creaked as he rose and stepped across the length of his trailer.

"We got word," Leo said, stepping up.

Anton smiled.

"The target was Hiroshima. We just heard. Around eight a.m. local time. Truman makes his radio address in a few hours. Eleven Eastern, tomorrow morning."

"No mistake?" asked Anton.

"It's confirmed. A city. Like we thought it would be. We're meeting later. You'd like a drink, I imagine."

"Congratulations." He offered out his hand.

"Yes," Leo said.

"You worry too much," Anton said. "Let's wait and see."

After Leo left, Anton sat back down and watched the desert

again through his window. He waited for the feeling of remorse he'd expected. He watched the desert and waited for a feeling that did not come. He had prepared for it. He would not, he had resolved, be taken by surprise. That was part of the deal he'd made with himself: do it right, no regrets.

He thought about the people he and everyone else here had saved by bringing this achievement to fruition. The war now would close. Fade like an exhausting nightmare. He would be going home soon. His wife waiting there for him. Everyone would be going home.

2

On board the SS *General Sturgis* a man named Oughterson, surgical consultant to General MacArthur, dictated a memo outlining the objectives of the scientific teams that were to arrive in Hiroshima in the following days. It was August 28, 1945. Anton Böll's team, the Manhattan District, was to take preliminary radiation readings meant to determine that levels were within acceptable limits for the scientists and troops following after them.

When he arrived at Iwakuni Airfield, near Hiroshima, on September 8, the smell he'd been told to expect still hung fresh in the air. He'd never known anything like it, this smell of burnt and decaying flesh buried under fallen buildings. He'd been shown photographs of the city, its streets once filled with people, all of it now flat as a razed forest. Sunburnt where awnings and trees and houses had once stood. But for those who picked through its ruins for scraps of food or in search of a family photograph or locket or spoon, whatever there was to be found, a silence deeper than dreaming lay over this island of burnt life. Only the rare building

remained partially standing; even these few beams threatened to
give way under the slightest wind. There was an alarming absence
of colour. To Anton it seemed as though he'd stepped into an old
film that, after a decade, still haunted him, *All Quiet on the Western
Front*, and here now such a world lay before him, charred black as a
nightmare. Not even a butterfly, he thought. That one last hint of
life before the sniper's bullet.

Under the command of Brigadier General Thomas Farrell,
Anton Böll and four other physicists from the Manhattan Project
back in the States moved through the crumbling town with Geiger
counters, notepads and cameras in hand, silenced by what they
saw. Within days the Joint Commission for the Investigation of the
Effects of the Atomic Bomb in Japan arrived, assigned the task of
figuring out in specific detail just how successful this great experiment had been.

1. A study of the effects of the two atomic bombs used in Japan
   is of vital importance to our country. This unique opportunity may not again be offered until another world war. Plans
   for recording all available data therefore should receive first
   priority. A study of the casualty-producing effects of these
   bombs is a function of the Medical Department and this
   memorandum is prepared as a brief outline for such a study.

The floodplain where the city had once stood became the petri
dish. The woeful Japanese test tube. This chosen lamb.

2. The casualty-producing effects of these bombs should be
   studied at the earliest possible moment for the following
   reasons.
   a. Much of the data must be obtained from the interroga-
      tion of survivors. The sooner this is accomplished the
      more accurate will be the results.

   b. Post-mortem examination of the dead may provide
     valuable information as to the cause of death. Three
     weeks or more will have elapsed and opportunity for
     post-mortem examination will be limited to late deaths
     among the survivors. It is hoped that some post-
     mortem examinations may have been done by the
     Japanese and that these records may be amplified by
     early interrogations of the Japanese pathologists.
   c. Accurate case histories by interrogations of the injured
     may provide the most reliable data. These should also
     be correlated with the physical findings and the neces-
     sary laboratory examinations.

They walked through hospitals and improvised clinics, relief
stations housed in tumbling school-rooms. They leaned over
corpses. They inspected and recorded children's scars, probing,
questioning the science involved, the finite series of chemical and
biological reactions initiated by the blast. Their mission did not
include providing assistance to anyone, not that they would've
known what to do amongst all that suffering. It was outside their
mandate, in any case. Anton himself was involved with monitoring
radiation peaks and valleys. He nosed around ash pits and makeshift hospitals and relief stations, walked over mountains of rubble. Imagining a city here. Watching the arm of the small tool in
his hands point and fall like the beat of his heart.

   4. The location of all casualties living and dead should be
     determined in relation to the bomb and plotted on a con-
     tour map.
   5. It should be emphasized that since the effects of atomic
     bombs are unknown, the data should be collected by inves-
     tigators who are alert to the possibility of death and injury
     due to as yet unknown causes.

Anton had his own camera, motion-picture, for personal use. It was something he'd acquired from an airman in desperate need of money on his way home to Iowa, via Sydney and Hawaii and however many other stops in between. The man showed him how to load and point the thing and threw three blank reels into the deal. Anton had held it in his hand and wondered about the images he planned to send back to his wife. He wanted to set it up and speak into it, though it carried no sound. He wanted to let her know he was okay. Ham it up for the camera if possible. Let her know he was fine. Maybe ask someone to get some shots of him eating well and having a nice time on one of those islands they stopped at on their way to and from. Life is okay, see? No need to worry.

The professional photographers who showed up not long afterwards—men from the AP, Reuters, UP—were there to document the scarring, and somehow make sense of it for the people back home. Rumours began to circulate that there was something beyond belief at such-and-such aid station, the Hesaka Primary School or Nakayama, maybe, or one of the hospitals outside the burn zone, and off they'd go with their Speed Graphics and measuring tapes and demand that all the bandages come off. Let's have a look at this kid, they'd say, bed number 16, the one with the elephant shape on his chest. Maybe a little horse-shadow or moo-cow leaping over the moon.

Some of them let their imaginations run loose those first weeks in Japan, once Anton's team okayed the area. He knew what most of them were up to. They were looking for something that would make a splash back home, maybe win them some recognition, at the least something that would explain things to the average American over his morning cereal. Perhaps even give rise to a patriotic rush, or tinges of sympathy. A picture that would bring out the best in people without taxing the brain or breaking the heart. It was an equation they wanted America to be able to make with its eyes closed. Power is comfort. Better them than us.

But the scars were never like that. There was no circus of shadows. Anton knew as much by now. No Mickey Mouse patterns, no jumping cows. But that didn't stop them. Most of the time they had to make do with polka dots and stripes, the clothing patterns that the blast imprinted on the skin. Sometimes sashes and buttons were melted in there, along with the afterimage. The boundaries of the physical world had suffered a fundamental shift, it seemed. Things were no longer where they belonged. He once saw an aged doctor scalpel something out of a fourteen-year-old girl's pubis. The man worked with quiet concentration. There was moaning all around him. A nurse held down the girl, but after the first incision her strength was not enough to control the patient. There was a shortage of anaesthetics. When she began to bounce violently, Anton hurried to the table and held her by the jaw and forehead and pushed her head into the table. Standing directly over her, he watched tears well in her eyes before she passed out. Though he kept his hands on her, he loosened his grip while the old doctor continued to work on her. It was as if he hadn't noticed the crisis he'd been working over. He was a sharp blade, Anton thought. He cut into her and pulled the flaps of flesh open and fished around with a blunt instrument. When he located the object, he went in with tongs. The zipper emerged from her body like a silver centipede reluctantly pulled from its dark hole. He threw it onto the floor.

In response, Anton looked to the mundane—people's habits and oddities, the disconcerting pop of an old man's knees—to ground him in the human or knowable. As a way of calming his thoughts, it helped him process the information that washed over him during the day.

They were all concerned with the collection of data, which would then be used to refine the instrument they had helped create. It was a language of elaborate beauty that Anton and his colleagues used among themselves, these symbols and equations they dealt in. Interpreters of the physical world around him, speakers of mysterious tongues that had defined the broadest sweep of the universe. The cold hard beauty of this language helped him to stop thinking for a time. It put things plainly and simply. But it was also incapable of stating the obvious: that this was not supposed to have happened.

When he wrote letters to Sophie he felt her there on the other side of the world, stirring a cup of coffee at the kitchen table. Reading his words to her, she left the rest of the mail, bills, bills, bills, stacked and piled at the corner of the table. He saw her mouth mirroring his silent vowels, touching his own lips this way. The more he wrote the clearer she became in his head. He smelt the coffee and heard the spoon clank against the smooth inverted bell-shape of the cup that sat before her, the light green one they'd bought at a five-and-dime together in Carroll Gardens—that's the one he always imagined, for some reason—and he saw the early-morning light come up through their kitchen window and touch Sophie's cream-coloured neck and dark hair, always perfectly dishevelled and spilling onto her shoulders so early in the morning.

This was all a terrible business, he wrote. He would rather not have come. He shouldn't have. It was using him up, draining him in a way he resented. This was not what he had expected. It was not time well used. He had to remember that he was a scientist, not a mortician. To get his mind off things he decided to look backwards. He couldn't imagine where all this time in Japan would take him. This is not a place for a man like me. My skills do not serve me here.

At night he reminded himself why all this had happened. He'd close his eyes and remember that there had been no alternative. Us or them. The sad fact of the world. A tragic inevitability.

As he wrote he remembered things they had done together, vignettes from their old life, brief as it was before he'd left. He wrote about how beautiful she'd looked the day they met. He used these letters to utter his deepest confessions. He wrote to her of the fear he'd felt that first day in Quebec in August 1943, because she'd seemed so much stronger than he was. Here he was, the free one, nice suit and hat, stiff leather shoes, the international scientist up in Canada because he knew something regarding the technical workings of the Auer Company, the War Office contractor responsible for the manufacture of refined uranium oxide at Oranienburg; and now he was intimidated by a beautiful nineteen-year-old refugee surrounded by old rabbis in a scattering of ramshackle huts on the shore of the sultry, wild, mid-summer St. Lawrence. He confessed this and many other things in his letters. In one he wrote of his desire to have children, which was the single true gift they could give each other, something he'd never really considered before seeing the face of so much suffering and death. Being in a place like this changed you, he said. It made you see things, the important things. What we fought for.

He wrote again how much he loved her and how desperately he wanted to come home to start that family—once he'd gained some understanding of this tragedy they'd been forced to live through. He'd need time, he said. Being here, you weren't able to understand anything. As he wrote he tried to call up the smell and taste of her skin. He closed his eyes, searching his memory. He shook his head with disbelief and marvelled at the thought that he'd convinced a woman as beautiful as Sophie to marry him; that they were able to make love so often and freely before he was called away to Chicago, then Los Alamos. Their first months had been a dizzying, exhausting time. As the weather turned in New York and the leaves outside their small apartment blushed and began to wither, they learned to leave their shame behind and explored the pleasures contained within the fingertips, the nape of the neck, the point where flesh was softest. It was nothing either of them had ever suspected, the bold requests, the gamely performance. The world of welcome acquiescence. Each one's delicious confessions of early fantasies and experimentation paralleled the other's. Their fingers and close breaths discovered in the opposite body the hidden temptations, and offered a liberation and confidence where once only confinement and shame had reigned.

He never made trips crosstown to check new stories of the magic shadows, and tried to stay away from the photographers. But those men were hard to keep clear of, discussing the circus of images, whether burnt into flesh or cast as shadow onto the surviving world, wherever they met. Sometimes a few of them were there at the mess hall, sitting in at dinner to pick the experts' brains. He kept his head down and tried to concentrate on his fork, on the truth of the matter. The fork moved, in, out, as he invoked the comforting refrain of *Us or them.*

"Well," he'd say in response to their questions, "this is a tragedy that will never have to be repeated. At least we know there will never be another war."

Mostly he said nothing around the press. He was careful to chew each mouthful twenty times, counting aloud in his head to help drown out their voices, concentrating on his teeth, on his heavy tongue, to push their words away.

They all had ways of dealing with what they lived with every day. A couple men he worked with stayed functionally drunk the entire six weeks. They would show up for work stinking of brandy and breeze through their day like bright-eyed interns. They wrote their reports over glasses of gin, then stood around outside the whorehouses after dark, working up courage. Others wrote letters into the night. Some volunteered for double shifts, seven days. He saw men, Americans mostly, picking through the rubble trying to uncover some hint of what this place might have looked like. Artifacts suggesting the genealogical tree of an extinct family. Some visited relief stations to lend a hand, but they never stayed long.

Soon the frenzied search for arresting pictures blossomed into something of an Easter-egg hunt. Who could find the most remarkable shadow cast upon some remaining section—wall or roadway or courtyard—of the flattened city? They began with the image of a man pushing his cart etched into the very structure of the Yorozuyo Bridge. But each day photographers reported new, amazing discoveries. The more bizarre ones got the *oohs* and *aahs* around the table, the raised eyebrows. These were the shadows that suggested things that could not possibly exist, optical illusions born of some geometric twist of fate and light, like the two-headed man that was said to grace the front of the incinerated Businessmen's Club; or the horn-headed devil figure with the canary—or some set of wings, anyway—perched on his left shoulder burned into the wall of the Chamber of Commerce, with the tail coming out his rear end.

Anton concentrated on his fork, in and out, in and out. Winning the war was one thing. Yes. Saving lives. His head remained lowered. But the shadows were something beyond this. During his moments away from the Manhattan District team he began to wander through the remains of the city.

This is what you get, he thought. This terrible lesson in humanity.

After three weeks Anton went to Tokyo for a weekend to study the effects of months of relentless fire-bombing. He wanted to make a comparison. He needed to know that the bomb had put an end to a greater crime. The second morning he got himself looked at by an army doctor. For two weeks running there had been a pain behind his eyes, and he wasn't sleeping. That, and the nightmares, he would report. He would ask for something to control the pain. As he sat, waiting for his consultation, he met one of the men who'd flown in that very plane. The man's arms were full of souvenirs. He seemed to be on the move. These knick-knacks would mean a lot to him, he said, some years down the line. He was on his way home. Just a quick checkup before going stateside.

"This is one hell of a place," he said, the statement accompanied by a suspicious wink. One that might have been meant to indicate the ancient intricacies of Oriental prostitution, or the exquisite mystery of Japanese gardens; Anton couldn't be sure.

The man had the drifting eye of a hungry tourist. "Jesus," he said. "I'll never be able to understand this whole business, though." A large shopping bag sat on the floor by his feet.

"Oh, yessir. A couple things to remember this lovely country by."

But there were things Ferebee, that was his name, had yet to acquire. He said he was in a rush. "You understand, I am the type of person who likes to get things while on holiday. Not that this was like any holiday I've ever been on before. Terrible business."

He had mementos from his postings all over the world. He understood the allure, now that his guts weren't sloshing around inside his skeleton seven miles up. It all came back to him. He told Anton this while waiting for something that would cure a certain ache he'd been carrying around in his belly the last month or so. "Minor medical condition," he said.

Anton nodded, desperately hoping a silence would fall between them. But Ferebee had heard about the fact-finding mission to ground zero, and could tell Böll was a part of it. "I am honoured. Truly. I believe I have seen your face in the photographs. Is that possible?"

"Not possible."

"I have a lot of respect for the sciences, you understand."

Anton looked away. On the wall was a poster of a picture he'd never heard of starring Hedy Lamarr. He'd been out of circulation too long.

"Yessir. Yessir. You know, when we dropped that masterpiece of yours, the plane bounced maybe fifteen feet up. Even a B-29 will do that when you dump four and a half tons of cargo in one go. Some piece of work, though. I'm truly honoured if you had a hand in that deal." He stopped and grinned. "You ever get lonely when you're here, sir, I suggest you try the local cuisine." Ferebee winked. "Local delicacies come cheap.

"But, you don't mind my asking, sir, I notice you have that accent on top of the American you speak so well. Congratulations—a hard language if you're not born into it, if you don't mind my saying. I can't help noticing that just a bit of an accent, Kraut, right? No offense. I admire a man who sides with the winner— mark of intelligence."

As Ferebee spoke, Anton saw in his memory the glow of the stars down in the desert, all the brilliant lights sparkling, and how he and Leo Szilard would go for drives into the cold, shining desert. He remembered, blocking out the man's voice, how they'd take the jeep out and drive and talk about their work. They were always talking, always looking. He was the first one Anton knew to do that. Think about the morality of it, the ethics of doing what they were doing. He understood the context of where he was.

Szilard would stop the jeep in the middle of nowhere, hills and sand and a century plant and hot hot hot. Heat waves glowing on the surface of the planet. He'd say in his deep Hungarian accent, "Anton. Anton, just listen to yourself. You try to understand yourself at one point in your life and you seem to be able to. You get the idea of who you are when you're doing something. Doing x. Anton washing his laundry on a Tuesday evening. You get a clear picture of this man doing his laundry. He's a man who can be understood clearly enough. Then you take this same picture of Anton and try to apply that to the picture of the boy who cried when his mother sent him to bed without his supper. This is the same person, the same genes and brain and fingerprints. Consider this, Anton. You cannot apply the same understanding of the same thing at different points in its trajectory. The principle of uncertainty." He stopped when he said that. "This is Heisenberg's principle of uncertainty. It is the same with particles and neutron fields and it is the same with human beings. Tolerance is necessary to reconcile the man washing his underwear with the crying boy, and the man who destroys the world."

The doctor in Tokyo had been unable to help with the pain that lived behind Anton's eyes; the nightmares got worse. After he got back to Hiroshima the taste of ash began to creep into his mouth while he slept. He awoke in the middle of the night, spitting out the taste even before he was fully conscious. It was dry and slightly bitter and seemed to move into the very meat of his tongue, a penetrating hole drilled into his flesh that sucked all the moisture from his mouth. He'd roll over and swish back the glass of bedside water and wait for his tongue to become his again.

But sometimes that flavour hung there long enough for him to watch the sun come up. Other times he would try to isolate a memory of his wife, create a box around her, and slowly the taste would subside. He drew a frame around her in his head as the sun edged upwards through their kitchen window, maybe, or as she walked past a vegetable stand in the market, a fish wrapped in the *New York Daily Mirror* under her arm. He invoked a familiar image to get him out of those tight spots. Sleeplessness, a bad taste in your mouth, doubts.

Sometimes the ash appeared in his mouth while he helped out the Japanese doctor. He'd started coming in more regularly after he'd helped subdue that girl. It had shown him that even the basic necessities such as anaesthetics were absent here. He could do something as primitive as this. Hold someone down. Sometimes he'd be cleaning up after the old man was through with a patient, taking out dirty bandages, slop pails, whatever, and the ash taste would be there again. Suddenly, out of nowhere. He asked some of the other men if they tasted the grey cloud that seemed to hang in the air, and most shook their heads and shrugged. Even though each of them had spoken about the smell of burnt flesh that never seemed to go away. He started walking around with packets of sugar in his pockets, lifted every morning from the PX. He found it overcame the taste, if only temporarily, like perfume in a slaughterhouse. He'd drain a sleeve into his mouth, then feel the ache rise in his teeth. But the taste would disappear. It was something he remembered from his youth, the treatment his mother prescribed for skinned knees and cut elbows, a childish balm transferred to adult life.

With the old Japanese doctor's muted guidance he started wrapping bandages. The scar designs he saw were sometimes beyond belief. That's when he came to understand how the patterns were formed on the skin, and the hideous attraction that had possessed the men with cameras. These were random detailed tattoos of fire, depending upon the pattern of the shirt or dress or skirt you were wearing the morning of the bomb. Horizontal bars across the back or front meant alternating dark and light stripes. Vertical meant suspenders. This code he could decipher easily enough. The bold round circles he found on certain women indicated a polka-dot dress. The white of the given material partially deflected the heat of the blast. The darker colours over that background absorbed the fire, which in turn drew pictures into the skin. The burns he saw were based on the clothes worn that last morning. They would never be removed. They were there for good, the story of that day told on the flesh like a living Braille for the blind.

3

He talked for weeks after he got back. He and Sophie sat in their small apartment, windows curtained against the world, each trying to find what had been lost. At first she listened, pushing aside her own worries. She tried not to fear who this man was to whom she'd given her life. She tried to be charitable. She waited her turn.

"It was successful beyond our wildest dreams." He clenched his fists, tried to squeeze the tumbling from his hands. "It was perfect."

She touched his face with the back of her finger, tracing lightly down over his hard cheek. She wondered now if they would ever get back to where they had been. If the physical passion they shared would ever return, if they could manage to turn their fears into strengths.

"Yes. It's done with." The finger continued, inviting memories of lost afternoons. It was meant as a consolation, a reintroduction of the gifts they had opened with such pleasure. "It's over and done with and we can start life again," she said. "You can forget it now."

"You think you just snap your fingers?" he said, suddenly vicious.

She'd tried to live with the news that had been coming out of Europe these last few months, hoping word might come through somehow, from somewhere. There was the slightest possibility. Every morning she hurried to the mail slot at the sound of the letter carrier. Maybe a neighbour from the old quarter or a distant relative would have word. Or something written in her mother's hand. *We are safe. We have tracked you down. We are coming to America.* But the letter never came. How could it? How could they know where she was, that she had married a German scientist who'd brought her to this foreign city, that she was waiting for them here, alone, with a man she feared she did not know?

But still there was time. Most days she took the Number 9 uptown to the Red Cross offices at Broadway and 66th, where hundreds milled about, checking the lists that were being compiled and added to, ever expanding. She was directed to a woman who headed the Austria offices. Information was still incomplete, she said. *"This is what we have. We are still looking."*

One day as she walked back out to the bus stop she saw a young Italian man from her neighbourhood. They'd met a year before, when, through her living-room window, he'd seen a rash shaped like a butterfly on her face. She waited for him now, and they walked on together.

He asked her name, and told her his. He had also lost people in Europe, he told her. He'd been coming to the Red Cross office since the winter of 1944. His English had improved since their first meeting. There was a class he attended week-nights, when he could.

"Why is this the first time I see you here?" she said.

"I come as often as I can," he said. He gestured to his own face. "You are better?"

"It went away."

"And when will you go back to home?"

"When I find my parents, yes. I want to go home."

"Yes." He was twenty-six years old. He was alone here, but for an uncle.

I am alone too, she wanted to say. I am alone.

He was the first person other than Anton she had spoken to in days. "Do you like your job?" she asked.

He delivered meat around the city. "Meat-packer makes good money in New York."

Both Anton and Sophie knew that variations of their hushed, nightly conversations were repeated countless times throughout the city. Everyone back from Europe or the Far East or Africa with stories of loss and guilt and fortunes changed. Boatloads of veterans were arriving daily down at the ports, carrying with them their pronouncements of faith lost and found. Vigorous promises to start anew. But the city had already entered upon one of its greatest eras of forgetfulness, working harder than ever so that the past might quickly disappear.

On her way downtown, after she saw Anton off to the New School, she walked in the cool shadows of the buildings that seemed to have sprouted up overnight. Businesses were founded. Entire families disembarked from ports. But a cut as deep as this would not heal simply because it had marked an entire generation. The searing pain could not be relieved or even dulled by the knowledge that their wound, or something similar to it, was suffered in common by so many. It burnt there in the darkness and in the light in its own particular way, regardless of the furious rebuilding and the need to look forward and not back and the legions with which they struggled along.

After work, late into the night, Anton told her what he could remember of his time with the Manhattan District. Sometimes he talked about his new position at the New School, where he'd been granted a full professorship. He talked about his ambition, about their finding a way in the world. But most often he returned to his time in Japan. He talked about the old man he'd helped out there, a man so old you could see through his skin. "The man with the funny knees . . ." What was his word? *Disconcerting?* The way they cracked, those strange clicking sounds. He told her they had all worked on the assumption that the killing nature of the bomb was indiscriminate. But it seemed this assumption was false. At least to him. He'd watched this particular old man lean over two small children, one holding the other's hand, and practically heard what he'd been thinking as he wiped the tears from his face. *Why not me? I am the old one.*

It was a country that had been turned inside out, a place where nature had been thrown on its head. He told Sophie about the bent backs and the crooked noses and rheumy eyes and knotted fingers still twisting with stubborn old life. He told her about the long-blind and the stone deaf who'd stared down over the perfect healthy bodies of the dead. The very old mourned the very young from the place they no longer wanted to be, a place that had abandoned them, turned to particled dust and irradiated ash and exploded atoms. It fell to them, still alive, to tend to the burnt lungs and melted fingers of the young and healthy. They leaned over crushed kidneys and blind-staring eyes, over medieval scar tissue that every so often re-enacted the blast in miniature by bubbling forth in tiny explosions on the skin, somewhere between red and yellow-white, causing shudders to roll down the length of the body. They leaned over crushed spinal columns and burst eyeballs, smashed ribs and ruptured spleens.

"But you helped end the war," she said, touching his neck. "You can't forget that." He'd barely touched her since his return, over a year now. Any contact between them she initiated, and when it came it was merely for comfort and not pleasure.

"You must think about the lives you helped save. The men in the invasion force . . . the fire-bombings . . . all those civilians."

He looked at her, his resentment rising. "Please." He took her arm in his hand and brought it away from him, holding it inches from his face and looking at it with the expression of a man examining a scab picked from a dry wound. Her fingers curled and she turned to cover her tears. He believed she would never understand at what cost the war had been ended.

"You've convinced yourself of something," he said. "I am suffering. Is that what you think?"

"I know you don't sleep. I hear you. You leave the bed every night."

"What does this mean?"

"You think about it. It's always in your mind."

"It's my work. They pay me to think. How do you think I pay

for this here? This place you live in. Do you think this just happens? In America everything costs money. You don't know that."

"I want to go to school. I want to learn English."

He waved his hand dismissively.

She would never grasp the forces behind the events he'd lived through. He was resolved not to let her pity him, or believe that he now regretted the role he had played. He openly admitted that his time with the Manhattan District had been disagreeable. For the first time he had felt fear. But he was back now. This geographical distance had helped provide perspective. It had returned to him a cool head with which the facts might be observed.

The necessities involved, the weight of responsibility—these were the things his wife was unable to understand. All the while she'd been here, at this safe distance, sculpting figures cut from the depths of her solitude. While he was away she'd begun carving small figures in soapstone, make-believe figures who now populated the apartment. It was like walking into an art gallery when he came home. It took him three days to ask what they were. While he was facing the unimaginable in Japan, she'd been getting on with her life, playing like an innocent. He had looked to her for strength. He had needed the memory of their life together to keep him focussed. But now this normal life repulsed him, and he resented her ability to carry on as she had always done.

He did not ask her about her family. Nothing about what she had lost. It was as if that blast had destroyed the ability to see beyond himself.

"You're crying?" he'd say, annoyed. "Why are you crying?"

She had not talked about her family with him, not once. She knew that he was incapable of listening at first, and that she would not be able to coax him with mention of her own needs. But she had not expected anger. She had not expected impatience. Silence, yes. But not that she would be expected to bear the consequences of his time at the war.

The secret, she finally discovered, was to apply herself in the midst of that dead time. Classes began soon after, in the winter of 1946. She looked forward to leaving the apartment every evening. She enrolled in a Brooklyn Central YMCA class, English for immigrants, the class filled with people like her, some older, others younger. They were everywhere, she discovered. There was a young woman from Vienna. They decided that first day to speak only English together. The Italian man from the Red Cross, the meat-delivery man, came in late her second day. She sat beneath a window that looked out over Remsen Street. He wore loose grey corduroy pants, white shirt and tie. His skin was brown, though it was still winter. As he took a seat he apologized to the teacher, and to the class generally, for being late. Sophie smiled at him across the rows.

But there was no escaping from the black air that seemed to infest the apartment where she lived with Anton. In order to breathe again, she began to shape in her head what she imagined he'd seen. She tried to understand him this way, all that disaster cut and buffed and displayed for her to walk through, look at from various angles and discover with a lingering touch of the forefinger. Her sculptures began to resemble the turmoil that kept him awake at night.

Sometimes on those quiet nights when she didn't have school she remembered her childhood, the years before she was put on that train bound for Germany. She had always lived in her imagination, and now, married close to four years to a man she did not know, she shaped the image of the old doctor her husband had watched so closely, a stranger he'd met at one of the aid stations. Once he saw him drop an instrument, a scalpel or something of that nature, and as he bent slowly to pick it up his brittle old knees had cracked.

Disconcerting.

"Like that," Anton had said. *"Pop, pop."*

How do you sculpt a word like that? she wondered. She'd lain on the couch, putting images to the stories he recounted from that time in Hiroshima. She needed to live through what he had seen.

Wasn't it a funny thing, he explained one night, a funny thing to notice in a roomful of mutilated people? Someone's knees cracking. He'd watched with the greatest fascination the manner in which the man held his back as he stooped to pick up the scalpel, stiffly erect, palm open against the spine as he bent.

He had seen the old man many times. They almost could have developed a rapport, were it not for the circumstances. He saw him at different work stations as he did his rounds, looking for tasks that would provide him with a sense of charitable accomplishment. Hopefully this would ease his conscience, moving from one station to the next. Patients died in great numbers in one neighbourhood and seemed to reappear in another like churlish, taunting ghosts. He worked with little sleep. Anyone with any medical training, no matter how old, was expected to mobilize. Most doctors had been killed in the blast. Soon after pinning that screaming girl to the table, Anton had rolled up his sleeves.

Sometimes Sophie would leave with Stefano after class and walk over to Rosalinda's, the diner with high ceilings and stools with spinning tops along the counter. On nights when Anton taught a late class at the university she stayed until closing time, and they drank Coca-Cola and coffee and he smoked cigarettes while he told her all the things he missed back home and what he would do when he returned. He did not tell her about the sad things. Just the good things. She asked him many questions about what it was like in Pescara, where he was born and had grown up. His father was a fisherman. One morning the Germans came to their house and took his family away. Stefano had been in the town across the mountains, studying painting at a small school.

"You are a painter?"

"No. I wanted. The war ended that."

"But the war is over. You can go to that school again."

"If I go back it will be as my father was. I will fish in the sea."

"You paint here now?"

"No." He lit another cigarette. "When I got back I found the house was empty."

"I'm sorry."

"Don't be sorry. I will find them. I will save enough money to return and they will be somewhere."

"They will be somewhere."

Sophie had never been south of Graz. They sat in a booth to convince the world around them to disappear, and she pretended they were in Italy and the war had never been. She had an idea of Italy, but she did not know how close or far off the reality was. It was just an idea. They were picture postcards in her head. She pretended that outside the window to her right was a street in Pescara and that the girl walking past was Stefano's sister on her way up from the harbour and that all the people around her were also from the village.

"Do you live with someone?" she asked, turning.

"I stay with my uncle, Faustino. He is twenty years here. The brother of my father. He works like an animal. *Animale.* He works in the sewer. All night he works. City Works Commission."

Sophie watched his hands and lips as he smoked and talked. His hands were small and delicate. It was easier to picture him holding a paintbrush than to imagine him gripping a butcher's knife or carrying a side of beef on his shoulder. When he held the cigarette in his mouth he squinted his eyes and pursed his lips.

"I can get lamb for you. Very nice cuts."

"Thank you."

"A delivery goes to DeLuca's tomorrow, the butcher outside your window."

"Yes, I know. I see you every Tuesday."

"You're very skinny girl. You need to eat more."

The uncle's apartment was small and cluttered. There were no curtains on any of the windows and no carpet on the floor but one circular rug in the centre of the living room, when you walked into the apartment. A balcony looked out over Charles Street, but no photographs or paintings or pictures of any kind were on the walls. He closed the door behind them and removed the scarf from his neck and took her coat and purse and tossed them onto the brown sofa by the circular rug. He removed his coat. They left their boots at the door.

It was a cold January evening but she still asked if he would open the balcony door. The cold air rolled into the apartment, and he walked into the kitchen and returned with hot tea. He placed it on the small table in the living room, beside a framed photograph of a child.

She returned from the balcony and took the picture in her hand.

"Who is this? Is this you?"

"This is the painter as a young man. Yes. I am nine then."

"You are a very handsome boy." She took his hand and placed it in hers and returned the picture to the table.

He kissed her shoulder and then her neck. It was cold in the room now. When he lifted her hair and kissed the back of her neck she had goose bumps there and something went up her spine and a knot tied in her stomach. His mouth was hot and she smelled the tobacco in his breath and tasted a slight sweetness of animal blood. It was in his hair and on his skin. When she placed his finger in her mouth she tasted the warm earth-smells of his work and the ruddy tobacco flavour. He circled his tongue to the front of her neck and she released his finger and she kissed his mouth and the cold in Uncle Faustino's apartment seemed to evaporate.

"Is it okay here?" she asked.

He nodded.

She slipped out of her blouse and dress and underwear and stood silently before him. She did not lower her head. She looked straight into his eyes and began to undress him and led him into the next room and they slipped into the bed together. When she returned home that evening she found the photograph in her purse, and hid it behind a stack of books in the storage room off the kitchen.

Port Elizabeth, 1995

1

The town Anton and Sophie ended up in was not particularly notable. Anton had lived in many towns and cities that were much better in every way he could think of, in every respect that counted, really, than the one he and Sophie had chosen as their last place on earth. But that was the point, of course. By mutual agreement they had managed to avoid the exciting and the demanding at this stage in life when, naturally, it would have been lost on them.

One night after supper in his seventy-eighth year, while Sophie did the washing up, Anton donned his winter coat and boots and walked the dark tree-lined streets of his neighbourhood, listening with an intense calm to the snow crunch under his steps. It had been a damp winter, as it always seemed to be this close to the lake, where temperatures were made warmer now and cooler in summer. Like the falling snow, the air was also thick and heavy tonight, though not, he was thankful, enough to threaten rain. The cold was sufficient to deliver the large leafy flakes to the ground intact, and the ground was sufficiently cold that the snow fell white on the roads and sidewalks and slowly overtook and filled in the patchy lawns and obscured street curbs and old footprints. The cold air, bracing, helped clear his head. The tree canopies he walked under were barren of leaves, naturally; yet the naked branches still managed to form the vague impression of a cathedral's arches, the length of which ran to the bottom of Spruce Street, breaking for traffic and sidewalks at the intersection with Lakeshore Road, and continued down to the water, the direction from which he had just come, where the street and its accompanying archway—full and green in summer, hard and stripped and grey in winter—opened onto the dangerous, endless surface of the great lake.

Anton walked up Spruce Street, fingering through his gloves the three packets of brown sugar he'd taken from the kitchen cupboard that afternoon. Before arriving at Lakeshore Road he turned left on Palmer Avenue, at the old McKaw house, whose front porch and cedar hedges still glittered with white Christmas lights. Before him stretched twenty or thirty paces of dark sidewalk, a sign that one of the house's eager shovellers had recently been out, as was usually the case, because snow was intently falling, as it had been for most of the day and seemed likely to all night. Anton did not care for shovelling snow, and even Sophie, who believed God gave us all the strength to stay active to the very last breath, said in her characteristic tone, half pleased, half condescending, "Don't borrow trouble," one of her favourite expressions in English. There were certain things she knew, absolutely, and this was one of them. She was the type who demanded busy hands from all those who surrounded her, possibly on account of her own condition, or what she had seen and lived through in her day. Yet something like this, a graceless task said to have stopped the hearts of men even younger than her husband, she knew this was one of those things best left to younger and stronger townfolk, of whom there were still quite a few, and, better yet, to the children, of whom there seemed to be even more. For this reason they retained the services of any one of the half-dozen teenage boys who came knocking on any given snow day—usually under-dressed in denim jackets and unlaced boots, shovels casually shouldered—in hopes of earning whatever change lay at the bottom of the clay jar on the key table next to the coat rack.

The crunching underfoot ceased as Anton crossed the exposed dark pavement. He pulled the scarf he wore neatly around his neck more tightly—black wool, a present from his wife from some distant Christmas, he couldn't recall how far back—and felt it catch briefly, weakly, on the slight grey stubble at his chin. His gloves were warm, his boots dry. This was an evening walk he enjoyed, as so often the old enjoy their rituals, and he understood, like the practised hand he was, that dressing for the weather made the difference between getting home and going home. He was in no rush. When it came time, perhaps fifteen minutes from now, to turn and walk back down Spruce and head up their walkway, not five blocks away, he would go round to the side of the house for the armload of firewood that would keep a soft glow alive on whatever presentation he was preparing at the time, prop open the side door, backfirst with the help of a probing right elbow, and there he would find things as they had always been. Sophie would fill whatever room she was sitting in, and most likely a few others besides, with her determined presence, perhaps mumbling under her breath, and with the lingering scent of whatever labours had busied her that day, and with the deep odour of beet soup and apple crumble, which he was now digesting as he stepped off the last section of shovelled sidewalk and continued eastwards to Jackson's Hill. In no hurry, he was in control of this fine night.

Well-bundled figures shuffled past, some of whom he recognized, partly hidden though they were in hats and scarves and winter coats. These were his neighbours, his fellow citizens. In summertime one or two might have stopped to ask after Sophie's health or if, by the way, he'd seen that old tabby named Samantha, "You know, the one with the cropped tail." But on dark evenings like this one, while enjoyable, no one stood still for street-corner chitchat, or even for simple questions that required merely a nod or a shake of the head. For most people, evenings like this were about getting home and staying home.

Anton customarily nodded his greetings as he passed, man or woman, boy or girl, and offered a smile whether he knew the people or not; though it was likely he did know most of them, at least to look at. And likely, too, that these people on their way home knew something in return about this pleasant old man. They might have known that he had been around here for a good long while, not all his life but long enough, anyway, to have seen some changes, and that he was known as Dr. Böll, or simply Doc, and most thought he probably would be a good man to go to if they cut a hand or had a persistent sore throat or trouble with the lower back—except that he was long retired and quite clearly a man well upon his golden years.

Most of the kids at Jackson's Hill, where he was headed that night, knew him only as Doc. If asked, they would've said this was because he was a medical doctor, which they all naturally assumed. At any rate, it was a name that had stuck, perhaps first spoken by someone who years ago had grown up and graduated from high school, or even moved away, taking the truth with him, and it was used, as they had always used their own nicknames amongst them-selves—Spider, the Pine, Speck—without any deeper meaning or thought that they were aware of. As Jackson's Hill was used. Who-ever Jackson was wasn't important, of course, whether he'd been the first owner of the closest house, or the first boy to slide down its steep incline on his backside, or to successfully jump the small gully that cut across at its base, at the bottom of which a stream flowed. No matter. He, too, was long gone by now. Of more impor-tant consideration on this temperature-perfect dark and snowy early evening were the bumps and moguls (a new and foreign-sounding word for most of them) that pocked its slick surface, and the imposing hard-packed snow-jump down below. Names weren't worth dwelling on. Not when life, urgent and real, wanted to be lived.

This was a sentiment with which Anton Böll would've heartily agreed. For it was the children who brought him out on these cold evenings when staying home and keeping warm would have been much easier. It was their need for speed, as he'd heard a boy say one day while they stood panting at the top of the hill, preparing for another run. It was the purity of their motives and the pinkness in their cheeks and the joy and thrill pulsing through their hearts when their sleds and toboggans hit the jump at the bottom and shot into the air and travelled almost magically, almost forever, over the small grey streak of ice and landed clumsily on the other side. It was the simple beauty of this evening pastime he loved the most; he would not think to call it nostalgia, because what he felt was more than the longing to recover what once might have been his and now was lost.

It was mostly boys, as was the case most evenings, but a number of girls as well ran and shrieked and zoomed down the slick hill, regardless of their brothers' bullying tactics. The toboggan slope was not like the brightly lit hockey rink on the other side of town, a ten-minute walk over the bridge. Parents did not flock here, paper coffee cups in hand, to watch their children. This was a dark, dangerous playground, unorganized, spontaneous, unburdened by rules. It was a vision of youth Anton treasured not because it bore some faint resemblance to his own, lost behind decades of clouded memory, but because he might never have known this beautiful and simple chaos had it not been for this place, this time, these children.

The clearest memories of his childhood were of listening to the stories his father told of the sodden landscape that had stuck to his trousers and seeped into his boots during his dreary days at the Great War. Even seventy years on, there would appear before Anton the image of his mother staring from the window of his parents' bedroom in the direction of the train station where she had welcomed home her young husband, still believing that their life might pick up where it had left off, or hoping that the man she remembered might one day jump down from a newly arrived train and remove the shadow that cast itself upon their life. But the young husband aged quickly beyond his years, and it became clear that the oppressive weight of the final months at Verdun and the ceaseless thunder of the big Krupp cannons he'd helped load and fire had hardened his heart against his fearful wife and young son, conceived so desperately in 1917 on the first night of a nine-day pass from the war, and all other men not witness to the life he had seen.

Anton was known to these children and they seemed not to mind him watching their rough and energetic games, as he did most snowy nights soon after suppertime, perhaps since they concluded he was here to make sure no one got hurt. He was secretly flattered that he was not clumped in with the amorphous blob that was their idea of all adults, though he never said or thought as much in such specific terms. He was simply flattered, and grateful. Standing here at the top of the hill, a bit to the side so as not to get in anyone's way or draw too much attention to himself, he thought of what he might have turned out to be. One of those old, bitter and silent men who sat their days away in darkened apartments or taverns, grumbling at the bad turns the world had taken. A life so desperately close to the one his father had lived. He was not like them—like him—thank God, and again, wordlessly, he thanked the children for their small contribution to his life, unconscious as it was, this gift of charity to his seventy-seven years.

A street lamp back near the sidewalk cast just enough light over the hill for the tobogganers to see by, but the far end of the incline was dark and the snow hump in front of the stream looked sharp and dangerous, barely jumpable. Falling snow seemed to hold extra light in the air, and at the north end, the light from the street lamp glittered against the gently falling flakes like flickering sparks—as if it were Christmas again, you might've thought, repeating its promises for a second time in under a month.

He took his position and watched the children clomping their way back up the hill, some eyes glimpsing the old figure backlit against the tallest cedar, one or two of those sets of eyes winking even, acknowledging. One of his favourite girls—Marlie, he thought he'd heard her called—waved shyly and looked back down at her green boots as she climbed. She pulled a small toboggan behind her, its snowbreaker, in profile, shaped like the top of a candy cane. The warmth of his home came to his mind then, as well as Sophie, his wife, and he saw an image of her sitting as she might be now, warming the house with her presence as she waited for him the way she did, without really waiting.

For Anton, waiting meant stopping what you were doing, or what you figured you ought to be doing. Waiting was an act in itself, exclusive of letter writing or cooking or the many dozens of tasks you busied yourself with. But at an early age she had learned a valuable lesson: waiting was a luxury afforded to those who knew the person they were expecting would show up. Both during the war and afterwards, his return to her had never been assured. You put your life on hold like that and what do you have left, she'd said, but an empty house and a broken heart. Of course, she had never understood his position. She had never understood the importance of his work, or the sacrifices he'd had to make in order to carry that work to its final conclusion. He did not blame her for this. She could never enter into the luminous realm that history had forced him to occupy. He had never criticized her limited grasp of the necessary evils. No, how could he? He had been away, and, like a young wife should, she had missed him. She had pined. She grieved. She grieved for him and for her lost family, and finally for herself. Then she got busy. She protected herself. She built a fire-wall between herself and his absence and everything that had been taken away from her, and that fire-wall, or a version of it, stood to this day. She had taken up the pursuit of her own life as a defence against the achievements of his own. No, how could he blame her? But nor did he blame himself.

The girl joined the roughly formed line that would lead her to the single groove of snow racing towards the ramp and, with any luck, a moment in time when she would feel the hard ground fall out from under her for the half-second it took to gain the other side. Some boys pushed and shoved, testing the limits of good nature, while others were simply intent on the task at hand, which was to cross the gully down below as bravely as possible, and, they hoped, elicit a cheer from the waiting gallery above.

Of course you didn't have to wait. Toboggans pushed off from the top of the hill at all points, some from the darkness at the south end, where the snow was fresher and there were no grooves. These were the older boys usually, thirteen or fourteen, who wished to distinguish themselves from the others by increasing the element of danger. Some of these crossed the hill at a diagonal; steering was difficult, and it was a long shot, but occasionally one of them came hollering out of the darkness, sometimes just a boy hanging on to the flaps of a garbage bag or cardboard box, which was even harder to steer and so almost always went off track, in hopes of hitting the jump.

The girl had taken off her wet mittens, which she held under her arm as she rubbed her hands together. She was talking with another girl—the same age, it looked—though Anton couldn't hear what they were saying. Maybe something about her cold hands. He wondered about offering his own gloves, clumsy and oversized for such small hands, but surely warmer than what she would be forced to pull back on as soon as the line-up thinned and she slid down the hill again. This was nothing serious, cold hands, but the reason he didn't offer was instead that he did not know this girl, despite the kindness of her smile, and he did not choose to force himself into their games. The enjoyment of children should not be dampened by prying adults. He buried his hands deeper into his pockets and followed the arc of sleds and toboggans down the hill from that safe, motionless distance.

The simple pleasure over which he presided was as much as he expected or needed, perhaps even as much as his aging heart could bear. In much the same way that these children might finally leave this small town behind and one day discover their limitations, Anton and Sophie had sought out this place for the implied guarantee that only so much life might be lived here on any given day.

But a new generation of children had arrived. On school days he saw them on their way to and from Brantwood, grades kindergarten to four; the high school was just beyond it, closer to the train tracks that cut across the top of the town, where the older ones drank and smoked cigarettes in summertime. There was another high school on the other side of the Burnt River, which was frozen now and also, like Jackson's Hill, a favourite venue for winter entertainment. Anton rarely crossed this river over either of its two bridges, one built in 1928, a year before the Crash, the second in 1967 as one of the hundreds of Centennial projects unveiled that year throughout Canada, when he himself was still teaching in New York City.

By the time they came to Port Elizabeth, he and Sophie had reached an agreement of sorts concerning the nature of comfort — an idea that had been refined over the course of decades, often at great personal expense and heartache. Comfort for Anton, at least at first, had always come second to achievement. He never said as much, but his wife's need, and what he took to be the meaning of this word for her, suggested if not a betrayal of life's powerful challenges then at least a measure of capitulation. He could not hold this against her. There had been a point in his life when he, too, had dreamt of raising a family. But their situation had changed, and when it became clear that the path chosen for them did not allow children, he was forced to acknowledge that his life's work would be done at the laboratory and university, not the home.

From the beginning, Anton's life in this unremarkable town had threatened to become the mere sum of past accomplishments. That was it. Leaving the university in New York, where he had been since the end of the war, where only the year before that first year on the lake he had been an active and revered faculty member, he'd still had a hand in shaping the young brilliant minds that reminded him of his own youthful genius. There was work yet ahead: imminent breakthroughs, discussions and conferences, papers to be delivered. Yet it was the feeding of minds he had always taken the most solace from, and the ready and ongoing engagements that academic life presented, which for so long now had held at bay the nagging question of his legacy.

Sophie, on the other hand, believed she'd finally got her husband back. And for a time she was right. She saw how quickly he learned to enjoy himself within these new limitations. The job he'd taken at the generating station—mostly in exchange for the daily exposure to bright young minds—absented him from the house eight hours a day, five days a week. Of course the work, which had him overseeing the upgrade of the four oldest reactors at the Pickering Nuclear Station, was challenging enough. The balancing of equations and flow charts was technically precise and demanding, but his position required little innovation and no creative thinking, at least for a man of his background. In the early days he still went to New York two or three times a year, and at least once every summer for the anniversary of the bomb, August 6, to speak at rallies and attend conferences. She knew he would never give that up, and she knew enough never to suggest it. Though less interesting, his new work satisfied his need for detail and study, and provided him with a schedule, without which he was simply no good. While the administration was boundless, he got through it. And now, at least, they were out of the city and away from that country where she had never felt at home, living in the kind of town she'd always seen in her head, and that, despite the hard times, and the diminishing years that remained to them, offered no small hope.

The house at the bottom of Spruce, then, had been Anton's concession to his wife. It was his sacrifice, one he made lovingly and without the shame and sinking heart he half expected, and even within a week, still months before the first winter freeze of 1980, he admitted that she'd been right all along, and that this change was long overdue. This, also, was a reflection of his generation. Stubbornness. He was sixty-two years old when he finally learned this lesson, and thank goodness, he thought, that Sophie's patience had outlasted his arrogance.

The Bölls had bought into a house and mortgage they could manage, based on his university pension and projected earnings from Pickering, in addition to what they'd saved over thirty-odd years. The sellers, who'd decided Florida was the place to be, especially since they had a daughter down there, had left the house itself well managed and maintained. But the inside was still filled with signs of children, pink paint on a bedroom wall, Big Bird wallpaper, phone jacks everywhere; corkboard in the basement, where one of the youngsters had practised his drums. The early renovations involved having all that cork taken down and burnt out back, stripping and painting the walls and ceilings throughout, replacing carpets that demonstrated that this family had gone through a number of pets. As it was October when they took possession, Sophie was forced to wait out the winter before she could get her hands on the garden, which was a sad and shabby affair, she thought, but whose potential she had noticed immediately and had swung the decision finally to choose this house over the two others, which were both somewhat more affordable but not on the lake and without much acreage.

The property boasted a gentle, barely perceptible lakeward slope where the carpenter who'd built the house in 1889—Samuel Richmond, a plaque by the front door announced—had most likely lounged during warm, long-gone summer evenings. Perhaps it was he who also had the good sense to create and nurture its surrounding garden, before it slipped away through neglect or a series of weak imaginations. Three principal windows on the main floor enjoyed a southern view to the lake, one above the kitchen sink, the other two in the living room and sunroom, as did a fourth, smaller one in what later became Anton's study. The master bedroom, too, on the second floor, looked out over the lake. It was a house whose inner and outer workings seemed all focussed, as they rightly should be, in that direction, for that purpose.

Out there the world seemed to come to a beautiful and silent end, Anton often said. As far as the eye could see, there was nothing except water and more water and the sharp edge of horizon, like a blue wall rising heavenwards. A slight westerly turn of the head as you washed dishes after a meal, or as you looped a tie around your neck at the foot of the bed, and you saw from one of those windows the narrow end of that great body begin its widening surge eastwards, and perhaps, small upon the horizon, you observed a speck of colour that was a sailboat, or an iceberg of grey steel that was one of the lake boats that every day crossed, laden and low in the water, from one end to the other, bearing mutely within its hold ore or grain or car parts destined for away.

After they finished the preliminary work, they began to think in earnest about which finishing touches were needed—a process Sophie enjoyed and Anton merely tolerated. There was only one sort of detail he was adept at, and this was not it. Over breakfast she told him her ideas, which he invariably agreed to, and then she saw to their execution. Light work, like the sanding of a particularly weary-looking section of bannister, she would do herself. The bigger jobs were left to a father-son carpentry team that had come highly recommended, Mr. Schmitt and his son Danny, who helped on weekends and after school.

That first winter, they worked on the transformation of the house, always under Sophie's watchful eye and exacting guidance, into what she had imagined it always should have been.

"Samuel Richmond would be pleased," she told Danny and his father the last day on the job. "The man who built the house. He'd be happy to see this place rejuvenated."

The boy blinked shyly and dug his calloused fingers into his back pockets. His father accepted the compliment with a smile.

"You know," Sophie said, turning to the boy, "you're part of its history from this day forward."

She poured Mr. Schmitt a glass of rye and watched him sip cautiously, then place the unfinished drink on the new countertop.

When the smell of new lumber and paint and plaster dust cleared away, along with the rare trace of rye that last afternoon, drifting out open windows in the kitchen and adjacent sunroom, the distinct flavour of spring breezed through the town's imagination and bore itself out in its citizens' manner of dress and lightness of spirit. Rubber boots and rain gear replaced winter coats and scarves. It was time Sophie turned to her main purpose in pushing for this house. She did not consult her husband on the direction she'd seen for the garden. Which, again, was fine as far as he was concerned. All he requested was a small square, preferably in full sun, where he could grow his tomatoes and peppers.

She commenced work the afternoon the Schmitts finished up, and proceeded to occupy herself with the slow, steady, concentrated vision that sustained her through to the end of that first summer. Back from the generating station twenty minutes from town, Anton would remove himself from the Plymouth and look for his wife in the maze of new and old trees that populated the back lot, amongst them piles of soil and pulled weeds and rocks and bags of fertilizer, and there he would find her, crouched over a clay pot or shovel or wheelbarrow, or consulting with one of the landscape architects she'd retained through the nursery up near Highway 401, where she bought most of her supplies, or talking to one of the two boys she paid five dollars an hour for their strong backs and tireless need to save for the coming fall's tuition. She would drop her gloves and kiss her husband's right cheek, sometimes leaving a dirty smear on his cleanly shaven face, and lead him around the maze of her labours to show him what she'd accomplished that day.

His acquiescence was due more to fatigue than to interest, and it was with a degree of pity and certainly bemusement and the slightest shade of impatience that he surveyed his wife's progress. What he could not understand was how she failed to see this, as he did so clearly, as the stop-gap of a bored housewife against loneliness. He searched for charity. Attempted to withhold judgment. But when so much needed doing in the world, what was it that pulled her attention to these stupid plants?

In time a single room of the house emerged as a shrine to the life Anton had left behind years before in Germany. Sophie had kept control of such things at the beginning, but slowly he had refashioned in the basement the long-lost country of his youth. The slow perfection of that room occurred over a period of years. He produced photographs to serve as templates for small adjustments, and Mr. Schmitt followed their lead to the best of his ability, which was significant, truth be told, as he still delivered some of the Old World skill his name had promised. Much of the wainscotting and shelving was crafted in the soft, curving pine that in Anton's mind was the truest image of *Heimat,* and was stained a rich brown to honour childhood memories of hiking vacations along the winding trails of the Black Forest. The furniture he found in Kleinburg, north of Toronto, at a small European shop run by Polish brothers. The walls were done in broad strokes of white stucco, which revealed (if only to him) small random portraits that seemed to appear and disappear mysteriously from one day to the next. Plaques and mugs and photographs and other odds and ends completed the decoration of what had once been the rec room, and some of these items, in the gradual shifting and organizing that occurs in a home, eventually made their way upstairs to the main floor and the study, where he did his reading, and finally to the guest room on the second floor, where they sat or hung unseen and forgotten.

As winters and summers receded into the past it became easier for the Bölls to accept certain facts that once had challenged their notions of marriage. Each found it possible to make amends for failures, of which there were many, they saw now, especially on Anton's side. Nevertheless, they had reached an implicit under-standing that neither believed the other could be blamed for any general failures in their shared life. After everything, they were still together; and in the world they had moved through, making such offerings as this somehow seemed enough. That was one thing they agreed on, deep in the bones—that happiness, pleasure, fulfil-ment were goals suitable only for the naïve and foolish or extremely lucky. They were none of these. True, one memory always threatened to resurface, a dull presence somewhere at the back of the mind. That single impalpable grey area that shifted between them was always there when either cared to think about it, long after the initial cause of mourning had passed, and after the failure of family and time. But it was manageable in these later years and so distant that the simple business of living had become the priority, the racking up of decades, and the memory not much more than an indulgence to be endured during occasional bouts of melancholy.

She had long since stopped accompanying him on his trips to New York. These were not as frequent as they had been even as recently as five years before. But he still forced himself once a year at least, she thought more out of duty than anything else, and because he needed contact with the younger generation of his sort of people. And, of course, the anniversary itself. There was wide-spread interest in the Uranverein, the Uranium Club, and not just among those who had been or were still directly involved. He told her he could not just give up a life's work simply because he was getting old. She knew she had no right to demand a role in that life now, as she once might've, had a child come to exist between them. As he would have no right to force her out of her wordless pursuits. It was enough that for her he had brought his career to an end.

His travel had more often than not intensified as summer drew on, as her garden did. While he was away she dedicated herself to its demands and pleasures, its Neapolitan geometry and bursting trails of flower and colour. The ache and confusion she'd experienced as a young woman in love never touched her as it had back in their New York days, and she'd resolved never to feel again what she had felt in those early years: what she'd once thought of as love, a hope for the future, the burning heart, a focus on just one man, good as he might be. This younger self had exposed her to a solitude and torn loyalties she had never dreamt would be hers to suffer. It had been even more painful than the separation from her mother and father, because Stefano Danella's exit from her life had been voluntary. He had gone back. She had stayed. Her parents' vanishing had been a staggering act of black magic, and one, she thought, entirely beyond their control. But the loss of her family lived within her still, as did the loss of her only chance at happiness, and it terrified her to think that she was expected to endure a similar separation from the only person she had left.

She knew well the limitations of any relationship. The trick, she discovered, was working around them and somehow discovering how to fill the holes. She was equipped for solitude, having prepared for it over some forty years. All women did. So, when the time came for her husband to leave her, again and again and again, for a week or two, he left knowing that her life would not be put on hold while he tended to his own.

2

Anton stood next to a cedar at the top of the tobogganing slope. In the time it had taken Marlie to get into position at the top of the lane that led down the hill towards the snow ramp, it had grown colder. He wiggled his toes and stretched his thin bony fingers inside his gloves, imagining how cold her fingers must be, back inside her wet red mittens. The boy in front of her whooped and hollered as he jumped onto a cardboard box shaped like a flying carpet, and headed downhill at full tilt. She waited until he got to the bottom in a spilling pile of arms and legs, having missed the jump by a good three body-lengths. The girl then climbed aboard her toboggan and wrapped the rope around a fist in the manner of a rodeo rider, her body a small bundle of tension and excitement. He saw when she turned her head quickly to her friend that she was smiling radiantly, and one of the boys behind her gave a shove, possibly invited, possibly not, which started her going.

He watched her small hunched form cut through the mist of falling snow, and the small whorls of snow she left in her wake. He knew she would carry these moments with her, most likely without knowing it, for the rest of her life. Long after she had grown up and moved away, or possibly was still here in this town and caring for her own children, she would gather strength from these simple nights when the plan of her life seemed somehow to veer off its mark. She might feel the pure rush in her veins and the comfort of unguarded friendship and the crisp knot of security that was the rope gathered about one red mitten.

He did not see the collision coming, only the second sled's slanting path from the darker, less frequented south ridge, and that it would surely intersect with the toboggan now hurtling in a straight line towards the ramp. When the slight human snap registered in his muffled hat-covered ear half an instant after the two sleds actually met, he began down the hill before anyone else knew what had happened, and soon was kneeling in the snow at her side, holding her squarely by the shoulders. She was crying.

He touched her leg gently, feeling for the break. "Does it hurt here?" He moved down the thigh to the shin. "What about here?"

He turned to one of the older boys who had gathered around and told him to run across the street and have Mrs. McKaw phone for someone to come from the hospital, to say that a girl had broken a bone at the bottom of Jackson's Hill. He turned back to her and began to examine her right side, where she had been hit, more thoroughly. She was straining to hold her leg as blood ran down her face. The gash was just above the right eye, which Anton wiped clean with a handful of snow. The boy who'd piloted the other sled stood sullenly just out of arm's reach, the long pompom of his green-and-red hat snaked over his left shoulder. His eyebrows were raised up onto his forehead, alert and defensive.

Anton did not explain to the girl that he wasn't a medical doctor, not wanting to undercut the comfort she might take from this misconception. But for a moment he believed he'd done all that was possible, and a surge of well-being rose within him. He had calmed her. He had taken her fear and assured her this wound would be tended to, that she was in good hands.

He had seen worse than this, incomparably worse. He had seen children suffer and die. Yet a child's suffering during peacetime, it seemed, was somehow different, more pathetic, the crying panic surrounding scraped knees or bumped heads. He felt for the break and unwrapped his scarf from his neck and told one of the girl's friends to push it down firmly on the cut above her eye. By now she had stopped crying. He brushed the wet flakes from her face.

He reached into his pocket, then removed a packet of sugar and tore along its edge. "Whenever *I* hurt myself," he said, "my mother used to give me a lump of brown sugar. This always worked like a charm for me. It was a very special thing to have sugar when I was a boy. The hurt always went away. Every time."

The girl opened her mouth slightly, her eyes still shut.

With a shaking hand he poured a small pyramid of sugar onto her tongue. "All right. Now close. Close."

He called from the hospital to describe what had happened, and when he was through Sophie said that, yes, it had been a kind thing to do, staying with the girl, but had he forgotten what day it was? Bela and Eva would be arriving at any minute.

He resisted the desire he felt to stay on longer. Having presided over this situation and seen to it that the young girl was looked after, he wanted to see it through to the end. To consult with her thankful parents, as a real medical doctor might have done, to offer them his comforting reassurances. Then he heard the doorbell ring through the phone line.

Sophie held the receiver away from her mouth and called out, "Yes, coming."

He told her to stall a bit, he'd get a cab and be right home. But after he hung up, he walked up and down the corridors, dawdling.

At home, Anton found the three of them sitting and talking at the bridge table. He told his neighbours about the accident, then excused himself and went around the side of the house to fetch some split cedar, which didn't burn as well as he would've liked but happened to be the species of tree that had come crashing down in the backyard two years before, affording the Bölls years of free, if spotty, fires.

The Szabos were the first friends they'd made in Port Elizabeth, and were ten or so years younger than Anton and Sophie. They lived three doors up and shared with the Bölls a modest though constant appetite for cards, the occasional drink on the porch in summer and a large, childless home. Hungarian, they too had been forced from their country of origin. The principal difference between these two couples, however, was that whereas the Szabos' children had grown up and moved on, Anton and Sophie had never had any, something neither Bela nor Eva ever mentioned after that first time they met.

Bela—a man with a broad neck and strong hands, the owner of a small real-estate business run from a street-front office on Lakeshore Road—had said something about finally getting the kids packed off to college, and wasn't it nice, the peace and quiet. When he asked if they had any grandkids, Anton gave without hesitation his customary response to questions about children, which was that they'd never thought it fair to bring any more people into this world.

Anton knew to expect one of two reactions. The most common was a sad nod of agreement, as if the heartache, compounded by all the uncertainties, what with crazy politicians and rogue governments and bombs that could wipe out entire populations, could not possibly be worth it. The second was embarrassed silence followed by some stumbling exchange quickly remedied by a withdrawal to another, safer subject. Though the Szabos knew not to ask again, of course they had their theories, which they were never unkind or unfeeling enough to test. Anton and Sophie were grateful for this restraint, and gradually the respectful silence hovering over this most glaring absence drew the four friends closer together.

In summertime their weekly bridge game trailed off and was replaced by more wholesome, outdoorsy pursuits such as gardening, fishing and weekend outings. Winter occasioned more frequent meetings, since warmth was found only at home on these cold nights—playing over tea or port by the fireplace. It was a pleasant thing to sit with people who fast became old friends, the snow falling outside, the rules and familiar lamentations and exclamations and gaming strategies filling in for conversation whenever it became thin or unnecessary.

Three months had passed before Sophie discovered that their neighbours were also Jewish, and that they'd accepted, as she had, the opportunity to leave behind family, nation and tradition when they arrived in Canada after the uprising in 1956. Of course, she felt obliged to add that day, she was not technically Jewish: this was her father's heritage. But when they learned her mother had been Lutheran, the Szabos did not dismiss her out of hand, as so many others had in the past. Only non-Jews considered Sophie Jewish; those on her father's side had looked upon her dismissively, so it was almost with regret that she carried this mixed blood within her. Her father was embarrassed at his people's reaction, and by the time of her exodus from Austria, when she was put on the train bound for Hamburg, he realized she was conscious of having somehow brought shame upon them. Even so, she was condemned to suffer along with them.

Coming to Canada had introduced the Szabos and Sophie to a clean, secular world where blood and faith were not studied with such obsessive rigour. This made sense, of course—they said sadly, and frankly—if you looked at the history. There was a tinge of regret whenever they spoke of such matters, which was not often, since they preferred to concentrate on positive things; and that regret seemed to grow as time went on. But one demonstrably good aspect of the past, they agreed, was that it *was* past. Gone.

Sophie, in particular, did not relish looking back on the old life. She had been alone in Carroll Gardens during the latter stages of the war, moving through the streets with haunting anonymity until she met Stefano. Every afternoon she passed by the neighbourhood shops of the second- and third-generation Italians,

stopping on hot days in the shade of lowered awnings to cool herself and take new English words into her mouth like the fruits
picked from the stalls on Court Street. The story of forced depor-
tation was her daily burden, one she had shared with no one before
Stefano. That would have cheapened it somehow, she thought,
putting it in the ears of strangers. It remained her private story
until she met the man who had seen what she had seen, someone
who felt the paralysis of the mass European exodus, the scattering
of families.

Anton had written many times from New Mexico that it would
all turn one day and he would get them back to where they
belonged, which, for her, meant Linz. Back to her old life and the
violin shop with its wood smells and big front window. But she
was abandoned in her solitude because of the work he had been
obliged to pursue, leaving for her only this solitary life and this
unpronounceable language. She wrote letters and posted them
into a void. At first not knowing they would ever be received.

America was a new world rife with pride, and it was as lacking
in compassion as it was in recognizable faces or voices. She walked
through her neighbourhood, moving between crates and boxes
and throngs of people speaking their different languages. Women
leaned suspiciously in doorways, holding dazed children by the
shoulder. She formulated her means of escape like a prisoner
dreaming of the outside. She waited for the moment she could
welcome the man she had barely got to know in the six months
before he was transferred, kissing the red desert skin of his face
and asking him that first night, close to his sun-blistered ear, when
they could leave this place once and for all. When real life would
begin again.

She'd been washing dishes when she heard the announcement that
a new type of bomb had been detonated over Japan. As soon as the

announcer interrupted the program she'd been listening to, *Fred Layer's Classics Hour,* she felt herself prepare for the shock. Somehow she knew what was to come, and that her husband had been involved. It was almost a physical sensation, as if he'd tapped her on the shoulder. Suddenly she knew that this was what his life had been moving towards, and that this day would hold one part of him hostage for the rest of their lives. She dried her hands on her apron and stepped back from the sink, unfocussed her eyes and concentrated on the voice speaking from the radio. She knew Anton would already have been informed. Of course. With her incomplete understanding of English she was able to follow most of the news bulletin, though some words were new, like *atomic,* and nearly meaningless. *Radiation* sounded too much like a mix of *radio* and *nation* to carry the menace it seemed meant to suggest. She understood *explosion* and *twenty tons of TNT,* and *Japs.* All these words she had heard too many times before.

As she dried her soapy hands on an apron, trying to translate the new words, she wondered if they might signify the end of the war and a return to Europe, might initiate the same train journey that had brought her here, only in reverse, so she could begin the search for her parents. When scheduled programming resumed she turned to the open kitchen window, still shocked, still thinking that this was her husband's life, and looked out to the street and saw a man making a delivery to DeLuca's. The meat truck was idling at the corner.

The man—wearing a full-body apron with brown blood-stains down the front—made a spirited gesture to the sky when he saw her standing at the window. He might have heard, too, Sophie thought. Everyone would have. The whole world would know by now. Still unknown, though, was how the bomb touched his life, too, how deeply it reached directly into the heart of this war bride living alone in the small apartment on the second floor.

He stepped down from the curb, stopped and squinted as if to look more closely, then crossed the street and peered up at Sophie through her window. He then drew his hand over his face, seeming to indicate that something was wrong. Believing that he needed help, she hurried out onto the sidewalk and took him by the hand and guided him back upstairs. She picked the few words of English— "The face is a red bird!"—out of his excited tumble of language.

When Sophie finally understood that it was her own face he meant, she crossed the living room and looked in the mirror that hung in the hallway. A red shadow, as if of a large butterfly, rested on her nose, its wings extending over her cheekbones. She could see now how it might resemble a bird, though when she tried to brush it off the shadow, whether of bird or butterfly, was not prepared to move. The rash, if that's what it was, caused no pain. But it was so plainly there, and red. . . .

She ran her fingertips over the skin to feel if her face had suffered any swelling, but could detect no difference. The man came up behind her and pulled her hand away from the rash. It would not serve to touch it, he had probably thought; it might be catching.

At length Sophie ushered the young man out the door. "Yes, hospital," she said. "I will go to the hospital." But once alone again she decided to wait this out, to watch in hopes that the rash would subside of its own accord. And next morning, standing before the mirror, she found the winged creature had vanished without a trace.

Not so much the religion as the old rituals were honoured by Sophie and her Hungarian friends. They were enacted more regularly now in the Szabo household, and more recently in Sophie's domain of the Böll home. On Fridays they shared the Shabbat, lingering over childhood foods; they clumsily mouthed, *She'ma yisroel, adonai eloheinu, adonai ehad,* remembered almost perfectly, nearly mechanically after decades; or, on occasion, spoke the first words of the prayer for the dead, *Yiskadel v'yiskadash sh'may rabbah.* These foods and prayers were as familiar and comforting to her as they were foreign and dangerous. This was home and exile spoken in the same breath. Bela and Eva accompanied her—and also, marginally, Anton, who sat in respectful silence as they spoke their prayers—on this return to the deeply confused realm of her past, which at the same time moved her closer to some hopeful future when her strange alienation from these traditions might become clarified, no longer tinged by the duplicity of her youth.

But Anton did believe that this partial rebirth of faith was one of the small blessings they'd found in coming here. Sophie had discovered in these people the chance to reclaim something she was forced to abandon as a child, no matter how difficult that reclamation should prove.

After a meal the four would sometimes discuss a certain susceptibility they all felt towards introspection, a looking backwards—something they all worried about, despite or because of their stated wish to stay positive. It was age, they agreed, and persistent memories of what had been lost in Europe. During these conversations over coffee Anton was careful to remember his place. He knew he had not suffered as they had. His loss had been of a different sort. He had chosen to leave his mother behind, with a full awareness of what often happened to the relatives of intellectuals who fled the country. Sacrifices had been required of them all, but his had been deliberate and foregone. He did have a choice. Still, he knew he was not judged at this table. His friends knew the outlines of his history, that he had almost certainly caused his mother's death in choosing to leave his post at the Kaiser-Wilhelm Institute at Dahlem. But that was a sacrifice for a greater good. To help end the world's suffering. They knew him as a refugee of conscience, not of religion or race, "and that," he said one evening as he returned the sugar spoon to its bowl, "is the free man's worst fear. The decision is his own to make. What if he chooses incorrectly, or for the wrong reason? He must live with the consequences."

"But he knows it's his choice," Bela said. "It is easier to live with guilt than with nothing at all."

3

Sometimes Anton watched the old films he'd brought back from the war, which he kept in a sailor's trunk in the shed. At night, after walking through his small patch of tomatoes and peppers, he'd seal the door behind him, blinking slowly like a man descending into a cold pool; waiting for his body to adjust to the dark, he would stand heavily, expectantly, in the midst of the silence that surrounded him, breathing in the odours of wood and sod and fertilizers. He observed the small squares of light falling through the dirt-stained windows to reflect off the collection of brown bottles gathered on the opposite shelf, which contained the developer and fixer he used to clean his old films and prevent their disintegration. Sophie's gardening tools hung against one wall—spades and hoes and work gloves and a green plastic hose coiled like a sleeping snake. On the plywood wall above his workbench, needle-nose pliers and screwdrivers and hammers sat snug in their Magic Marker outlines. Under a white sheet on a small table beside the developing table and the sink sat the Bell & Howell projector. On these nights he might remove the sheet and hang it delicately on two nails over his tools. Then he'd open the large trunk under the window and slip into the past.

When the good weather came, after Sophie went to bed, Anton sometimes stayed out in the garden, facing the lake, sipping his melted ice water and waiting for sleep to come. Sometimes he wanted to ignore the films and instead walk along the yard's twisting trails, marking time. Avoiding those memories housed in the shed. He found this helped, especially on top of his usual walk through town after supper. But that dark path he travelled, like most things he did, sent him back to his Hiroshima or New Mexico days, to moments and desires like details taken from a large canvas, then expanded on, enlarged by the gaze of memory.

One night he saw an old Pueblo Indian he'd once known down there—the only people who truly belonged in that world—step out from the darkness and point along a narrow path.

"Yes," Anton said, smiling.

Then the man was gone.

Anton imagined the simplicity and ignorance of the world as it might once have been before all their atom-splitting machines and blue-grey industry and military secrets arrived at that place. He had seen the landscape transformed into a graveyard of junked cars and trucks, airborne flakes of burning red rust tingeing the winds a soft swirling pink. Smashed liquor-stained bottles sparkled in the sun, dulled and polished smooth within weeks by drifting sand. Where century plants had grown, stinking privies had been erected, one for whites, another for blacks, wafting their stink over the land. This segregated community where democracy marched onwards against fascism.

Often he lost himself there, eyes almost shut as he wandered along the garden paths; and when he stopped and focussed himself, looking through the dark, he wondered what he might find before him. It was a sort of trick he played on himself. A small adventure to be enjoyed on a warm summer night as he beckoned sleep. Sometimes he'd step off the herringbone brick path and notice a shape that he hadn't seen before, in that particular light, at that precise angle. It was a maze he never seemed to manoeuvre himself out of the same way twice. He saw things his wife had never seen or meant to be seen; and later, when he told her what he'd encountered, she would laugh and tell him he should be sleeping at such hours instead of lurking about the property like some prowler.

On occasion it occurred to him, depending on the strength of that night's memories, there might be more to these shapes than the small amusement he gained from them. He wondered if there was something to be learned about his wife. Not that she was expressing herself in any overt or defiant manner, or to any specific purpose. But he did wonder how she'd come to fill their yard with small animals of all sorts and sizes, and what possible motivations she possibly could be driven by. He expected the garden didn't actually possess the complexity of shapes he imagined while he was out here waiting for sleep, but certainly it had long since passed the point of an eccentric hobby. Visitors—the few they had, mostly colleagues from the plant, before he left—were generally charmed, impressed and confused, usually in that order. Who could blame them? What his wife had wrought was strange in a benevolent, puckish fashion that suggested she'd always been rather different from what he'd believed her to be, a notion he found both comforting and disturbing and wildly contradictory. It was like discovering in your wife's closet, beneath shoe boxes and old suitcases, several unpublished and dusty manuscripts whose heroines, you discover upon reading, serve to remind you of the joyful girl you once knew and thought you'd lost forever.

Was there something she meant to tell him? But if that were the case, wouldn't she say it directly? Ask, or even demand, what it was she wanted? Anton himself never asked her what, if anything, this population of odd shapes and animals might signify beyond the obvious interest in plants, the simple pleasure of dirt under her fingernails and the continuation of the soapstone sculpting she'd devoted herself to in the early years. Perhaps it was merely her means of occupying herself. But, however much he wondered about those leafy green surfaces in the solitude of night, the next morning he never put his questions to her, because the garden, in daylight, was different, and so was his need to understand.

On warm days, before breakfast, Anton and Sophie often walked into Port Elizabeth on an errand. Usually there was milk or coffee to pick up, or the papers, but when nothing was needed they sometimes went anyway, with no purpose other than to stretch their legs of a morning. They walked together along the main street, all three blocks of it lined on both sides by small family businesses; at one end stood the Anglican church, at the corner of Lakeshore and Elm, and at the other, the red brick Lutheran church with the lovely roses out front. Smack dab in the middle they would pass Bela's office, and at least once a week they saw him hurrying across the street juggling coffee and Danish to open for the day, and they'd wave or call out.

Sometimes these walks served as an opportunity for Anton to talk about people he'd met down in New York, or discuss his ideas for a conference he was set to attend.

"Yes," she would say, "yes," thinking to herself that he was too old for all this, they were both too old to be running around in circles. *Does a man like this ever rest? Can there ever be peace and quiet in this house?* But she knew he would never be able to rest, given his expertise and the cachet still attached to his name.

She would have liked him by her side more often, hoping that perhaps there was time yet to thin the lasting grey fog that had settled between them. But what was the use? She had long since relinquished any right to demand. She had foolishly pursued her own life, she thought, foolishly and necessarily, and now she could say nothing. She believed she had denied herself that right.

Nor could she help but admire his devotion to his work, no matter how deeply she had been hurt by it. This was his life, after all. She believed that his inability to give it up was due in part to his belief that once he stopped he would never be able to start again. It was an old man's fear that stirred him, so he went on not in spite of his age but because of it. It was his fear of stopping forever that drove what he called the restless pursuit of his principles.

And so they would walk through town on a spring or summer day, their soft German cadences trailing behind them like footprints leading to no specific destiny, and she would resolutely take his hand in hers, a gesture that demonstrated they were together after all, that this was the main thing, despite principle, despite memory, despite failing health. Despite the things that would not go away.

And they never did. The stupid and meaningless along with the poignant and terrifying. They never seemed willing to leave him, or Sophie. It was as if neither of them had been able to escape the shell of that burnt city. The memories played themselves out over and over again under their sleeping eyelids like a looped news-reel: his version, the days spent there; hers, the days she had been denied. She knew it was her desire to understand what he had seen there that destroyed what they had. The more she tried, the deeper his resentment became. It was an impossibility.

With the passing of years it began to seem that their lives had happened not to them but to other people. It was as if they had been privy to the intimate details of strangers, the hopes and failures, the sideways glances and regrets, as well as the profound loves. Such was the curious bending of memory, for, when they did remember, it was never the event or memory in question they saw or felt but simply a snapshot of themselves from that time, posed, impersonal, young and stiff and unformed.

Anton was always more interested in his legacy, in any case, which for him seemed more a question of the future, strangely, than it did of the past. Even into his seventh decade he felt his work wasn't yet completed, and in 1979, on a cloudy afternoon in May, when he delivered his last talk to a crowded lecture hall at the New School—a consciously humble farewell made with no mention of his greatest achievement—his heart had been filled with a dizzying sense of pride and sorrow. Pride that he had been here as long as he had; and sorrow that he was leaving. That speech was one of his best, he remembered, possessed of the proper balance of humour and gravity, dignity and warmth.

He was going north, he'd said, at the behest of his wife. As a man who had devoted his life to science, and to the discovery of the hidden magic of the physical world, he felt it was time to concentrate on perhaps the deepest mystery of all, which was the chain that bound human hearts. With that he'd wished his students luck, folded his notes and stood for a moment before the lectern as the assembly rose in unison, an entire hall of glowing faces, and showered him with a rousing ovation during the length of which he recalled, with a certain satisfying nostalgia and very few regrets, the twenty-seven-year sweep of time he'd spent here, humbled, deeply humbled, and alive. Standing there, he saw the image he'd had as a boy of Moses preparing for his crossing of the Sinai. His retirement might prove to be his greatest challenge yet, he thought, a sort of soul cleansing.

"Yes, the mystery of the human heart," he said. "Isn't that, more than any science, the greatest mystery of them all?"

Smiling, he bowed when the clapping finally fell to a thinning rhythm of individual hands, then looked up into the rows of seats one last time, to the young, departing faces, to the signs of hope and ambition he had helped inspire, and left the stage. And as he departed he was braced by the memory of his first leave-taking, in 1940, when he'd walked out of his hotel on Rue de l'Odéon one July morning, and forever left behind Erich Bagge and the other scientists from the Kaiser-Wilhelm Institute who'd come to oversee

the reconstruction of the Paris cyclotron. That morning, before
the sun rose, he'd met Varian Fry, the American journalist in
charge of getting intellectuals out of Europe and into America.
Over the next three weeks, he moved south between safe houses
and finally, in early September, he carried his secret over the Pyrenees into Spain.

The belief that he was preparing again, at this late stage, at the
age of sixty-two, for yet another momentous and most probably
final change filled him with a renewed and powerful sense of
courage. He would devote himself, as he had not done in decades,
to the conundrums of the human heart. Isn't that what this was?
His last and most enduring challenge, the guarded and cautious
heart of his wife. This was his resolution. It would prove a long
desert crossing, but he and Sophie would make it through to the
other side—blistered and limping, perhaps, but absolutely and
fully together.

Emiko

I had been taught to believe that the American doctors had seen something in my condition that could be treated. Nothing more, nothing less. It was not me they were caring for but the curious medical condition my skin represented for them. By the age of fifteen I was already used to the idea that I was not special, so this knowledge did not disturb me. I was accustomed to the doctors and their tests, and to the whispered taunts that followed me wherever I went. *"Oni,"* the other children called me, something like "ogre" or "blackface." I cannot say I blame them; ignorance and fear had made them treat me this way. I might even have reacted the same way if the shoe had been on the other foot. But it was not.

So I was a young girl chosen because I could be turned into a favourable statistic. For me the chances were better than for many others. Girls with scars worse than my own were ignored because they were beyond repair. As disfigured as I was, my scars were still within their limited grasp of medicine. I was not far from believing that there was a science to distinguishing who fell within the acceptable limits of ugly and who did not. Yet I never complained. Look at me, I thought to myself. I made it. I was going to America to get my new face. Wasn't that good enough? I was one of the fortunate. I should be thankful, I thought. A person misses a flight and when the plane crashes into the ocean she thinks there is more to it than blind luck. Not me.

I think sometimes about how I might've turned out if I hadn't been selected as one of the twenty-five girls to be sent to America for reconstructive surgery. Sometimes even now I see myself as an old crone sitting alone at a half-opened, soot-covered window on the outskirts of some dingy Japanese suburb, a lifetime of suppers for one in a cramped one-bedroom apartment chiselled out of a bomb survivor's pension. I think I always knew too well what life held for a woman like the one I had narrowly avoided becoming. The constant invocation of courage had soon become a numbing refrain. This was who we were. We would accept our lot in life. Once beautiful, radiant children, we now were fairy-tale monsters best stoned and run out of our city. The only possibility of escape, the route back into the world, was in the care of men none of us knew and had no reason to trust, who lived and worked their scalpels somewhere on the other side of the ocean.

My grandfather, the one person I left behind, told me he'd rarely met a foreigner he felt he could trust in all his many years, not even when, as a young man, he went to England to study medicine, where he'd met many dozens. But he said he trusted even less than those foreign doctors what the future held for a little girl who looked like me. Though that might sound like a terrible thing to say to a fifteen-year-old, I had lived almost ten years with that face by then. I understood the truth about being ugly and in constant pain. No one could look at the scars on my face without being overcome with revulsion. At the time I hated my grandfather for saying that. I also knew he was right.

We were expected to provide the small bodies required for repair, and the time this repair would take. Nothing more. We were told to prepare for eighteen months. By then we were used to the pain in our bodies, and what worried me more was being over there. The doctors who had conducted the primary examinations lacked the brusque manners of the Japanese doctors we were familiar with. But I also knew they were special emissaries and, as such, must be kind and respectful. All of Japan was watching them. For a brief time, before leaving, we were in the Japanese newspapers. The American doctors spoke respectfully of Japanese medicine and the practitioners who'd cared for us to that point. Careful not to offer offense, they said they had made tremendous advances that would be able to help us. But I knew I could not gain a true understanding of the place they came from based on their behaviour in our country or what they said in our newspapers.

The night I was told I'd been chosen for the program I lay in bed beside my grandfather in our partially reconstructed home, trying to imagine the new face they would give me. I was still very young, and very silly, I know, suddenly fearing that I might end up looking like one of the foreigners who had done this to me. I did not have any firm notion regarding race then; but the thought of becoming like them, with their clumsy size, their aggressiveness, troubled me. I did not want to look different, only how I used to look. I didn't have a clear idea of the nature of the surgery, simply that I was supposed to feel privileged to have been chosen over so many other girls. All I could really be sure of was more pain in my small body, more bandages, more time in the hospital. During the interviews they conducted after the initial examinations, they had talked of recutting and grafting. They explained what awaited me, but I cannot say I understood clearly. Even to my grandfather's ears much of what they said, in translation, was strange-sounding, almost impossible. These were groundbreaking techniques, developed in America. But soon enough, words I had never heard before—*cicatricial ectropion, split skin grafting, defatting*—would become familiar to me, whereas now they seemed as odd and terrible as the monstrous young girls they would be applied to.

The foreigners explained to my grandfather and me how they would open up the left eye again, which had been closed by the large flat keloid scar that had formed rapidly there, and the methods they would use to remove healthy skin from my thighs and the right side of my back to replace the dead skin on my face. I knew nothing about these procedures. What if they rebuilt me in a way they wanted, I wondered that night, rather than as I wanted? I feared they would turn me into someone else, perhaps for their own purpose. In my mind I saw myself stepping into another girl's skin, a pink and puffy sort of skin that sagged horribly about the ankles like a baggy pair of pants. I listened to my grandfather snoring through the wall. I wondered if he would recognize me when I came home, or, for that matter, if anyone would.

That night I imagined my own death. This in itself was not unusual for me. I had often wondered about the place where my parents and brother had gone, and whether it might not be in everyone's best interests for me to hasten my own departure. But that night I went there, actually *into* that place where I believed them to be, and saw that my parents and little brother did not recognize me when it came time for us to meet. Their ghostly shapes walked blindly past, unable to see their daughter, his sister, with her new American face. For the Obon festival in July my family had always offered prayers to our recent dead. Now I knew I would never be recognized on that day. It was, I thought, a fate worse than death. I buried my face in my pillow and cried. I could not go through with it. As ugly as I was, I was not prepared to lose what little I had left, which was the chance of meeting up again with my family.

The next day I told Grandfather of my fear. He thought carefully before speaking, then looked at me squarely. "Do you think your parents and your brother would know you now, with a face like that?"

One of the few things that remained for me before I left for America was the duty I felt toward my grandfather, who seemed to be aging as rapidly as I was growing up. The need to take care of him, despite my own physical limitations, gave me my strongest sense of purpose. With him I knew what was expected; it was a last piece of my past life. I knew how to prepare his meals and boil his laundry, the same way my mother had done. Only I knew how to ease the pain in his knees, which grew more stiff with arthritis by the day. These were the last certainties in my life, as insignificant as they might sound to someone who has not lost so much in so short a time, and without them surely I would have failed to get through those days.

I also knew the broken maze of our neighbourhood and the one oak tree that had somehow survived, near the vegetable stand where my mother used to shop. I knew some of the schoolchildren who'd been away from the city on the day the bomb fell, on the Family Plan Evacuation. These were the ones who called after me in fear and disgust, "*Oni, oni,* go back to your cave." I knew their names less well than I knew their faces, each just as perfect and beautiful as mine once had been. I was unable to speak with them because of my shame, and because of the names they called me. One day I mustered enough courage to attempt to join in the game they were playing, which was called Special Train, after the many spacious railway cars reserved for the occupation forces. In Special Train the girl conductor seated only those pretty enough to board. Of the group gathered at the base of the small wooden crate she stood on, I was the only girl she would not permit on board. That they would've ended up like me, or worse, but for their relatives in the countryside, did not matter to them. I was different from them, and they would never let me forget.

Mostly I knew the other girls in the Red Cross Hospital where I stayed before my grandfather came to take me back to what remained of our home. I had dreamed of that day for years. But when it finally came I was sad to leave the girls I'd come to know as friends. We promised to see one another as often as we could. At first I visited once a week. But eventually even my grandfather explained that I would have to move my life forward from this point; now that I was out in the world again it was not a good idea to associate with those girls. I should find normal friends, "girls like yourself," he said. But I never knew if he truly believed I could ever be normal again, or if he said this simply to lift my confidence. For a short time I was blinded to my condition by his ambition for me. Once I returned to school, my classmates took it upon themselves to remind me definitively that I was not like them and never would be. Those were also things I would always know.

There were many other things I had known before the war that in America were no longer of any use to me. I was taken aback by the most mundane of discoveries. To my surprise there was something here called a washing machine. Even the nightly ritual of knee-rubbing—the time I would devote to easing my grandfather's chronic rheumatism—was forgotten. My first host father was a young man in no need of my hot-water bottle and strong hands. The same was true of my cooking. The food I prepared on rare occasions for my American family, for certain Japanese festivals, was consumed politely, in small quantities if at all, then pushed aside. Not even my well-rehearsed sense of gratitude and deference meant much in my new home.

Every Sunday I was expected to attend church. The day of our first visit, once everyone had taken his seat, the pastor introduced me to the congregation. My host mother gently nudged me and I stood, briefly, and bowed to the assembled. Someone started clapping, which then set off everyone else. I blushed and sank into my seat while my host mother took my hand and smiled and kissed the good side of my face. I had prepared myself for such public demonstrations, knew this had not been an attempt to embarrass me. It was meant to welcome me into their community. I was told back in Japan that such public displays must be endured if we were to fit in with these people, whether we understood them or not. I was respectful and silent when the pastor spoke, and gave him my full attention. Of course I could make no sense of his words, but that didn't matter. Afterward we stood on the front lawn of the Church of the Holy Trinity, accepting everyone's best wishes.

Even though I grasped so very little during those first few months, at the worst of times there was always one thing I was sure of, the one advantage I'd brought with me: the silence I had perfected and used to protect myself. I did not show pain. I would not show pain. There are forms of discomfort the body grows familiar with, and I recognized them all. By now I knew my damaged skin as intimately as I did my old bombed-out neighbourhood back home. It was forever scarred and blackened, so that bombing it all over again would hardly make any difference. Somehow it never smelled right, and visitors no longer cared to stop and admire it as they once had. They could punish those old houses, and the bruised and scarred little girl living in the deepest and darkest of its basements, only so much. Ultimately it would not make any difference. I would continue on as resolutely as she always had, the world be damned.

This silence, this refusal to give in, was my sole tactic in this unknown world. I could not have survived the reconstruction of my face, or the enormous tests America presented to me, without it. Perhaps I was a strange child. Silence came out of the cracks for me. How can I say this? I saw it everywhere. I saw its shapes in the large elm tree outside the bedroom window of the house of my first host family, of which I had six over those eighteen months. I saw it pushing purple-and-black animals through the sky like ghosts from the past. Sometimes it came in the cloud shapes and tree shadows I stepped over on the sidewalk. Always it appeared as pictures before my eyes. I saw things. I thought this was a consequence of the act of drawing that by then had become for me more a need than a game. Often the quiet came at night, when the refrigerator fell still and my host parents went to their bedroom and I was more alone than I thought I could bear. I would close my eyes and wait with a pounding in my head, balling the bedsheet in my fists, and out from the cracks in the wall, or perhaps through the window that looked over the yard, a silent calm would appear to me, a feeling of peace not rightly my own, and it would sit like an old friend at the edge of the bed and wait there reassuringly until I fell asleep.

I learned that I possessed this advantage early on, back home, when my brother and I were still in the hospital together. After his death the silence that fell over the ward threatened to overwhelm me. I had no one to rely on except Grandfather, but he could not come to visit at night, and he could not come to visit me now. It was a difficult time to be alone, so I learned to live without fear in the midst of that silence because I realized it would always be there, taunting me, unless I found some way to welcome it, which finally I did in the form of my drawing. I was like a girl who convinces herself that a cut on her finger doesn't really hurt at all. I found that if I drew it it went away. If I looked directly into the eyes of the monster under my bed, it too went away. That is how I looked at things in those days, because there was nothing else to rely on. Especially when the men brought me into the operating room and started putting my face back together.

Initially I did not believe I would ever get my face back. The day we arrived in New York City I was more doubtful than ever. After our reception at the airport we boarded a bus and drove down Fifth Avenue, the rain streaking in a diagonal line across the window until the bus came to a stop, waiting for a light. Gazing outward in wonder, I turned my head at a slight angle to avoid touching my scar to the cool glass. As the motor fell to a soft rumble, I saw a group of black men, a thing I'd never seen before, standing in a loose circle around a cardboard table. One of these men wore a wool hat with turned-up earflaps. Small beads of silver rain sparkled like mercury over the cloth, and I watched with amazement as his dark fingers darted through the air. It was an image of exotic and frightening beauty. He looked in the direction of the bus idling at the intersection, flanked by a police escort. It was simply a glance, not even focussed at first, just a movement of the head—then we locked eyes. In school back home we were taught about the shameful injustices suffered in America by the poor, and the Negro, and I felt certain there was something prophetic about this first encounter. I saw my own fate running parallel to his. I saw his astonishment, the shock in his eyes like a flaring match, and the strange articulation of his facial muscles. I was the object of this surprise, as he was the object of mine. I painted him quickly in my imagination, as if capturing a bird in flight, trying to hold on to that astonishment. His eyes moved over me, and in his own way I knew he was making his own picture of the strange little girl with that dark shadow on her face.

The gears ground as the bus started slowly to life again and the man turned back to his circle. I watched his shoulders, my neck turning with the receding scene until he was gone. Once he was out of sight I returned my attention to the silver puddles in the street and the bright American flags snapping in the wind as they hung from the building façades, as if from the bows of ships.

Despite our exhaustion there was much conversation among the girls on the bus that morning. Giddy and nervous, we talked quickly and quietly and called hushed exclamations of surprise to one another. Even though Helen Yokoyama, our interpreter and guardian, had grown up in San Francisco, she seemed encouraged by our curiosity and high spirits and tried to answer what questions she could about this city she'd never lived in. At first I tried to listen to her speak, but there was too much to see.

Earlier that day our plane had landed at Mitchell Air Force Base on Long Island. I had emerged haggard and groggy along with the other twenty-four girls, aged between eleven and twenty-two

years, after a five-day trip from Japan via Wake and Johnston
Islands, Hawaii and San Francisco. Some of us wore scarves to hide
our scars. Unsure and shaking in the chill early morning, I wove
my fingers together and looked down at the tarmac. I knew only a
few words of this language. Already I missed where I had come
from, and the only person I had left there.

The cameras had gathered around us before we were fully off
the plane. We were used to a certain amount of attention. I had
expected perhaps the same level of interest on the part of the
newspapers here as in Japan, but what greeted us that morning was
nothing I could have imagined. Dozens of reporters clustered at
the bottom of the gangway, asking questions and taking pictures,
their flashbulbs reflecting off the shiny tarmac like lightning bolts.
Dr. Barsky and the others from the hospital greeted us all with welcoming handshakes. The reporters continued snapping photographs and hurling questions through the rain as we waited to
offer our small hands, questions that Reverend Yasaka, the organ-
izer of the program, attempted to answer.

"Why only girls, Reverend?"

"The decision was made," he answered.

"Is it something Japanese? Are there no boys who need this care
in Japan?"

"There are many. More than you can imagine."

That evening, one of the doctors hosted a reception for the new
arrivals. All the Americans were dressed very finely. We wore the
secondhand dresses that the Salvation Army had provided for us
earlier that day. Unlike the clothing we were used to wearing, these
dresses were clean and unripped and close to the right size for our
ages. My first dress was the colour of a blue sky, with white trim,
tracing the hem- and necklines like clouds. Turning slowly, I
admired it in the mirror in the community-centre basement.
Hardly any of us could remember the last time we'd seen clothing
this pretty. But Sachiko, one of the younger girls, had unknowingly

been given a dress whose polka dots mirrored the scars on her body. She became upset and began to cry as she stood in front of the mirror I was sharing with her. We exchanged dresses, and though the new one didn't fit as well as the blue dress, I was happy to have it.

Before that night I had never seen rich people. All twenty-five of us stood to one side of the room and waited to be told what to do. Some of the women, even those with long gloves pulled to the elbow, tried to talk with us through Reverend Yasaka or Helen Yokoyama. One woman pointed to me, with her eyes more than anything else, through the crowd of cocktail drinkers. She smiled as if an idea had just then popped into her head. I'd seen her talking with the reverend and Bernard Simon, a surgeon from Mount Sinai who had volunteered his services to the project. I lowered my eyes, as was natural for a girl to do, afraid that I somehow had offended the woman. I wondered if she'd noticed that my dress, too small, made me look large and awkward and my figure prematurely developed. I attempted to wish away the interest she seemed to have taken in me, but in a moment they were at my side and she began to speak.

She had large teeth and blond hair; very beautiful, I thought. She was polite enough to look directly into my good eye. I was fearful, though, having no idea why she had found me of any interest. With the help of the reverend, she began by asking me about our journey to America.

"Do you like America?"

"I have not had much opportunity to see America," I said, after her question was translated for me.

"But do you like America. Americans?"

I smiled and nodded, as I had been told to do when I didn't know how to answer a question.

"Do you know what television is?"

"Yes." I nodded.

"Have you ever *seen* television?"

"No."

"Not back home, either?" she said.

"I am sorry."

She touched my shoulder lightly and smiled, then she turned and walked away.

The next morning, the reverend and Helen came to the hotel and told me there was a TV program in Los Angeles that was interested in our story. I asked why these people should like to know the story of a group of deformed and hideously ugly girls. I was sitting on my bed. He sat beside me. "Don't talk like that, Emiko," he said. "Show respect. The Americans can be people of compassion. They can be like us. Many of them regret what has happened. Almost ten years have passed now. There are people who want to help ensure that the bomb will never be used again."

"But it was used," I said.

"Yes. It was. But we can help show people that it is a terrible weapon. We can show people what it does."

I said nothing.

"They want to help us," he said, "by raising money that will be used during our stay. They will give us the opportunity to tell America our story. Once our story is told they will never use the bomb again. Takako has already agreed."

Takako had sat next to me on the plane, and we'd shared a room during our stopover in Hawaii. She'd been visiting relatives in Hiroshima when they dropped the bomb on us. I liked her and thought she would be a good person to visit Los Angeles with, despite the bad leg which forced her to walk at an exceedingly slow pace, and to sit and rest often. Although the surgeons could do nothing about her smashed leg, I envied Takako for the fundamental difference between us. She had gone alone to visit her uncle and aunt in Hiroshima, which meant her parents were still alive in her hometown, and when I considered I decided I would give up both legs, not just one, for the same to be true for me.

"Yes," I said, bowing. "I will help."

I didn't know how far away Los Angeles was, on the other side of the country, back in the direction we'd just travelled. I was sixteen now and, though severely scarred, I still had the energy and boundless curiosity of any girl that age. By then the burns on my face and back did not limit my freedom of movement. Of course I could smile only out of one side of my mouth, but my general mobility had not been affected. This was a time when such a long trip was a small sacrifice in exchange for television. Although I knew only a few words of English—learned from my grandfather, who had picked up some of the language during his stay in England, and from the postwar radio program called *Kamu Kamu Eigo*—I believed this might be the reason I was chosen. We were mostly uneducated girls with no foreign languages or particular skills between us, myself included.

I had touched the real ocean, not just the bay on which my hometown was situated, only once before in my life, barely four days before, on our stopover in Hawaii. However excited I was at the prospect of doing so again, I chose not to reveal this, because I knew that the trip was considered an important job—though I did not yet have a clear picture of what it entailed—and that it must not be sidetracked by a young girl's whim to gaze upon the ocean that was her link to home.

The day we landed in Los Angeles was beautiful and warm, unlike the one we'd left behind back in New York. A man from the television show greeted us at the arrivals gate, holding a cardboard sign spelling out "Yasaka." Without acknowledging me or Takako, he shook the reverend's hand and tipped his hat to Helen, then led us to his car. I couldn't understand any of the conversation he carried on with the reverend and Helen. Instead I watched the grey highway and the speeding new cars driving on either side of us and wondered where were the Japanese my grandfather had told me about—those who had tried to convince the people here not to harm our city. It seemed now that those people had been no more than an invention of his imagination. I asked no questions, because none was asked of me.

It was during that ride, however, that Takako and I began to guess something more regarding our involvement here. We had been invited in order to help raise money for our stay in America, but exactly what our role should be was yet to be explained to us. Helen sat in the back seat with us, leaning forward slightly as she listened to the reverend and the driver speaking. Occasionally the driver looked at me and Takako in the rearview mirror. His smile was embarrassed and uncomfortable.

We sat quietly with our hands in our laps. Barely able to contain myself, I shuffled my feet on the floorboards and fiddled nervously with the pleats in my dress. I raised my eyes from time to time and saw the flash of the driver's teeth in the mirror, and his pink cheeks bouncing in time to the bumps in the hard road beneath us, and the cars speeding past outside the windows. I wondered if his eyes could tell me anything more. He spoke very quickly. I thought even Helen, who was from here, must have difficulty understanding him. Takako and I exchanged glances.

"Enough of that," Helen said. "We will be there soon."

I still did not have a clear understanding of just where it was we were going. I could see Takako was as eager as I was. We smiled and rolled our eyes and shook our heads, staring into our laps, still full of disbelief. We could not comprehend the gravity of what was slowly dawning on us. After Helen returned her attention to the conversation in the front seat, Takako spoke behind her back in a whisper, but I understood perfectly. I shook my head with a clipped motion that was meant not to be detected by the adults. *No, no. Not us. They would not put such ogres as us on the television.*

2

Their names were Mr. and Mrs. Forrester. Sitting fully dressed at the edge of the pool in the backyard of their home in Harristown, outside New York City, I tried to understand what my first host mother and father were saying to me. I looked along the row of houses that faced the yard, some with their own sheets of perfect blue water, others with oddly shaped pagodas and winding paths, and an American-style rock garden of a type I had never seen. I regarded the glint of sun on the grass beside the cement patio and looked down through the water and remembered that it was impolite not to look into people's eyes here, even of your elders. I tried to, but couldn't. Despite all we had been told before arrival, I forced a deferential smile and turned away.

My host mother smiled for me in return, and her husband took her hand and repeated something I still did not understand. Mr. Forrester spoke softly, and his wife gestured toward my face. Naturally I understood what was being asked of me, but I pulled the scarf tighter over my nose and looked at the ground, then pushed my feet together and held my knees in my hands. Each spoke my name again in that impenetrable language. I turned my head up and tried to smile. When I nodded my refusal Mrs. Forrester leaned forward and patted my knee. She stood then and went into the kitchen, returning with a tray she set on a cast-iron table, a glass of juice for each of us.

Birds sailed over our heads. I wanted to die. Lifting the scarf away from my mouth, I sipped from my glass. Though not thirsty, I believed I was expected to accept this offering. Hiding my face was not something that had concerned me when I was living with my grandfather, and only with strangers did I take such care as now. I would never have thought this could be mistaken for vanity or arrogance. I simply wanted to protect people from the embarrassment and shame of witnessing such a monster. I was sure the Forresters had not known what they were getting into, offering their home to our cause. Nor did they understand that I was ashamed to bring this disfigurement into the house of strangers, and that my hesitancy marked my respect, rather than a defiance. I was resolved to keep my face hidden those first days. The unmasking would be gradual, for their benefit as well as mine.

That night I lay in my new clean-smelling bed and remembered the old cot I slept on at home, and the many sleepless nights after I returned from the Red Cross Hospital in 1946. My grandfather had begun drinking the terrible *kasutori shochu,* which the black marketeers began to manufacture after the war, and which now seemed to accompany him most nights while he worked. He would sit at the kitchen table with the bottle beside him and drink long into the night, rolling new cigarettes from the discarded butts we collected during the day, which he would later sell to vendors in the market district.

Just before nine o'clock, soon after I had rolled my quota for the evening, I carried the radio into my room, turned the volume low and listened to a program called *Missing Persons.* Every night the same disembodied voice read names from a list of relatives who had been separated during the war. Also read out were the names of towns and addresses anyone listening could make contact with to get information. Lying on my cot, I would listen for hours, waiting to hear my mother's name spoken to me out of the darkness. Perhaps somehow there had been a mistake, I thought. It was someone else my grandfather had seen in the garden outside our burned home on the day of the attack. Perhaps she had been spared and years later was still looking for her family, as so many people still seemed to be doing. For months I listened to that program, quietly hoping against what I knew to be true.

For a short period too I listened to a similar program called *Who Am I?* This was for people who'd emerged from the war with no memory of who they were. Many of their stories of disorientation were terrifying, and as I lay on my cot listening, watching the soft glow of the radio tubes on the wall, I wondered what it would be like to feel such a sense of mystery about who you were. Not knowing where your family was out there, or if you were the last of your people. When, finally, the program ended, I would turn off the radio and listen to the quiet, remembering things, and from the next room the sound of my grandfather's muted sobbing would come through my door, to stay with me through the night.

Mrs. Forrester took me into the city for my first consultation three days after I'd arrived at their home. The community of Harristown was forty minutes from Grand Central Station, and from the train that day I watched the landscape come alive before me while Mrs. Forrester busied herself with the macramé she'd produced from her handbag. I watched with great interest as the procession of small towns rolled by the window, and when the train stopped at each town in turn we waited while a second and third and fourth wave of men with briefcases and hats came on board. Outside, the trees and bushes near the tracks moved in the wind we created while rumbling past. It was mid-May now and almost always warm and pleasant, unlike the dreary weather that had greeted our arrival, only a week earlier, from Japan.

Mrs. Forrester and I were the only women on the train, it seemed. Some of the men who boarded would smile and tip their hats and mutter good morning, but other men would turn their eyes away once they saw us. Soon the only unclaimed seats were the two directly across from us. Clearly, no one wanted to sit near me. Finally a man in a dark suit looked up and down the car and, seeing no other seats, reluctantly took one of these. Abruptly he opened a newspaper and began to read. When the train began again, its motion caused his paper to bounce unevenly in his hands. He tried to pad the bouncing and jumping by raising the newspaper over his lap, making it hover in such a way that his arms seemed to float above the turbulence.

Some minutes later the train slowed again and stopped, and a man with a long narrow face and large blue eyes walked up the aisle and sat directly across from me. He seemed to know not to pass up a seat this close to New York, for he didn't bother to look any farther. Turning my head away to watch the window scene begin to change as we pulled out of the station, I saw the first man lift up his newspaper again while Mrs. Forrester continued her stitching.

The blue eyes landed on me then. I felt them roll over my skin and lift like wet stones and swing in my host mother's direction, then return to me, disbelieving, quizzically, disgust gathering somewhere beneath. I believed he was wondering if we were together, calculating this attractive young woman's relationship to the Japanese girl whose face was covered by a red scarf. I tried not to pay attention, as I had practised in my mind so many times before, and watched the landscape scroll by outside. I imagined the colours and swirls and the speed of our train and the spring landscape, as I did whenever something fascinated me, seeing it in my head as a painting, hoping this would return me to the silence that so often was my refuge in those days. I painted the lives contained within the small houses and farms we passed, and in the lovely little towns, tucked between distant hills, that seemed more like postcards than real places I could observe and step into.

Desperately I painted the memory of my brother climbing with me onto our grandfather's shoulders as he did his morning exercise. Together we shrieked with joy and pulled at his funny tufts of hair and twined our limbs with his until he fell backward onto the bed with an exhausted yelp. Somehow I even captured the close, warm smell of his skin as he emerged from sleep every morning. I painted this with colours I'd never seen before, the pleasant old-man smell that seemed so natural, and the powerful strain on his body as he worked to lift his two grandchildren, and the sounds I felt echoing through my own bones.

I turned briefly to see if the man had stopped staring. If my silence had worked. His eyes looked like beautiful cold stones. He did not turn away. He grinned and leaned forward. I wanted to rake my fingers across his face when I heard him say "Jap"—a word I knew—and Mrs. Forrester's expression hardened. He motioned to me with a slight nod and pulled at the loose skin on his cheeks with his fingers. Presently Mrs. Forrester began tugging at my hand, pulling me up out of my seat and pushing me gently but urgently into the aisle. When I was safely clear she turned and confronted the man, who spoke again, a sentence I didn't understand at the time but retained in my memory until I came home later that evening.

"What is that *thing* with you?"

The slap of her hand against his face forced all the others in the car to drop their newspapers and cut their eyes upward. I watched the hand come down in slow motion. It was slight and feminine and it met the man's face with a loud, ringing clap.

"A child," she said. "She is a child."

He straightened his back and smiled, as if she'd just confirmed everything he'd always suspected. He shook his head then, and my host mother grabbed my hand and marched me down to the far end of the car, where two men offered us their seats. She shook her head no. We stood the rest of the way.

After we finally arrived we took a taxicab to Mount Sinai, where Dr. Barsky, the head of plastic surgery, and his assistant, Dr. Simon, were waiting with our interpreter, Helen. I had not seen either of the doctors since the reception the day we landed, when the lady had asked me about television. Mrs. Forrester was shown

the lounge while I was led to an examining room. Dr. Barsky patted
the table with his right hand and Helen told me to hop up, that
they would begin with my cheek, followed by my eye, then my
back.

"You may remove your scarf," she said.

I unwrapped the cloth and bundled it in a pocket, then Dr.
Barsky lowered his face to mine. Feeling the heat and freshness and
health of his skin, I averted my eyes and sat quietly, awaiting further instruction.

He tested my skin. He tapped and pinched and probed. Helen
stood in the corner of the room, her arms crossed. I moved when
she told me to. Even translated into my own language, much of
what the doctor said was incomprehensible; it was a technical language invented to describe creatures like me. When he was
through with my cheek and eye, he told me to remove my shirt and
to lie on my front. I felt the smooth, cool touch of the examining
table on my stomach as his hands circled the scarred area and
probed the lower back and under my arms. I could not count how
many strangers had touched me in this way. Such examinations
had become little more than other common daily or weekly rituals, much like eating or going to the bathroom. I knew this was one
of the necessities that came with the conditions of my life. I could
not recall a time I had been free of this casual manipulation of my
body.

When Dr. Barsky's hands withdrew, Dr. Simon, a younger man
with curly black hair, seized the opportunity to lean in close. I was
thinking about the train ride now and searching my small vocabu-
lary for a way to apologize to my host mother. That incident had
been my fault, I thought. I, the ugly one, had been the cause. I
searched among the few English words I knew. I didn't even know
how to say something as simple as *I am sorry*. The words did not
come.

Dr. Barsky then outlined the procedures I should expect in the coming months, while Helen translated. He told us of the series of operations, what each would entail and how far apart they would be spaced. When I had asked all the questions that occurred to me, Dr. Barsky left me in the hands of Dr. Simon, who was to conclude this initial consultation with a general physical. I was told to remove my dress and underwear.

"Why?" I said, when Helen insisted.

She told me to do as the doctor said, that other girls were waiting.

I climbed back up onto the examining table, naked but for my socks, and lay as instructed on my stomach. I waited, eyes closed and teeth clenched, for him to begin his test. A cold instrument of some sort touched my skin between my buttocks and began to push into my rectum, but instead of crying, which is what I had believed I would do, what I wanted to do, I swatted away the hand that held it. Then I sat up and covered myself with a sheet.

Once I had collected myself it was explained that this method of gauging body temperature was normal for children here. I asked Helen to remind the doctor that I was not a child; and that, in any case, I should've known that such a barbaric place as this would treat their children in a pitiless manner.

"Well, go on and tell him," I told Helen desperately. But only silence followed my outburst. "Tell him his country is a barbaric, monstrous place I should be happy to leave as soon as they let me."

Helen refused to translate my angry words, but I believe Dr. Simon had understood. The meaning in my voice was clear enough. He seemed acutely embarrassed and apologized several times. That was when I learned how to ask forgiveness in English, and did so as soon as we left the hospital together.

My host mother took me to Coney Island later that day, after this shaming episode. When we emerged from the fascinating adventure of our subway ride, we walked into a cool knot of air that enveloped the coast. This was the first time I had seen the Atlantic Ocean from ground level, and it seemed to me a wondrous thing, endless in its possibilities. Far out of sight Portugal and France rose from her waves, and Spain and England and all the other magical countries I had seen represented on the maps of my childhood. But now they were like my own, still smouldering from the wars that had visited them. I had known them only by their colours and shapes; but now I also understood that many of those dark, imagined shapes had been part of the history that had changed me.

We continued along the boardwalk, the ocean and her secret continents to our right. We bought hot dogs and Mrs. Forrester showed me how to dress mine, all this without words, squeezing ketchup and spooning relish and sauerkraut, and when I bit into its centre she smiled and repositioned the bun lengthwise in my hands.

At the marine aquarium we watched the bonnethead sharks and imperial angelfish, surrounded by the sputtering of filter pumps and trickles of water, turn their saltwater loops. We saw a purple sea squirt take his late lunch of plankton while a convict surgeonfish picked at purple and red coral, and the grandfather green sea turtle stirred small hurricanes at the tips of his scarred flippers. These were colours I had never seen or hardly ever imagined to be possible. My life to this point had been lived amid the grey rubble of my broken city. I watched the perfect white Florida manatee nose across the glass wall that contained him. Bright-purple ribbon eels craned their necks from rock caves, searching and gnashing their teeth. I skimmed over the strange names engraved in brass at the base of each large tank. These words were impenetrable to me: raccoon butterfly fish, Moon jelly, *Chaetedon lunula*, *Pelagia colorata*. I tried to imagine what they would sound like in my ear; but I had no understanding of the pronunciation of individual letters, much less whole words. Never had I seen anything as beautiful.

Journeys, 1938–1957

1

Sophie reached down to their outstretched hands from the compartment window, but their fingers did not meet. Her father smiled confidently as he withdrew his hand and blew her a kiss. They walked beside her, at first keeping pace with the train; when they began to fall behind though, step by step, they eventually stopped and Sophie saw the train's rounding belly finally push her parents from view. There had been a great effort to hold her tears, trying to believe what her parents had told her, that they all would see one another again soon. The three had dressed for the occasion. Her mother's dark-blue hat was tilted just so, her double-breasted jacket fastened tightly at the neck, her chin held high with resolve.

Sophie knew this journey had been forced upon her as a result of the star painted in white on the front of her father's music shop. He feared the men roaming the streets, shattering windows and knocking people down. He said it was not safe for her here. When the problems eased she would return. She would be sent for when those men were rounded up and brought before the courts, when things got back to normal.

Her father, a luthier, had learned his trade from his father, and his father before him had learned it from his. This shop sat on a quiet street called Hildestraße, in the old quarter, near the Temple. When she was a child one of Sophie's greatest pleasures had been to sit at the shop's front window and feel the sun warm her face and listen to her father working in the back while her mother dusted the completed instruments or knitted patiently, waiting for customers. The air was always rich with the smells of distant hardwood forests and the stains that were used on their precious wood. Before she had learned to speak her nose had been able to distinguish oily East Asian teak from the South American rosewoods and ebonies that her father kept stacked in neat piles in the storeroom. Slowly, back there in his workshop, he shaped five-hundred-year-old planks into instruments of perfect tone and astonishing beauty— violins mostly, but cellos and guitars, too—which were later strung and sold to the town's klezmer musicians and students from the conservatory and members of the Linz Orchestra.

On that train she sat across from a fat man in a grey suit with a double chin. She did not want to speak. She watched him lay out a blue-checked handkerchief on his lap and carve a piece of sausage with a pen knife, then a big yellow apple, and pop both into his mouth at the same time. He chewed with his eyes staring straight ahead. The train cut slowly north through the delicious spring-green pastures of Swabia, through Augsburg to Stuttgart and on again into the Odenwald. Sophie believed she saw the fabled Black Forest in the large, dark storm front that approached from France. She imagined crooked-backed shoemakers pulling water from deep, cold wells, and the bud-shaped hands of the elves known to live there. She knew the fairy tales of this Germany, enchanted and dark but not long for this world, like a taste of sweet jam on her tongue. The pleasures of her excitement when she had read those stories of lurking monsters and club-footed dungeonmen and magic weavers and lonely kings returned to her as the darkness gathered on the western hills and the train continued north. Wasn't she herself one of those heroines lost in the wilderness? She hoped for the good fortune she'd heard about often enough in those stories her mother had read to her years before. She remembered also the meanness, the men who ate the bones of children, and then tried not to look at the man across from her, who had since finished his meal and fallen asleep.

That night, in Frankfurt am Main, a porter shook her awake and told her she must change trains. Ten hours later she awoke to a

Importance of Storytelling !

taste in the air she had never smelt before. Her back was sore from
the journey, her eyes were tired and burning. She could think only
of food, and of her already distant mother and father. She rose
from her couchette and turned to the window and there, beyond
the grid-work of metal trees which soon cleared in her eyes to
become loading cranes, beyond crates the size of houses and large
grey ships the size of apartment blocks, dark and high in the water,
beyond this tangle of metal and steam and men in overalls and the
single gunship emerging out her train window to the right, she saw
the long narrow finger of the sea pointing deep inland, ending
where she was now. The train whistles blew and the station outside
her window blurred in a mass of pink-and-white faces until the
carriage once more jumped and finally settled and seemed to sink
ever so slightly into its tracks, fused to the metal of the rails under
her feet. The sign outside her window announced Hamburg. People shouted and more whistles blew. Sophie gathered up her bags,
then found the porter who had shaken her awake and asked which
exit she would take for the port.

Later that morning she boarded the *St. Louis,* along with nine
hundred and thirty others, who had no reason to believe their
entry visas to Cuba would not be honoured.

The crossing did not erase the pervading image of home from
her thoughts, or the pain of leaving her parents behind. She hid
herself from the hard winds of the North Atlantic, and when those
winds turned warm and the sun became persistent and welcoming
she hid from them too. One day the island appeared outside the
small porthole in her cabin and she beheld the pale-blue harbour
and the low brown city, confident and lazy under the May sun. For
two weeks they remained at anchor. She saw palms moving slowly
in the wind and small dark figures at work on the shore. They
straightened their backs and waved to the distant ship as they
smoked and shuffled their feet. With amazement she watched
what she had been told would be her new home and heard her

mother's voice inside her head. Confident and soothing, it floated behind her right ear. "Do not give up hope," it said.

And her father's clean, smooth face smelling of bathwater and soap came to her. For some reason she sensed his presence here, sitting now at the edge of her bed, and realized that the headboard was of spruce, and she was suddenly back there among the comforting smells of her father's shop. She cried herself to sleep every night aboard the ship. She remembered the simple mornings before going off to school, how her father would cradle her face in his rough callused hands and sing "My Princess and Me" or "Upsala Upsala One-Two-Three." She remembered the sweet smell of his bath soap, which was never diminished at the end of the day but mixed with the wood smells he returned home with. Now there was only the strange smell of the sea and the promise and threat of an unknown city somewhere at the end of this journey, its odd rhythms and smells of fried plantains and dark tobacco drifting like an unwelcome promise through her dreams.

She awoke on the third morning into the second week of waiting with an unknown stickiness to her legs, as if someone had stolen in during the night and spread her lower body with honey and jam. She placed her hand on her belly, then between her legs. She opened her eyes into the morning light of her single room and found a griminess there she had not seen before. She removed the hand and examined it closely, then smiled. She knew what this was. She sat up in bed, pulled back the covers and, inching away from the dark stain on the sheet, looked at the full length of her body. She walked to the bathroom and looked at herself in the mirror and examined this new wetness on her thighs. The air was already heavy with her body's smells. She could not stop the flow, and watched as a small dark bead searched its way down over the pale winter skin of her right leg. Below her belly button the slight shadow of pubic hair was matted flat against her body. In a burst of confidence she put her hands on her hips and smiled into the mirror. She cupped her small breasts in her sticky hands and lifted and tried to look like her favourite movie star. She laughed and turned in a circle and felt the dark bead spin off and saw it splatter against the enamel of the bath.

After she got cleaned up and dressed she took the sheets and held them to her chest in a large rumpled ball and stood in the middle of the room, wondering what to do with them. Of course she did not want them discovered. She did not want a stranger to take these sheets from her and let it be known that this had happened to her, here on a ship of strangers, alone with this delirious secret, and it was then that she remembered where she was, trapped in solitude, and she sat on the edge of her bed and cried.

There were new rumours every day. Tuesday they were landing, Wednesday they were sailing on to New York. Thursday a German U-boat had entered the harbour and was preparing to sink them right there and then. Friday they'd be steaming back to Hamburg, Saturday Roosevelt was arriving that very evening to take personal control of the situation. There were reports of spies on board. She had sat in the cafeteria over an unfinished plate of rice and baked fish and listened to four men talk of plans to seize the ship and steam for Miami. Already, one man—a tall, thin Jew from Cologne—had slit his wrists and thrown himself into the harbour. Could he possibly have known, she wondered, of some terrible fate arranged for them all? Why would a man do such a thing if he hadn't been assured a death worse than drowning? But he had been fished out, treated and returned to the ship and was now, she figured, condemned to see what he thought his eyes could not bear.

Smuggled newspapers found their way onto the *St. Louis*. She decoded their headlines with the rudiments of English she'd learned from her mother. In Linz she was accustomed to reading the words *Juden* and *raus* in the same article. She was surprised to find no such words now, only *diplomacy, unresolved* and *international* in the copies of the *New York Times* and the *Miami Herald* she found ripped and tattered, discarded in stairwells or pushed slowly over the wooden deck by a hot Cuban wind. *La República* she understood hardly at all, but her smattering of Latin helped. In any case, she preferred the American papers. Soon she found herself looking more at photographs of movie actors and for incidental pictures of American life than for news that might determine the ultimate destination of this voyage.

Nearing the end of the second week at anchor she noticed a stiffness in her fingers she had never felt before. She was sitting in one of the cafeterias, watching the island through a portside window, when a mild paralysis seized them like a clenched fist. She stretched her arms out across the table and watched a paleness begin at the tips and creep up their length in a strange constriction. In a short while the ghostly shade had turned a light ocean blue, cool to the touch when she tested her fingers against her cheek. In another climate she might have suspected it to be frostbite.

Her first thought was of her period, wondering if there could be a connection. Maybe there were so many strange events that happened under the skin at this time in a young woman's life that you could not be expected to foresee every twist and blood-letting turn. Strange and unseemly events might occur, particular to each person, that her mother had not yet been able to prepare her for. *My dear, your fingers will become numb and pass from pink to pale to blue.*

She retired to her room when the blue became noticeable and she detected alarm in people's faces. Someone might insist she see a doctor, a kind old man who was unfamiliar with the intimacies of the female body. This man would probe her, putting his fingers where even her own were too timid to search. While she sat on the edge of her bed imagining this assault, the blue of her fingers turned deathly, which then brought to mind the reason she had been placed on this ship of strangers destined for the New World. She lay back on the cramped bed and closed her eyes.

Maybe she was dying, she thought for the first time in her life.

Maybe she already was dead. The mind holding on a few moments longer, able to observe the tide lowering as life was drained from her body. Maybe this was death's great secret, its one last offering to the passing soul.

But she knew she was not dead when the fingers began to throb again. All the blood that had been absent seemed to rush outwards on the verge of exploding, filling her fingers with pain. She lost all desire to understand the mystery of this condition, consumed as she was by the fire it had sparked. She did not want to solve the riddle. Just that it would stop. That was all she needed. That would be enough. And slowly—as though someone had been listening, waiting for this simple request, *Please make it stop*—the burning sensation cooled by degrees and her hands again became hers.

2

When Anton saw Sophie standing in a doorway at Camp L five years later, in 1943, on the banks of the St. Lawrence near Quebec City, he believed immediately that something more than mere chance had brought him here. He wanted this to be a journey of fates. He walked slowly towards her, shooing flies as the sun scratched its way across the wet dirt. He stretched the bones of his fingers against the air, excited to find such beauty in a place like this. A surge rushed up the length of his body. He recognized— even in this baggy camp uniform, denim trousers and shirt with the red dot sewn into the back—the shape of a beautiful woman. His dress shoes, bought at a small shop in New York, at Fifth and Seventieth, gave him away for the visitor he was. He smiled at her from across the compound. The early-morning air was hazy still after a night-long summer rain, and down the hill, beyond the camp gates, the great river, emptying the five Great Lakes above it, began to sparkle under parting cloud.

The streets here were ankle-deep in mud, if those pathways that crisscrossed between huts could be called streets. He tried to step around puddles as he watched the young woman, just a girl really, stretch and yawn as though she had just risen from sleep. She leaned against the rough-shod door frame, held within its embrace of shade. She bit her bottom lip, ran her tongue over its surface.

More than coincidence, he thought.

She pulled a cord of dark hair from her eyes, curled thickly after a week of damp air which had culminated in last night's rain, and swatted away a fly. She closed her stiff fist and looked across the compound and watched him back. She often dreamt of being taken away from here. Awake, she understood these dreams to mean she should take any available offer. A nice boy, maybe, who would provide a safe place to hide. She knew worse fates. She stepped out from the shadows.

The camp warden, an army colonel named Higgins, introduced them. "Our youngest internee," he told his visitor. In a camp full of old rabbis, he explained, she was his favourite.

Anton introduced himself in English, for the colonel's sake, though he knew most of the internees were German speakers.

"Yes, Professor Böll, of the New School in New York City," interjected the colonel, "is our honoured guest. He is a man of influence, a great mind."

Trailing behind after that brief introduction, she wondered if this man might be able to get her out of here. She gathered from overheard snippets of conversation that he'd come to speak to an important group of people regarding the war in Europe. That he might have some sway over the people who ran this camp. He might be a man emerged directly from her own dreams of escape. She watched eagerly, looking for clues, though she had no idea what form they might take. She observed the young man greet with due ceremony the youngest son of the Crown Prince of Germany, Prince Friedrich Georg Wilhelm Christoph von Preussen, he too delivered here like another head of cattle. And then, suddenly, he was alone. Perhaps this was not a sign, a clue, but she saw it for the opportunity it was. She strode across the compound and said quietly, directly into his ear, "There is a place to go outside the fence. Would you like to see it?"

For a moment he was puzzled. Then he smiled. "Yes. But how? You cannot leave."

"I can get myself out. I walk out there always after dark," she said. "There is nowhere to go, so I always come back."

After dinner in the mess hall, a large barn-like structure which also served as the recreation centre, he sat for hours over a cup of cold weak tea and listened to the stories of the internees who'd stayed to talk after the meal had ended. He brought them news from the outside world, as much as he knew about it, anyway. As they shared their stories, he was struck by this small community. A prince and fourteen rabbis, as well as academics from a dozen European universities. They'd even set up their own university here, a small shack at the far end of the compound. An optometrist had made a camera while living here behind this barbed wire. The man showed Anton some of the photographs he'd taken with film stolen from a guard.

Near dark he excused himself from this company of men, saying he wanted to stretch his legs before returning to the city. After a measured walk around the perimeter of the fence, eyes moving from ground to guard tower, he found the shallow dip in the hard-packed earth and slipped beneath the wire fence, then stepped quickly down to the edge of the water and waited for her in the tall grass. His mind raced through the possibilities. From here he could still see the guard towers on the eastern and western edges of the compound and the silhouette of a man leaning on his elbows smoking a cigarette, his rifle leaning against the wooden rail like a garden implement. By now it was almost fully dark. His head crowded with versions of the next hour. He could not be sure what he was to expect. He saw the ember glow in the night when the guard inhaled, and as he waited, crouching in the grass, he remembered in his knees the heavy lurching he'd experienced as he'd descended the mountain into Spain more than three years earlier, en route from France to Portugal and, finally, to New York.

He had taken the same mountain pass as Alma Mahler and Marc Chagall had, only a few weeks after. Anton had heard the story. That Mahler had carried with her an original Bruckner manuscript, which turned out to provide some welcome propaganda for the American papers. By the time Anton arrived they'd dubbed it the Path of Great Men. The *Mirror* called it the Path to Freedom.

After a week of walking he made it to the border and sat among the rhododendrons and watched the border guards down below, on the Huesca side of the Pyrenees. One of them got up from his tree stump and relieved himself a few steps away, then walked into the shack and came back out a moment later carrying a wine skin. He lifted it in the air and squeezed the wine into his mouth. Anton could not see the purple stream from where he sat, but he knew it had gone in because the man wiped his mouth, passing the skin to the other man. They were having a nice time of it, Anton thought. He wondered if they'd ever killed anyone. He knew something of the Civil Guard, and that their war had been the proving ground for what was happening back home. He watched them for an hour into mid-morning, waiting for a sign.

The men stopped idling when he finally stood, and observed him moving down the mountain. It took him ten minutes to reach them.

Buenos días.

The older one, a short, fat man in his mid-forties with a small nicotine-stained moustache, took the *tricornio* up from the table, placed it on his head and, stepping forward, said something Anton could not understand.

Did the man speak French? he asked. Or English?

When the guard gestured for him to come closer, he resisted the temptation to run. Reminding himself that he was now a French citizen carrying an entry visa to the United States of America, he found courage and stepped closer. The younger man rose from the table and stepped back, within reach of the two carbines leaning against the wooden shack.

The man stretched out his hand palm up. *Pasaporte,* he said.

Anton pointed to the knapsack on his back and the man nodded. He slipped it off his shoulders, dropped to his knees and began loosening the clasps, all the while trying not to look at the boy beside the rifles. He held open the mouth of the bag to show the guards that there would be no surprises.

He reached in and retrieved the passport and the transit visa and crisp white scroll of paper with the red ribbon tied at its centre. Apparently uninterested in the visa, the guard took the scroll over to the table and looped the wine skin over his shoulder. He spread the paper out on the table, which was rough-hewn and fashioned, it looked to Anton, with an ax. The man said something to his partner, then stooped over and found four rocks and placed them on the corners of the document. Only now did he lower his face to peer at the paper, which shone brightly in the sun.

He cannot read, Anton thought, watching him pass his hand over the scroll. The guard closed his eyes and smiled gently. The stubble at the corners of his mouth rose like a cat's whiskers. His index finger slowly circled the raised wax seal in the top right corner of the scroll, lingered upon it, red and swollen, as if it were a woman's nipple. Finally he pulled up from the paper and slipped the wine skin off his shoulder and said wistfully, "*À l'avenir.*"

Anton believed he might stick out in the city when he finally arrived, dressed as he was in rags. His clothing had already begun to sag noticeably after only fourteen days' walking, though it felt more like fourteen weeks. But Madrid didn't notice. There he saw worse rags than his own. Small children dressed in hardly anything. An old woman, anywhere over seventy, sat on the steps of the Tribunal metro stop, a curled hand resting on her knee, her face turned towards the sweating plaster wall, feet wrapped in cloth. He stopped and dug into his pocket for a coin and held it up to the shaft of daylight coming down the steps from the exit. People streamed past her. He was not yet comfortable with these coins, not having had time to learn their value. She didn't look away from the wall when he placed it in her palm, and the hand fisted slowly, automatically, like a flower closing at the end of light.

When he arrived at the restaurant he'd been told to look for, he found the Portuguese alone, halfway through his meal.

"Hello," the Portuguese said in English, already standing. He wiped his mouth with a white napkin and gestured for Anton to sit. The other place was already set. "I only have this moment to eat."

Aristides Seixa da Costa summoned the waiter, then glanced at Anton. "Do you take lentils, I hope? That's all there is today."

"Anything is okay."

After ordering, he told Anton the news. The French had just detained Varian Fry—the day after he got Anton out, he added. Da Costa broke some bread and offered him half.

"What happens to him now?"

"Nothing. They just send him back to New York. It's everyone else we have to worry about."

Anton slept that afternoon. For the first time in seven days he was able to close his eyes and not be awakened by dew working its way under his clothing, or a farmer's prodding pitchfork. He felt a desperate need to slow down the pace of change. To indulge at least the temporary illusion of having a place waiting for him at dusk. Before da Costa returned in the evening he stood on the Portuguese diplomat's balcony, his hands gripping the iron railing, and watched the night descend over the city. More than a year after the war ended here, Madrid was red clay rooftops, askew at every angle, torn and slanting. Where a building suddenly disappeared into shadow, he knew a bomb had fallen. Entire neighbourhoods were still in ruins. He knew this was where the Germans had tested their Junkers, Heinkels and Messerschmidts before flying them over the rest of Europe. In the twilight he saw holes in the sidewalks, enormous walls of cobblestones stacked and waiting to be replaced. Everywhere the earth seeped through the pavements, churned as if a great plough had been pulled through her main streets. He knew this was what awaited the rest of Europe. He shifted uncomfortably on his feet.

The electric lights were being turned on below him in the Glorieta de Bilbao, single lamps and pork-fat candles flickering at small broken windows. From the bar-cafés a murmur of voices rose through the air, punctuated by the screech of metal shutters clattering in their guides. He could make out the conversation of coffee spoons and ceramic bowls and then wondered, from up above, warm in the falling evening, how all this would end, Africa so close, and a wind perhaps from as far away or close by as Algeria or Morocco pushing past his face. He breathed deeply and closed his eyes.

When da Costa returned they discussed his departure on the ship from Lisbon to New York. "Don't worry," he said. "If you've got this far, nothing will go wrong. Now you are a French citizen, and the French are treated decently here. The Spanish don't like them, but they treat them well. If they think you're French you will have no problem. Your French is fine."

Anton Böll nodded.

"Then you might know the Spaniards look up to the French. Rather the opposite of how they treat the Portuguese." He stood. "Would you like a drink with me?"

Anton said he would, and the diplomat walked to the kitchen and came back with an opened bottle of absinthe, two glasses with ice, two sugar cubes and a spoon with small stars cut through its centre.

"Most of the Civil Guard can't read, you see. They will be impressed by the formality of your papers, and hardly any know French. They did a good job on them."

He fixed the spoon so it sat snugly over the mouth of his glass, then placed the sugar cube in its silver cradle. "Like this," he said. "It's too bitter otherwise." He took up the bottle and poured the green liquor, which smelt of anise and turned milky white when it touched the ice, over the sugar. Anton watched the cube dissolve.

"You don't get this in France anymore," da Costa said. He leaned forward and passed the spoon to Anton. "This cannot be called the advancement of civilization, when the French take away the workers' last refuge. I believe this. In this country there is at least some respect left for the small pleasures of the common man." His smile fell away. "Despite what has happened here."

He leaned back again and sipped at his drink. "Now," he said. "You've got something up your sleeve. I can only surmise this, as you are here."

Anton studied his eyes, waiting. The diplomat's English was more idiomatic than his own. He didn't know the expression. He shook his head, unsure how to respond.

"The reason they want you over in America," the diplomat insisted. He waited again, took another sip. He watched in silence as Anton prepared his drink.

"Good," he said. "I don't want to know anything about it. Keep your mouth shut. Some of my charges feel they are safe to talk with me. You are never safe here. I do not want to hear your story."

• • •

The next morning railworkers dressed in blue monkey-suits, picks and brooms and shovels raised over their shoulders, watched Anton and the Portuguese board a train at the dead-end of a railway line. The air was still cool. The sound of metal shutters opening in the cafeteria opposite the track clanked against rusted rollers in the breaking daylight.

The two men took seats in third class among ragtag businessmen and domestic migrants and visiting relatives. There was no money and no work—Anton saw this in the eyes and the clothes around him, the hard stares and silence—but still there was the need to move. There was a better place to be than here, and he waited with them for the change that would bring their lives into proper alignment. He saw the envy of motion and of great distances outside his window in the listless attitude of the workers, leaning against the reassuring pleasure of their morning tobacco. They smoked and watched passively as the train began to pull away from the station and slowly the car Anton and his guide were to travel on through Castile, over the frontier and then to Lisbon, emerged into the half-light of the rail yard. A hard grinding of wheels echoed up through his limbs and rattled the sleep from his eyes with the eternal and impossible promise of departure.

His own solitude came upon him then as hard as he'd ever felt it, turning as real and physical as the coins in his pocket. A secret brought up from somewhere, dark and surprising and slick.

You are a walking bomb, he thought.

His knowledge was something he had shared with no one other than his colleagues at the Institute at Dahlem and at the Army Ordnance Department's Gottow Laboratory. But there had been few takers. No one of authority—neither Dieber nor Hahn nor Heisenberg—supported his split with Walther Bothe, who believed the neutron absorption of carbon would never sustain a chain reaction. When the decision was made to shift the program's focus from graphite to heavy water, Anton protested. He insisted an error had been made in Bothe's calculations, that graphite of a greater purity could be achieved, and he would show them exactly how in under a year. Perhaps eight months. They considered his ideas fanciful, his methods unorthodox. Bagge had already begun scaling back his access to vital resources, and after his break with Bothe things only got worse. That's when he'd decided to get out. He would not sit on this knowledge, not when he knew the discovery could be his.

Soon after, when the carriage began to fill with cigarette smoke, he moved to the section between cars where two metal floor-plates shifted under his feet with the sound of grinding jaws. He stood at an open window and let the wind rush over him. His mind was still clouded from last night. By now more than a year had passed since the Spanish war ended. That morning he believed he felt the awed silence of a people trying to understand what had happened to them. What they'd done to themselves. This was a contemplation not yet possible elsewhere in Europe, burning as it was now. Here they had started early and finished early. He saw a bombed-out farmhouse on a hill, once alive with flapping laundry and pecking chickens, now abandoned to silence and self-condemnation. As his own country would be one day, he thought.

Around noon they climbed down and took a beer in the station cafeteria in Salamanca while the train waited for track clearance. An aging woman sat behind the bar shelling sunflower seeds.

"You know," da Costa said, sliding the empty glass across the stone slab of the bar, "it's usually Jewish intellectuals. You are not a Jew. That's obvious." He gestured to the old woman, and waited as she refilled the small glass at the tap and pushed the glass back to him. "Yet I appreciate that wartime is often a time of great scientific achievement. Jewish or not."

Perhaps Anton understood the limits of conversation better than this man. He had been warned: say as little as possible. But he wondered how the Portuguese knew. His hints, the leading statements. *Scientific achievement.* With this the man had already crossed into a dangerous area. If either one of them was stopped, now or at the Portuguese frontier in three hours' time, something as small as this might prove fatal.

But it was difficult to fault him for it, he thought. In a situation such as this there was a longing for detail, the need to assign a value and importance to his work. How proud he would have been to conduct Thomas Mann or Albert Einstein. Famous men. Men of stature. So far the feather in his cap had been Marc Chagall. Yes, the hunger for facts beyond train and boat schedules was completely comprehensible; it was one man's cry in the dark, his attempt to understand his own significance in the face of a necessarily dense layering of prevarication and silence. But people would die were it not for this prevailing sense of ignorance.

And if I were to tell him, how would I say something truthful? That I am a walking bomb?

"Silence," da Costa said as they started back to the train. "That's good. You are getting used to your new life. After a few years this is something you will do with your eyes closed. Second nature. Some people it takes longer. One day you'll see what it is to live where no one knows you. Where you're a stranger. That's where you are going, isn't that right? No need to say anything. I'm not listening. The life of an exile. This war makes exiles out of all of us. What they want you for over there in America assures it. Whatever it is. You'll see where it makes you go for company. You'll see the dark spaces you're forced to reach into."

A small rustling came now, then the thin squeak of the wire fence being lifted to accommodate her small body. In a moment she was beside him. She came close through the dark, her breath like the thick swirling of the river just out of sight.

She crouched and spoke softly. "I feel like a spy when I come out," she said. "Maybe a submarine will sail up here and take us away." Then, after a moment: "Can you get me out?" Her accent was distinctly Austrian.

He hesitated a moment, surprised. "I can do nothing," he said.

He asked how she had come here and she told him about her voyage across the Atlantic, how they had next been shipped to Scotland after being denied entry to Cuba and then, finally, to this place.

He wanted to ask if she had family left, but knew she would have no contact with them. She was cut off, as he himself had been.

"When it's warm out," she said, "I come here. It was beautiful after the rain last night. It reminded me of home."

"The Danube?" he said.

She nodded. "When I die I want to be buried in a place like this, near a river that goes on and on. The moonlight shining on my grave." She reached into the dark, picked up a pebble and tossed it. Without speaking, they watched the water break, ripples gathering, then fading again.

"Being out here with me scares you," he said, finally. "I make you nervous."

"Maybe you're different. I saw you talking to everyone. They seemed to like you." She tossed another pebble. "When did you leave home?"

"Three years ago. I was in hiding in France."

"But you're not a Jew."

"No."

"Why were you in hiding, then?" she said. Such a possibility had never presented itself to her before. "Only Jews hide. The colonel said you are a professor."

"Yes."

"What do you teach?"

"I am a guest lecturer at a university in New York established for people like me. People escaping the war."

"My father taught me all about the stars. We used to look at them. You are meeting Churchill tomorrow? That's what they're saying in camp."

"Who is saying that?"

"Everyone. Yes, Churchill and Roosevelt."

"People know those men are here. They're convening in Quebec City."

"Why are you meeting them?"

"Because I know something very special about Germany."

"But so do I."

"Then maybe you should come, too."

"I would convene a swimming event for those men who started this war if I had the chance, and the one who doesn't drown, the last one still swimming, will win the war and that will be the end of it."

"Then we could all go home," he said.

"Yes."

She stood and unbuttoned the denim shirt and unfastened the rope that held the baggy pants on her hips. They fell down her legs easily, and she slipped her feet from the bundle and removed her underwear. He watched her outline against the night. She stepped away and entered the water as quietly as a deer drinking at the edge of a lake. The water moved up against the pale form of her body until he could see only her head moving in an outward V into the current, then she disappeared.

He stripped away his clothes and felt the water's coldness. When it licked at his genitals he wanted to get out and wait up on the bank for her to swim back, but instead he kicked out his feet in a brave push and paddled to where he thought she was. The current pulled hard to the left, and, stopping for a moment, he felt the absence of bottom. He didn't call out, because his voice would carry over the bank to one of the sentries.

It was possible she was already waiting for him back on shore.

With his arms and feet sweeping and kicking, he turned his body in a circle, trying to keep fixed in his head the point of land where they'd entered the river. He knew the current had moved him downstream, but only a short distance. He turned another slow circle, eyes scanning the flat surface of the water to where, an arm's length away, the water disappeared into blackness, and suddenly her body moved against his and she laughed under her breath.

"Did I frighten you?" she said. The warmth of her breath pressed against his neck, and together they swam towards the bank where they'd left their clothes. His foot touched bottom and they stood in water up to their thighs, the air balmy against his skin. Breathing deeply, they watched the sharp ripples of their wake disappear in the river's black sheen.

"I came out here tonight," she said, "thinking I'd do whatever you wanted with me. I thought you'd take me away."

"There's nothing you have to do," he said.

"It wouldn't have mattered what you were. It still doesn't matter. I was going to do whatever you wanted. I've been here too long."

He told her he didn't want what she was talking about, however much he was secretly excited by the suggestion. He lifted his foot up from the bottom and brought it down and felt the sand stir up and settle again over his toes.

"I'm sorry," she said. "I thought about what it would be like, being here with you."

"That's all right," he said.

"No it's not."

He didn't want this, either, standing here ridiculously naked and talking nonsense, each of them feeling remorseful and craving release, whether in the form of escape or lust.

"Maybe you were just looking for a swimming contest," he said. "As you said before."

"Then I would've won the war," she said.

"Yes," he said, "you would have."

A drop of water at her temple came free from her hair and ran down the side of her face. By the light of the moon he saw it clearly as it ran down her neck and pooled on the ridge of her collarbone.

"My name is Sophie Heinemann."

He shifted in the shallow water, and she lowered her hand to the river and brought it up again holding another pebble and tossed it out into the current. The guard in the nearest tower turned in their direction, his silhouette stark against the night sky. He might have thought the sturgeon were rising to the new moon, taking dragonfly nymphs as they sputtered into the air.

He touched her shoulder, shining with damp. "You could come with me to America," he said.

3

The near impossibility of the agenda at the Pugwash Conference, at which he and his colleagues would attempt to define the precise state of their science at that moment in 1957, was overwhelming. He marvelled at some of the other academics, awed by their cool theoretical approach, as if they were debating Zeno's paradox, nothing more urgent. There were men who had not actually been there—for whom all that fire they'd learned to unleash might be philosophical in nature, merely a problem of ideas. Sherry and polite conversation followed suppers, talk of young grandchildren, new automobiles. Still, the strange calm helped him to focus. He knew he was party to an historic event, so now it was a question of getting him up and out of that history, to redefine himself however possible. This is how he would be remembered. He thought of those women he'd heard about in a park in New York City, a small gathering from which something grand and lasting had emerged. A significant pride would follow. Something he might orient himself by, and use to bring himself back into the world.

In New York, just a year earlier, he'd waited for Bertrand Russell's first announcement regarding this conference. Neighbourhood boys were shouting down below in the street, and from the corner opposite his window he heard a high adolescent voice call up "Olly Olly Oxenfree" and the larger, general shuffle of sneakers on pavement. When he heard the truck he leaned his head out the window and watched three men unload the meat. They carried the produce on their blood-stained shoulders, large sinewy beasts fresh from the slaughterhouse, into the butcher's at the corner. The men laughed and joked as they inhaled the cooling animal scent into their throats, far enough back in the truck that their lungs misted in the cold, even in the heat of that late June, and one of them stepped into the street and said, "Stay in school, girls," and slapped the meat on his shoulder and laughed as he walked into the shop. The butcher stood at the entrance, Mr. DeLuca, a round man and balding, ticking off the order in his head, the joints and pounds of beef and veal and lamb he would carve and dispense in this neighbourhood of Carroll Gardens.

Anton pulled his head in and returned to his desk on the far side of the living room. He tried to focus on the task at hand, scribbling notes for the lectures he would deliver later that month. He stopped and looked over at the radio sitting on the bureau, turned low. He looked at the clock on the kitchen wall, listening to the blur of sound issuing from the mahogany-cased box. He never used music when he worked, finding it a distraction, but he'd tuned into this channel and wanted now for the music to end.

A gust drove crumpled issues of *News of the World* down the street, and plumed the thin skin of cotton over the window. Had

Sophie remembered she would not've busied herself with the shopping today. By now he was in an excited stage of dreaming possibility, and couldn't make out what music was playing for all the racket, laughter and clanging garbage cans, coming in from the window. His agitation mounting, he again peered down over the slabs of red meat riding the men's shoulders below, and the kids gathered around and bald-headed DeLuca standing at the entrance like he usually did when the truck came, pushing the sawdust to and fro with his feet.

Anton returned to his desk and looked at the clock and got up a third time and turned up the volume, then the radio crackled once and the introducing voice loomed clear like a sports announcer's and he moved to the middle of the room and began bobbing forward and back, head tilted, while he listened to the announcer switch over to the live news conference from London. Upon hearing Russell's voice, he thought: This is it, this is the voice of possibility. The pacifist. A man who'd gone to prison for his ideals.

Two weeks earlier, a half-dozen women had gathered in Bryant Park and refused to leave when the test air-raid sirens went off. It was a form of protest he'd never considered, this simple disobedience. They argued that hiding under the stairs or under the bed wasn't going to get you far. Not with a bomb like that. The city was in training for a new era, like a winner-take-all track meet. Ten thousand miles of streets had been vacated in under eight minutes. New York had become an instant ghost town but for a few young mothers and babies who'd sat down in the park that day and waited for the air-raid wardens to come and tell them to hurry along; but they'd just crossed their arms and enjoyed the sun and said to the reporters the next day that they didn't accept what the government was doing. Or saying. They weren't going to be tricked into believing the bomb was anything you could shelter from or live through.

That's what the manifesto Russell was announcing now was

about. Helping to understand what would really happen, to counter the government propaganda.

The door latch turned and Sophie called out for him to help put things away, but Anton shushed her from the middle of the room. She remembered then the news conference on the short-wave. She began unloading the grocery bags in the kitchen, half listening, and he turned the radio up because of the rustling bags and the sound of tins and jars being set out on the counter, and still the noise of children playing outside. Before she finished she came out from the kitchen and leaned against his desk and listened with him to the end of the speech.

"That's him holding out his hand to you," she said when it was over. "This is your offering of grace. This is God's finger pointing down at you. That's as good as a personal invitation. You're not turning your back now."

By this time the test grounds at Yucca Flats had been turned into a great outdoor theatre. Sophie, as well as Anton, knew what the government was doing. The crystallization of desert sand into a hard blue souvenir glass had become a tourist draw. They were making the bomb into some sort of spectacular event, a reason for sunburnt vacationers to congregate on safely distant bleachers and revel in it, cheer for it, as if at a football game. The plan was to take the fear out of the bomb. Make this into a wondrous science, this wholesome, fascinating spectacle of technology.

It was something to see. Russell knew that, as did Anton. The impressive mushroom cloud would seduce anyone lucky enough to be sitting outside its killing radius. This was the ignorance he was talking about, and the first attempt to organize the scientific community, to oppose the idea that the bomb was easily managed, a picturesque desert pastime, the defining measure of the free world's domain and divine right. Anton closed his eyes. He knew Sophie was right. He could not turn his back on this opportunity. But the responsibility he felt for August 1945, as well as the pride, was accompanied by the need to dissolve the mythology of the bomb. He would meet with these minds, he thought, learn from them, present them with his own thinking. This was a chance to educate those who did not understand the burden of their times. He was fully aware of his unique position: refugee of conscience, Manhattan Project veteran, member of the Manhattan District. He needed to meet these people. To make his ideas known to them.

Sophie left him alone and resumed unloading the groceries in the kitchen. She was reaching up to the top cupboard when he came through the doorway.

"If I get invited I'll go. He's pulling a conference together. You gathered that."

"You won't stop talking about it if you don't go." She stood down from her toes and turned to him. "I'm serious about what I said."

Failing health had forced Bertrand Russell to withdraw from the conference, but a group of men from seven countries had taken his concept and made good on it. Anton received confirmation in December of 1956, and the following summer he and Sophie took a train up to Montreal, where they caught a connection going east. They'd decided to make a trip of it. Find a small cabin somewhere in Nova Scotia after the conference, just the two of them, and get to know each other again. Or maybe, truly, for the first time.

There'd been a time when hope had been their initial and easiest reaction to the world. On their way to Pugwash he considered this, that instinct fell to the positive. Wasn't it funny, how this shifting had occurred, this departure from what you once believed was your prevailing nature? Or in fact did your ignorance protect you like a shell until your abilities to deal with the complications matured? Now he understood the difficulties, or at least he thought he did.

Their last night in that small provincial town he watched Leo dance with Sophie. A stocky man who carried the scent of after-shave and a nick of blood on his collar, Szilard was one of the first men to argue against using the bomb. He'd helped to perfect it, and now here, amid the seagulls of coastal Pugwash, he had joined a community of scientists attempting to dispel the notion that simply taking cover in the basement would be enough to save your skin. There were some festivities, too, not just sober dreams of ridding the world of its means of mass destruction. Anton stood back and watched Sophie spin across the room, shaking his head in wonder. She looked back, eyes filled with radiance, as old Leo led her around the small floor. He looked to Anton and smiled a compact with him, then winked. An agreement between gentlemen. He leaned back against a table, his shirtsleeves rolled to the elbow. A ball of sweat snailed down his neck, salted like the sea crashing a hundred yards from the door. Leo stepped forward and gently took Anton by the elbow.

"In the old days," he said above the music, "when I was a boy, the matron used to patrol the dance floor up and down, up and down, looking for anything suspicious. God forbid a kiss! Of course, you first practised dancing with a friend. Then, when you understood, you got to dance with a girl. A *real* girl!"

Anton smiled and touched his shoulder, then turned and put his face into his wife's neck. They danced through their first song together, and she leaned strongly into his arms when he said something in her ear.

"Remember this," he said, but she couldn't tell if this was meant as an imperative or a question. She just pulled closer and smiled into his shoulder. Outside, the deep Atlantic tides cooled the shoreline. She pressed an ear against his chest. This was the entirely physical nature he had always needed from her, that which had initially attracted him. She filled any space she walked into, any room, any riverbank or dance hall. It was something you couldn't turn away from. Like the way she had become for him, in the camp, every beam, every blade of grass, every shadow. And the hours that filled their first night.

"Do you remember where you took me?" he asked, still dancing. "That first time."

She smiled. "Don't make yourself sound so innocent." This is all he needs, she thought. Coming up here and rediscovering that first enthusiasm, that optimism they shared. To be able to end the war.

Later, they stood by a slightly opened window; the room was beginning to heat up, despite the comfortable cool sea breeze. Night sounds carried beneath the strains of music. Someone brought drinks around. Anton pressed her hand and she smiled.

They walked into the dark down a stone path, the music following in their wake. When they rounded a tall rosebush, the sounds from the party and Benny Goodman and distant laughing all became small, almost galactic and flickering. They continued along the path to the water, where it was still but for one wave, then another, rhythmical and perfect. Lights cascaded down the lawn from the hotel and lay in strips and pools in the harbour. The music continued but they were outside of it now. They were outside its influence. A halyard slapped lazily against a flagpole or masts somewhere in the harbour, singing through the dark. They watched a wave break on the shore and dissolve in foamy silence.

"What if you did your work here?" she said. "Nova Scotia even sounds lovely." She spoke the name slowly, in her heavy accent, the words coming pleasingly off her tongue.

"Say it again," he said, putting his open mouth on her throat. She repeated the name for him, and her voice resonated against the bones of his mouth.

"If we can't go home, I mean. If you need to stay in America. Because of life. But just think," she said, stepping away. "We'd be living under the stars." She spun a dizzying girlish circle, throwing her voice skywards. "You never see stars in the city. This is so good for you. For us. Neither of us likes living there. It changes us. Look

at this." She offered a gesture, that he should open his eyes to what
surrounded them.

"If I were an astronomer, maybe," he said glumly.

A wave caught the illumination from the air in the moments it
took to spill apart on the shore. Anton took his wife's hand and
held it against his cheek.

"I can't leave New York now. I'm still not ready. Not yet."

He had meant for Sophie to understand he was not yet ready
professionally. But as he heard himself say this, standing there
looking out over the harbour, he realized that his actual meaning
was something entirely, fundamentally different. Only in New
York, he now realized, could he come to terms with what he had
done with his life, and with what remained for him to do. He did
not know until then, as the halyards clinked and chimed above the
dark water and he bent to give his wife an apologetic kiss on the
cheek, that he was waiting for something, as indeed he had been
ever since returning from the war; and although he didn't know in
what form it would come, it would come no matter, and he was
not free to leave that place until it did.

"We're getting better now, right?" she said.

He nodded. "Yes," he said. "I'm back."

She was the standard he would judge the rest of his life by. He
could feel her able grace and her determination to find peace,
almost like a palpable warmth.

"Yes," he said.

The flashes of brilliance that had awakened him in his youth had
left him long before then. The dreams he'd experienced back in
Tübingen as a boy accompanied visions of the trajectories of the
shells his father fed into the cannons he'd maintained in France,
their exploding radiance and incendiary, mud-vapourizing powers, to a point where he almost could have drawn their twenty-

mile arcs in the night sky outside his bedroom window. Now the thinking had became rote, but the equations and formulas he'd mastered years before still swirled in his head. He felt his creative mind freezing up, and this was something he would've, if there were a God, thanked Him for. There was already enough to keep him wondering another ten lifetimes. That period of fevered creation, two years of cold sweat under a hot sun, and now he had the rest of his life to answer for it. A lifetime of trying to understand the consequences. There was no end in sight, and it stretched out before him like train tracks leading in every direction, with Anton himself standing at the hypocentre.

They travelled west by rail to Quebec City, where they got a car and drove out to the Plains of Abraham. The route came back to him as he drove. He'd always had a head for directions. He was able to get inside distance—the relationship between objects—and figure out the perfect mathematics of arrival. He didn't see it as the best way there, really, or the fastest, but as a statement of harmony; any variation and the relationship crumbled, a dissonance created, as each body exerted its forces of push and pull.

They found the camp exactly where he'd remembered it, bordered on three sides by horizons of corn and barley. The hollowed-out structure rose out of the afternoon like a dark giant up from the earth, an orphans' holding pen, collision of fates. He parked the '49 Ford at the main gate and they sat there without getting out, she with her hands folded timidly in her lap, like a cross; he nervously picking at the steering wheel with his thumbnails. They watched the hard-packed dirt compound for movement, empty but for a carpet of weeds that the fences and wire had been unable to withstand, waiting, possibly, for a ghost to swing open one of those wood-shack doors and rustle the tall weeds with his invisible feet.

Everything of any value had been carted away. Doorknobs were missing, hinges, window frames. Scavengers had come to pick through the remains to aid in the construction of some shack or other along the river. The barbed wire had been liberated, only to be wrapped around unseen lives in neighbouring townships. The door leading into one of the cabins on the right—had it been hers?—hung open and moved in the wind, as if the forms that haunted her memory lived on, persistent and invisible, still pacing from room to room. Shafts of light fell through the splitting wood of buildings uninhabited this last decade. The silent guard towers that had watched over the internees cast afternoon shadows along the dry earth.

He pushed open his door. "Do you want to go in?"

Days here had possessed the slow drudgery of an imprisoned life. Her mind had occupied a different world from the one she and her husband now looked over. While she was interned her imagination had spread out across sea and country in search of her parents. She'd cast her memory backwards over the length of her journey—Scotland, Cuba, Hamburg, the fat man on the train in Linz—to the point where she found herself sitting at her parents' kitchen table, as she often had as a young girl, listening to her father tell stories of when, as a young suitor, he'd brought flowers to a certain address in town and left them at the window, every Sunday for six months, before Sophie's maternal grandfather even let her acknowledge the boy he was in those innocent days.

And she remembered the tinge of sadness her father was never able to hide from her, too, the regret that lay heavily in his deep-brown eyes as he shook his head and smiled in telling these stories. On these occasions, he always spoke in a way that reflected the depth of their love, the story an example of how nothing could have kept him away from Sophie's mother. But the more she recalled while shut away behind barbed wire—performing one of the chores the internees had organized for themselves, the endless laundry, the kitchen duties, her studies—the clearer she saw her family's divisions played out over the map of Europe.

Anton pointed through the windshield. "We could get in through there."

At first she seemed not to have heard. A silence dropped between them. Finally she shook her head. "Inside, no. I don't want to go in there."

But after another moment she was out of the car and walking along the fence's perimeter, dragging her hand lightly across its sagging wires. A fine dust rose. He took her hand and led her down to the river, to a clearing that resembled the one where they'd met, possibly that very place, and watched the river as they had done back near the beginning of their lives together. He unbuttoned her blouse and ran his hand over her and she released him from his trousers as he deftly manoeuvred her—half standing, her body resting in the firm cup of his folded arms—in a manner that would hardly have been imaginable to either of them their first visit here, and finally lowering her to the sand, legs up, laughing together quietly at the thought of their irreverence, then not at all, just breathing.

4

A week later they drove on to Toronto and stayed in a cabin just off the Old School House Road, north of the city on Stony Lake, which they rented from a man who ran the gas station in a nearby town. It wasn't much more than a shack. Which was fine by them. They were looking for silence. The day they arrived they boiled water on a wood-burning stove and placed their groceries in an icebox in the pantry. The next morning they stripped down and bathed in the lake, washing each other's back and toes in the cool water; and in the late-evening sunlight, as the world hung suspended in the pines and maples that hugged the shoreline, they swam out to a submerged island and climbed ashore, panting and exhilarated, and rediscovered the boldness in each other's body they knew from their early days in New York.

Back on shore a small dock jutted out ten feet or so into the water, with an iron ring a pirate might have worn on his ear bolted into one of its planks, and tethered there was an old rowboat. After an evening swim they would take it out onto the still lake and navigate parallel to the shore, entering small inlets and bays where Anton tried his luck at fishing for the bass said to live there. Behind stands of birch and maple and pine hid cabins similar to their own. During the day they sometimes used the boat as a diving platform; or Anton might take it out early in the morning to fish those quiet bays, thinking about nothing in particular and admiring the beauty of the world reflected back to him on the dense black surface. The mind gloriously free. One morning Anton came back with two bass, which Sophie insisted he clean as far from the cabin as possible so as not to attract the animals she heard foraging in the night. She watched him from the verandah. "Farther," she called. "Away. Away."

He nodded his head, smiling, and walked deeper into the woods, where he found a fallen tree trunk that could be used as a table. He cut off the heads and opened the fish and tossed their insides into the bush.

That evening they sat close by the fire pit, the lake lost in darkness now, and watched the flames cast their sparks through the air. Here the bugs were not so bad. The breeze shifted in off the water and made the fire crackle, and a pale late-night glow dropped from the leaves around them in pink, then orange, then grey beads of light which finally turned deep blue and black and hid them from everything and everyone but themselves.

"It's hard to believe anything else exists," Sophie said.

"It's marvellous."

"It makes me want to believe in God."

"You can believe in God."

"You believe in what you do," she said. "That's something I don't have."

"What we believe doesn't matter much," he said.

"But to the believer?"

"You can never know what someone thought about something until he's dead, anyway," he said, putting another branch on the flames. "When he no longer has the luxury of changing his mind."

They slowed life down here as best they could during those fine summer days. They listened for the rustling of leaves overhead and the hollow thumping underfoot, which Sophie fancied echoed up from deep caves beneath them, evidence of Indian dwellings or burial sites. Who knew? she said. It was a strange and beautiful land. She had never seen anything like it. For hours she'd sit and watch the summer sun sparkle the surface of the lake, and delight in the antics of the younger cottagers on the opposite shore. She enjoyed the sound of a joyful holler when it came to her ears a second or more after the boys playing on the tree swing let go the rope, and the sound of the splash that lingered in the air, impossibly longer than those thin, tanned bodies.

But it was the sun she was not used to. The butterfly rash she'd suffered years before returned in a new set of markings on her skin. Not at all similar in shape, the red, disk-like shadows on her chest and arms and back reminded her of that day she'd heard the radio broadcast about the bomb. One morning at the lake she awoke in pain, scratching. Anton pulled her hand away, thinking this was a particularly severe case of sunburn, or maybe the bite of some insect. In order to see herself in the small bedroom mirror, she had to stand on an old crate. Wincing at the sight, she observed the circles on her skin where once there had been a butterfly. But these circles were raised and rough, almost scaly to the touch. It was the pain, though, that got her attention. Years before, there had been none, but this morning the burning had brought her out of sleep. Now there seemed to be small bits of smouldering fire buried deep within, a fire waiting to be released from her body.

She ran her fingers over one of the spots. Though the rheumatologist had long since provided his prognosis, there remained room enough for doubt in the absence of a definitive test, and the symptoms, when they came, had appeared and disappeared without pain. It had been a secret easily kept, almost forgotten about during the years when her skin cleared. But because there would be scars now, it could no longer be kept from her husband.

This condition wasn't caused by the sun; she knew, however, that the sun had a harmful effect, as she'd been warned a year after the butterfly shadow appeared. She had not told Anton. At first she thought he didn't need to know, and later she became afraid of telling him. A visit to her dentist had revealed a host of mouth sores. The first guess, syphilis, had proven inaccurate. It took three doctors several months to finally give her condition a name. The last doctor asked her questions, leading her back through her history, looking for clues. She remembered the "frostbite" she had suffered off Havana. The rheumatologist listened closely, checking off the symptoms, and then listing others she might experience.

These were all signs, he said, of systemic lupus erythematosus. He described its severity, and explained that if it didn't kill her within five years she might learn to live with it. People did— though rarely, if truth be told. She would carry it the rest of her life. There was no cure. The doctor asked if she and her husband had planned on having children. She told him yes, this was something she had always wanted. When she finished asking her questions, he told the nurse to give her a pamphlet on adoption along with the usual information from the SLE Foundation.

So she knew, and simply had been waiting for another eruption to occur. That summer—a world away from the rheumatologist she'd discreetly been seeing off and on for years—it came. Though she had known to expect one or more of eleven diagnostic criteria, now that it was upon her Sophie had no idea what to do.

"We'll find a hospital," Anton said. "It's probably nothing. Some skin allergy."

He only half believed her when she said it was not to be worried about and thought this was her way of masking her fear, which it was. But it wasn't the disease that she was frightened of, that kept her atop that creaking wooden crate, deflecting Anton's offer to drive her to a hospital in Peterborough while she touched and stared at these painful red circles, each one counting as another unborn child. Each spot an infant unconceived, undelivered, impossible.

"No," she said. "I don't want to face a doctor."

"They will give you an antihistamine. It will be no problem. We'll be back for lunch."

She shook her head. Burnt alive before they could be born. Each circle another reason for her husband to leave her, or else for him never to know. What devotion could she expect if she were unable to give him a son? Wasn't that his right, anyone's right? To bring something better and more permanent into the world than the sad legacy of his deeds? Look what I've become, she thought.

She would not ruin the first good time they'd had together in years.

"No, no, darling. It's nothing."

When they got back to Brooklyn she saw her rheumatologist. She was given quinine, an antimalarial, to help clear up the cutaneous lesions that had settled over her arms, chest and back—but not, she was thankful, her face. She couldn't hide what was happening any longer. She met Anton at his office at the New School, something she rarely did, and told him what the episode at the lake had meant.

"These marks aren't going away," she said. "The doctor says this is lupus. I look like a leopard now. The spots don't go away. The doctor said that I'd have them. . . ." She stopped, trying not to cry.

Anton stood.

"The kidneys can't clean the blood fast enough. That's how the doctor explained it. You drown in your own toxins. I've had this since I was sixteen—symptoms anyway. Once I had a butterfly on my face. But the ones on my arms and back now, those are scars. They stay with you. But he said people can survive this, and lead whole lives."

When he put his arms around her, she sensed a hesitation in his touch, an equivocation, as if a third presence had edged between them. She pulled back slightly to look into his eyes, and tried to smile. "It's not catching," she said.

There was something he didn't understand: that she had kept this secret, that she must believe he could not be trusted with the burden of this knowledge. She had held this worry close for ten years. She had managed this degeneration of her body—the carefully arranged medical appointments, the hidden symptoms—all with the deftness of a cheating wife.

"Why wasn't I allowed to know this before? You thought you'd get better?"

"I was afraid."

"Afraid of me knowing?"

"I didn't want to tell you because of those letters you used to send me. Because of what you talk about when you talk about the future."

He shook his head impatiently. "What?"

"How you talk about family. Raising a family."

He held her arms tightly. "This means you cannot have children?" he asked.

She shook her head.

Spring 1995

The trees arrived before the lake emerged from its morning fog cover that day. Sophie watched the men unload them from the truck and directed them round back. She hauled out her work pants and thick flannel shirt from the upstairs closet, both dusty and mothball-smelling after seven months of close proximity to the old suits and dresses of their younger lives. She'd stopped a moment and run a hand along the length of an old cocktail dress, blue-sequined, not sexy but thoroughly daring, as far as she could remember. The dress—and the matching shawl she'd worn to hide her scars—had been bought for a New Year's Eve celebration at the house of one of Anton's colleagues. She examined the dress's hem with a finger, then raised it closer to her face to regard the fabric. Champagne, interesting guests. The apartment had offered one of those views you see in photographs meant to capture the majesty of New York, lights sparkling, the Brooklyn Bridge spread out far below like a model in a toy shop. That view had stayed with her: so specific, and so solemn. She sighed as she let the dress fall back, after all these years on its hanger.

Through the window halfway down the stairwell, she saw Anton's feet sticking out from under the car, which he'd been tinkering with off and on all morning. She watched him for a moment before setting to work on the trees, wondering about his tireless efforts to keep everything—the house, the daily routine, the car—well oiled and running smoothly. She believed this simple industry was something he'd learned from her over the years; it was an important outlet for a man like him, trapped as he was in his own head, retired now these twelve years. His booted toes bounced awkwardly, maybe to some old song running through his head.

The air was still now at the edge of the lake. A light dusting of mist clinging to the shore gradually thickened as she gazed out into the distance, maybe a couple hundred yards, where it solidified into a white wall. Sophie filled her lungs deeply. This was better than any cocktail party, she thought, thrilled by the smell and possibility of wet soil. The new sun, punching weakly through the clouds, felt lovely in the cool air.

She fetched her work gloves and shears and wheelbarrow from the shed, uncoiled the hose and twisted it onto the spout at the side of the house, then ran it along the winding path to where she planned to plant the two new trees. Presently Anton wandered up, wiping his hands on an oily rag. Standing in front of the first juniper, now sitting upright in its hole, he kicked the fresh soil and shook his head. "You're crazy, is that it?"

"You can help," she said. "These are heavier than I thought." She looked at the hole she had already dug for the second tree, its wrapped roots bulging like a baby's diaper.

"This damp's not doing you any favours, either."

He took up the shovel and planted the second tree for her, stamped down the soil and put away her tools, from time to time shaking his head in disapproval. She walked back inside to sit at the kitchen table and watch the lake, then he joined her and made a pot of tea.

"Did you change the oil? Is that what you were doing?"

"That was stupid," he said, ignoring the question. "You know you shouldn't be doing that sort of work. Nothing like that." Then his tone softened. "Are you sore? Do you need a bath yet?"

He pushed aside his tea when she said, yes, she did, and unlaced his work boots, which he placed beside the glass door. In the upstairs bathroom he drew the bath, added the oils and readied the creams he would apply to her skin.

She had a minute yet before she'd go upstairs. Another two months must pass before she could begin the shaping, the actual clipping, which was the stage she most enjoyed—that along with the designing. Pencil in hand, a steaming cup at her elbow. This was how she first came to see the new figures her garden might contain. But by this time of year, still so near the edge of spring, she couldn't help but get excited about the coming season, and even the pain in the old joints and general fatigue would not knock any sense into her head. Though she understood Anton's frustration, she was reluctant to give in to it. This was something they went through over and over again. He worried; she played it down.

It was a matter of course by this stage in their lives to enquire after each other's creaking and wheezing, and the half-dozen other irritations that assaulted them on a daily basis. More than alarm, it was a form of ritualized curiosity and caring. He had maintained his health for the most part, and quietly accepted the mild discomforts that often arrived so suddenly. The distant ringing in the ears, the increasing frequency of bathroom breaks. There had been a slight stiffness in his right leg for years now, and he walked with a suggestion of pain that was just shy of a limp. But this was not worth worrying about. Worry was for the truly ill.

His old skin still shone with the memory of youth and its pleasures. He had got out on the river three weekends last summer (hardly enough, if you asked him), and with this winter's first snow he had snapped on the old skis that hung from the rafters in the shed out back and moved through the pine forest east of town that ended abruptly at the wide expanse of Lake Ontario, the deep cliff dropping at the curling tip of his skis. His breathing was laboured, a song that followed him through the trees like a bird call; but he'd moved over the snow with an old man's determined pace, despite the creeping hesitation in his right leg. At trail's end he would stand at the edge of the cliff, the lake reaching out before him, and listen to his heart moving quickly in his chest, grey temples pounding with exhilaration, then try to match his breathing with the natural rolling rhythm that spread out as far as the eye could see. He'd watch the churning swirls leap up from the dark mass one hundred feet below, and finally the song in his lung stilled and only the wind persisted. Or when he was crouched over in the small vegetable garden his wife had allotted him between the shed and the rosebushes, knees sandwiched into his chest as he plied the earth at the roots of his tomato and pepper plants, the hollow whistle in his left lung also sometimes sounded, but he never thought this was anything to fret about. One thing he'd been given was a healthy body. For that he could be thankful, that he was well enough to look after his wife.

They were each as active as their abilities and health allowed. When he brought down his skis in winter, Sophie would busy herself in her own way. She knew how to minister to her failing body's needs. She needed rest. It was a matter of management, something she had learned to adjust to over the years. That's when she would concentrate on refining her garden's design, sitting there in the kitchen. It was an interest he could not understand, but he knew it gave her strength. Though she would never enjoy the feel of snow crunching under her boots, or the simple, indescribable pleasure of a well-placed dry fly, her none-too-physical pursuits, acceptable to both her doctors and Anton, afforded her body its necessary rest.

Then there was the work itself. Not its rigours, not the strain it brought to his wife's body, but the fact that she never seemed to repeat the motifs she bent and twisted into shape with rolls of stainless-steel wire from one year to another. Last summer the theme had been animals of the forest. Some of those tortured winding shapes were still held within the branches of the winter-beaten evergreens that dotted the property. Atop one bush he still could see the remnants of a fox's head, or what he thought had been a fox's head; and inside the large ivy bush that leaned into the bird-watering station, a deer seemed to dip its ragged antlers. Over the years she'd carved rabbits and squirrels in the smaller shrubbery that bordered his vegetable garden, and lined the walkway that led down to the water; and in a cluster of yews by the arbour she had fashioned a swinging monkey and—improbably, with the help of one of the local boys—a giraffe's head at the top of the highest cedar.

What about a simple cone or sphere? he often wondered. The perfect truth of geometry, of balance? But he never asked, for two reasons. The important thing was rest, no matter what activity she pursued. That is your scientific brain talking, she would've said. Which was the second reason.

She had spent that winter sketching fish, all sorts of them leaping and swimming in schools through her notebooks, spitting green gaiety and blue daffodil fountains from puckered mouths while standing on the tips of their tails. She sketched standing at the kitchen window while cardinals and starlings and chickadees tapped with their beaks at the feeder Anton put out and tended to regularly in the cold months. She sketched fish from memory and imagination, trout and salmon and pickerel and fish she could not have seen, not here anyway, such as those she saw in books checked out of the town's small lending library.

Often she worked in the sunroom, on the oak table Anton had found at a garage sale in Cambridge Bay. The room was a clutter of wire bundles and metal files and wire cutters and pliers and potted plants; magazine clippings of designs that had caught her eye over the years were pinned to a corkboard above the workbench. When the skeletons of these small shapes and animals were complete they were set in a planter, and the holly or boxwood or snakeskin plant or rosemary was placed in the soil or moss, and slowly the plant filled the wire frame as it grew to maturity. When the good weather came it was transplanted to the garden, and set among the larger shapes along the herringbone pathways that wound and twisted between the house and the lake. Now wire skeletons of fish cluttered the room, each standing in its individual oversized pot and already green and white with the flower she had chosen to concentrate on this summer. They were now ready to be taken outdoors.

She never considered doing a sculpture before she knew what it would entail in real terms. Some were technically impossible, she knew, because of size (she preferred full-scale) or some other concern she was always thorough enough to discover before it was too late. She found pictures and weighed the technical demands that each animal would pose, the layering of scales or delicacy of fin construction, and whether it made sense to portray the individual fish or a whole school.

The older junipers and yews and hornbeam that walled the property and walkways had long since taken on their precisely anonymous cloud shapes and would require only trimming. Of course she could not coax new designs from such shrubbery each season, but the smaller plants she'd been nurturing for the past few years—the wild hawthorn and Leyland cypress and holly and creeping ivy—were ready to be massaged into the creatures she'd imagined over the winter. Long before the last April storm broke apart along the shoreline, she had decided what this summer's figures would be, and the strength of her confidence surprised her. This was an ambitious project. She envisioned entire schools of exotic and indigenous fish that, by mid-August, would be splashing their way up the property from the lake. She would have little time to tame such a demanding surge of life, and this wily chaos of fish shapes in constant need of pruning and clipping would be the concern that would keep her busy while Anton, who still travelled too much for her liking, was away.

A sliver of lake glimmered through the long avenue of cherry trees. She rolled out of bed and pulled the curtain back and looked out over the water. She dressed quietly on her side, then drank her coffee standing on the terrace, watching the garden come to life in the new light. The parting blanket of mist left a tumble of shimmering diamonds scattered about the lawn, and she tried to focus on the work that awaited her. She would manage a little, anyway, before her mid-afternoon nap. She'd been through the worst of it, she hoped, and now was out the other side.

The smooth sheet of glass stretched out before her, cool and deep and perfect. She placed the empty blue ceramic cup on the patio table and came out to the street by way of the side lawn. The grass, thinner here, would need reseeding. She stepped onto the sidewalk that led up to town and waved to Eva, whom she saw standing at her kitchen window, then turned left onto Lakeshore, the main street, where she planned to pick up a paper and some cream.

Within five minutes she was sitting on the bench in front of the Anglican church, concentrating on her breathing. Maybe she'd take that nap when she got back home. Only these few blocks had tired her. As she often did at times like this, she pondered what it was in her bloodline that had brought this on, what family legacy had remained untold when she was separated from her parents. There were no survivors to enquire of; no one was left. She wondered now if this most recent flare-up had come on account of the digging, the strain she'd put her body under after a winter of inaction. Old body, old joints, maybe something as simple as that. Such pain was entirely understandable for a woman of her years, but she knew this was not the case. She knew exactly what state of decline her body was in.

She rose slowly, testing her feet, then she straightened her trousers and pulled her shirt snugly down over her hips.

Around mid-day she was confident again. To be sure, she would avoid heavy work. She would be reasonable. She would take her husband's advice, as well as let her nephrologist know, a few weeks from now, at their next meeting. The pain, as it often did, had already become a memory. Now it was merely soreness and a swelling of the feet, an ache, an irritation. The sunlight was too beautiful; there was too much to do, and to think about. She believed in the strength of her determination, and even her body.

She wore sunblock outside, and always long sleeves and a hat. No part of her ever touched the summer sun. That was her enemy, she knew, as one of the books Anton brought home had put it. But today the sun was only a warm hint of the season to come. For a brief, glorious moment she enjoyed its caress on her forearms and the back of her neck and was able to remove her jacket and roll up her sleeves, and for her this signalled the true beginning of her gardening. Fatigue or no fatigue.

That afternoon Sophie rested frequently between trips out to the edges of the garden with the wheelbarrow, which she pushed with deliberate contemplation over the brown grass; but the discomfort did not return, and she was able to transplant most of the topiaries before Anton—her embodiment of common sense—appeared from around the side of the house to ask if she'd lost her mind.

"I feel better. Look, I'm going slow."

"You're going to rest now."

"Just wait till you disappear and start flying all over the country. Then we'll ask who's overdoing it."

"I won't be going anywhere if you keep this up," he said. "It's not me who was moping all day yesterday."

She smiled and shook her head. Had he really said *moping?*

But again, the following morning, she awoke stiff and in pain, the joints in her arms and legs truly pounding. Anton turned and touched her forehead, the only part of her he knew would not hurt. They decided it was bad enough that they should drive to the hospital in Cobourg, the Northumberland, where she'd gone three times a week for dialysis treatments before they were able to secure a machine for home use.

After the exam Dr. Stephens, her nephrologist, took Anton by the elbow and directed him to where his wife was waiting. As he shuffled over the buffed white floor, the echo of his steps bounced off the polished walls and his heart pushed hurriedly against his lungs. He felt flushed and forced a smile when he saw his wife sitting on the edge of the examining table. He was surprised to see how small she looked.

"Come sit here," she said after the doctor left them, and patted the cushion beside her. It was covered by a sheet of paper, thin as a delicate chocolate, with one long rip down the centre. "People are always sick in hospitals," she said.

"What did he say?" He saw she might cry.

"The kidneys are going fast." She put her hand on his knee. "I'm just a fussy old woman. I don't mean to make problems for you. I'm just an old fuddy-duddy."

"Did you tell him about that stupid tree?" he said. "You were straining yourself," he said. "That was hard work."

"He said they want me to consider a transplant."

There was a pause, ended when she shook her head. He didn't even have a chance to ask; they'd already talked about it, and she would have none of it. She would be no one's experiment. They'd been through the arguments—and the statistics—numerous times, but there had been no changing her mind. He placed his hand in hers. "Then why do you have to stay?"

He noticed his twisted, elongated image reflected back to him on the uneven metallic surface of one of the contraptions the doctor had used in his examination. He looked down at her feet hanging in mid-air.

"He wants to keep me on a little longer. I'll be home in the morning. You know I can't stand it here."

There was no window to look out, only posters on the wall in front of them about drinking and driving, and smoking, all the dangers to one's health.

"They're getting a room ready for me."

He drove back to the house. He would stay with her tonight, but there were things they needed: toiletries; a clock radio; a few items of clothing; maybe a book, if she had the energy. He knew what she usually took along during these brief overnighters. He packed a single suitcase hastily, not liking to be alone in the empty house under these circumstances, then carried the suitcase outside and put it in the trunk. Next he went back to make sure everything was turned off and locked up.

He walked up the street and told Eva what was happening. His neighbours knew from experience what was expected. They would keep an eye on the house, she assured him, not that anything would occur in the twelve or so hours they would be away. She nodded, said that, yes, Bela would be sure to go by tonight and double-check.

He drove back into the city and parked across the road from the hospital. Sophie didn't wake up when he entered her room, by now mid-evening. The reading lamp on her night table, switched on, reflected against the shiny surface of a magazine on the bed beside her, its spine turned up like a wave. He closed it, leaned over her and placed his palm on her cheek, then her forehead. The temperature seemed normal, he thought. He pulled the blanket up under her chin and sat back in an old green recliner to watch her, his hands on the armrest, both feet on the floor. A low sound, whose source he could not identify, hummed on the other side of the wall. He closed his eyes and waited.

Once her condition was revealed to him, years before, they had managed to live within the confines of this illness. He had steeled himself for the inevitability that one day he would lose her. That he would not be the first to go. The likelihood of her dying due to this illness was always there, but somehow in all these years it had never been quite real. The idea of a dark shoal or reef jutting out of the otherwise deep, silent water of their twilight years. Couldn't this be just another setback, he said to himself, another near miss they could sail past? Nothing permanent, nothing unexpected. Lupus presented complications that you might prepare yourself for. It was a matter of getting through it, of re-establishing the equilibrium.

It had seemed a whole lifetime, now, this degree of peace they'd finally achieved together, carried away again and again when another wave dislodged any tranquillity from their lives. But they had always waited, made their fearful hospital visits and agonizing blood-lettings, as she called them, and that peace had afterwards returned, in every case. These times reminded them most profoundly of their connection to each other. It was deeper than a lover's commitment, though that, of course, had been there. It was deeper than family or any other shared history could have provided. It was what they had lost that linked them. And the inevitable surge of fear that broke the peaceful silence quickened their sense of duty and reminded them of their perfect vulnerability, like unclaimed orphans able to rely only on each other, for all that had been lost.

It was the necessity of survival that held each in the other's radius. How they had looked up at the stars and known it was marvellous that they should be there at all, clear in the night sky, because they were so easily forgotten during those early years in the smog-choked city they had spent most of their life in.

What they had wanted together now was a slowing of time. They had almost been happy. Their careful management of the illness had both slowed and magnified the intensity of daily events, helping each of them catch up with the other. Walks down to the water's edge, where they set their lawn chairs in the sand and read under the striped umbrella, read and looked without speaking over the flat distance. And Sophie, always the one to get up and walk over the sand and stones to enter the water slowly and stand hip-deep, would cup the surface and splash Anton with an open palm,

egging him on—"What are you waiting for, next summer?"—
before folding her legs beneath her and, with the radiant glow of a
child rising from sleep, disappearing beneath the surface.

Anton opened his eyes and watched her. The hospital made its
unknown hospital sounds. A lamppost outside, half covered by a
spring maple, shone like a flower coming to bud. Beyond, in the
parking lot, cold shining steel collected the night's dew. He observed
the light on his wife's face, the wrinkles softened now, all the tension released.

She seemed her normal self that next morning. The dialysis
machine had worked through the night. He got up and drew open
the curtain, sat again and took her hand in his, squeezing gently.

"You didn't sleep here, did you?" she said. "You should've gone
home."

He knew she was grateful, as he would have been.

After they checked her out and were on their way home she
told him about her dream. "Everything was so green," she said. "It
was hot and children were everywhere, such beautiful children."

They were headed back east along 401, a twenty-minute drive
in good traffic. The dreary grey pavement and office buildings on
the edge of Cobourg gave way to green fields. Farmhouses flew by
outside the window as she talked about being back on that ship to
Cuba when she was a girl. But in her dream, as opposed to the reality, she was able to escape. She told him how she'd slid into the
warm harbour waters and swum ashore and walked barefoot
through the magical streets of Havana under a large moon, mar-
velling at this elixir that was freedom. That's how it felt. A child
again, and free. She followed a circuitous route through the dark
city streets and finally came to a secluded grove heavy with a
strange, beautiful fruit, as if a spell had been cast over the land. She
knew in this dream that she was supposed to pick a great abun-

dance and this she did, and later she carried the fruit to the edge of the orchard, where began a steep hill, and rolled each one down. As they spun away into the dark, the fruit became running children who bounced and laughed and turned to her smiling as they disappeared within the folds of the evening.

Emiko

1

Of course I was surprised to hear from him that second time, given how he'd left our initial interview. In something of an old man's huff, I thought. I didn't usually make trips like the one he was proposing, but after two days I came to the conclusion that I might find something unknown in his life that might prove interesting.

It was muggy and claustrophobic the day he came to my house in Park Slope. I knew he was apprehensive about being shown in a bad light. He'd said as much to me the day before, at Fayerweather Hall, where I'd caught up with him. He was worried he was being positioned for something that, if manipulated just right on film, might expose him as the villain he most likely thought I considered him to be.

He sat on my couch in the living room, facing the window that looked out over the street. I'd asked him if he didn't mind taking off his shoes, explaining that I knew this wasn't a very polite thing to ask a guest, but that I had someone living in the basement apartment and the hardwood floors amplified the sound. He crossed his feet at the ankles, and I noticed his big right toe stretched out nervously.

"First you get to interview me," I said. "That makes sense to me."

So I answered his questions about myself, where I first began making short films and why, what schools I'd gone to, the usual CV sort of thing. I suspected he knew something about me to begin with. This was not my first project in the field, and I imagined he would've been familiar with some of my work. We, the two of us, occupied opposite ends of the same spectrum. I was surprised when he professed to know nothing about me. I elaborated on my particular interest in this project. I stressed the point that this was not a personal rampage. A professional documentary filmmaker, I would not cloud my work with my own stories, which, such as they were, were of interest to no one but myself. I explained my vow never to stoop to confessional ranting, and he seemed to listen to me intently.

"Of course," I said, "that doesn't mean I just walk away from this history. It is a history that will always fascinate me. It's my subject, and I can never imagine another as important or as definitive of who we are. The difference is that I don't turn the camera on myself, that's all."

I went on for a time like this, then showed him a couple examples of my work. He watched in silence until the two short films were over.

"I'm not saying you'll make or break the idea," I said. "I've interviewed more than fifty people over the last six years. I have hundreds of tapes, stored A to Z. I have seven more people lined up in the next few days."

"Mostly survivors?"

"No. I have Edoardo Alder. Pierre Brody. Vannevar Bush. I also have average Americans remembering what they were doing when they heard the news. A couple of young kids who never even heard of Hiroshima."

"I can't imagine you're not going to push it in a certain direction. I say that with respect. And that's your right, too. But I mean slant it in a direction that suits your purpose. Editorialize, even proselytize?"

"Everyone's got a message, right? This is a document I'm building. It's a collage. But I understand what you're getting at."

"Maybe I'm not precisely the best person for this," he said.

Was this more confession than humility, I wondered, or the other way around? Or simply a moment of fear? I noticed his right toe began to bob then.

"I think I've scared you with the idea of a last act."

"Sorry?" he said.

"You don't want to make any final declarations. That's my guess. Reluctance to stick your neck out. It's not all that unusual. Sorry, it's not an accusation, just a fact."

"How long have you been here?"

"Remember what I said, Professor Böll. I will not turn the camera on myself. That's my only rule. What matters in this project is your interest here. Ultimately, like I said, you won't make or break what I'm doing. I thought your point of view might interest some."

I saw immediately that I'd upset him. He unlocked his hands and prepared to raise himself to leave. It looked like I'd lost him, so I had no reason not to continue. He was going anyway.

"You know it's true," I said. "You must know your research position could've been filled by any one of two dozen other scientists in the time it took to get a plane out of Chicago or New York. You are a footnote. You must know that. Which, in some ways, you must be thankful for. It must lessen the guilt."

"Enough," he said. "Enough!"

"Being there, in whatever capacity, though," I continued, "is probably enough to keep you awake at night. Am I right?"

He turned in a fury and began toward the door. I almost felt sorry for him. He seemed ridiculous and pathetic, simply an old man in stocking feet.

Then he stopped and turned. "You are a surprising woman," he said. "I didn't know what to expect when it came time to finally meet. I thought I might like you. But I see you are a fish in a glass bowl, with only one view of the world around you. That is what I can see in you. You are no different. And that is a shame. I expected more. I had hoped for more. I will tell you what frightens me. What frightens me is the thought of what would've happened had we not succeeded. What would have happened if we'd failed. That is what keeps me up at night."

• • •

I rented a car at International Arrivals and drove to his home in that small town three-quarters of an hour east of Toronto, where he lived with his wife, Sophie. He met me in his driveway and came to the side of the car.

"Trouble finding the place?" he asked, pulling open the door for me. "It's an easy flight, isn't it?"

"It was easy enough," I said. "You can hardly call it travelling." I stepped out. "You must have flown it a hundred times."

"Let me help with this."

"It's not much," I said.

He stepped back and I reached across the seat, took the single equipment bag, which contained my video camera and blank cassettes, and swung the door closed. I was glad he hadn't offered to pick me up. This way I was not beholden. I could leave whenever I wanted to, which I planned to do the following day. The fewer niceties, the better. My luggage stayed in the car, because I'd be sleeping at a roadside hotel I'd passed on the way here. I'd brought only one change of clothes with me, and my return flight was booked for the following evening.

He led me into his study on the main floor, whose walls were covered with books and maps and an old print of a labyrinthine garden somewhere in England, I guessed. There was an old Bell & Howell projector sitting in a corner of the study on a small stand, dust patches spotting its grey cast-iron surface.

He touched his finger to the stack of film reels that sat on his desk. "Straight to it, then," he said. "I made these while I was in Hiroshima. October of 1945. Late September. I'd bought a camera from a serviceman, a 16mm Pailard-Bolex. A good little handheld model. I doubt they make them anymore. I could hide it easily enough, which I was obliged to do occasionally. I got these out without anyone knowing. I remember a group of Japanese film-makers were thrown in jail for doing the same."

He checked to see if the projector was plugged in, drew the curtain and turned the machine on. He pulled the screen down by a cord which hung from a canister placed horizontally a foot shy of the ceiling, and the white box of light established itself squarely in the middle of the wall.

I'd already looked at hundreds of hours of Hiroshima tapes. Always edited, censored by some military board in some forgotten New Mexico outpost or some such place. I knew how the sanitized version went. It was meant to be consumed in classrooms and public libraries across the land, nothing nearly as hideous as I'd known it, graceful in its platitudes to the suffering of the Japanese people, but still unrepentant. *This was war,* after all. *Remember Pearl Harbor.* Some of these films showed brief shots of the destroyed city, some bandaged children receiving medical treatment from American doctors and food supplies from international organizations. Normally they didn't mention, much less focus on, the festering wounds, the destroyed families, the orphans.

But at the very least what he was about to show me might prove to be a unique point of view, I thought. I didn't expect great things. I hadn't come all that way for someone else's documentary. But as I watched the people on the screen it became clear quickly enough that this first reel might be a document not to be entirely disregarded, although aesthetically, of course, it bore many of the beginner's trademarks. The images came in jerks and clumsy bounces, sloppy home-movie style, sometimes a forty-five-degree slant, sometimes just a foot walking, just plain ground and someone's mud-splattered army-issue boot crunching gravel. Then a line of faces, moon-eyed and empty, staring up from their hospital beds, so familiar to me. I wondered for a moment if I would see myself or my brother lying there in one of those beds, or my grandfather shuffling up the aisle. I felt myself stiffening, preparing for an assault. But I did not see those memories in his films.

What I did see was raw and completely unedited. These film reels did not carry any sound. That's why the films, as he played one after another, began to seem important. They were dirty and harsh and completely true.

"How long after the bomb is this?" I asked. "October, you said?"

"Three weeks or so. Maybe late September. I was there a month and a half. I have dozens of these. Each one's just a few minutes long. I don't know how many I've lost. I think quite a few. They didn't store very well. Some are in pretty rough condition, probably totally destroyed. But I have reels from all over. Others I haven't even bothered to develop."

I didn't speak. For a time I just sat watching, enthralled and horrified in equal measure.

"I've carried them around like family portraits in a way."

I didn't say a word. My excitement was growing. I could do something with these. I'd come hoping that some unknown history would pop out of his gentlemanly exterior, this proper old European, that I might discover something about myself in this strange old man—and suddenly all this was coming at me in the hyper-real colour that put heat and light into the objects and people they focussed on. They all seemed to run a millisecond too fast, in the fashion of earlier film. A man onscreen walked through the ash garden of the city with the approximate gallop of a Charlie Chaplin film. It was like watching the past trying to catch up with the present. Most of the reels stopped and started in the middle of things, broke away, went blank. Some sputtered and jammed.

There were no scenes, no secrets given away, no narrative. Just a day walking through the city, charred and anonymous. It looked precisely as I'd remembered it, the film clicking there before me. There were makeshift hospitals and a man squatting in the ruins with his pants at his ankles; half a minute of two well-dressed officers of the conquering army striding down the middle of the street; and an American with a Japanese girl on his arm and a bottle of liquor standing at a street corner in Tokyo's Omori district, maybe, having a fine time, the sign over their heads shouting out DANCE DANCE DANCE in flashing red.

"No one knows about these?"

"These have been out in the shed since we came here."

"You haven't looked at them since when?"

"Oh, only once in a while, at least since we left New York. Fifteen years. Seeing you reminded me."

He stopped himself.

"I wanted to put them to good use. I never knew how. There's other stuff, too. I went to Palomares in the sixties, when the four bombs got dropped by accident. Mid-flight refuelling. I was interested in documenting certain things. I wasn't as organized as you are. I read about it in the papers. One plane clipped another, and they both went down. I got over there as fast as I could. I doubt if anyone else got that on film. Franco and the Americans kept it relatively unknown. I've got pictures of army dump trucks carting away radioactive Spanish soil. Then I followed it to North Carolina, where they dumped it. I used to try to track down accidents. Cases of nuclear negligence. I was trying to do something for the New School, develop a course, but I never finished with it. That's when I taught myself how to develop this stuff. I didn't want anyone to know what I was up to till it was all down. I've been carrying it around ever since, but I never have made anything out of it. Now it's just wasting away. And those undeveloped reels."

When I told him I could do that for him, restore the damaged reels and develop the rest, he said they were a sort of diary to him. Very personal, he said. He wasn't sure he wanted just to pass them over to me. He'd have to look at them, see what they were. Then he could decide.

He drew back the curtain when we were through, revealing the lake, and raised the screen. I blinked in the light glaring off the water. Sophie, his wife, standing in the yard amid a cluster

of creeping rose and lilac bushes, turned to the window and
smiled.

He took me outside and introduced us. She was dressed in
work clothes, a gardener's hat and gloves, totally protected from
the sun. She didn't seem surprised to find me there. I assumed he'd
told her that they were going to have a visitor. She looked fragile
and pale, although it had been a bright and hot summer, in New
York at least; but she seemed comfortable, too, in those old, baggy
work clothes.

"I hope you had a nice trip," she said.

I told her that I had, that I was glad to be here.

We were standing in the middle of a marvellous garden filled
with bushes and hedges cut into strange animal shapes.

"What do you think of my husband's work?" she said. "He's
very pleased to have you here, you know. He needs this more than
he knows. He's tried to get me interested in his studies."

"It might help with my project," I said.

"I've never wanted to look at them, those films, myself. I don't
understand the fascination. That was a terrible time."

Anton managed a smile and asked if we'd like something to
drink, then turned back to the house to prepare something. His
wife led me down to the edge of the property, where the grass
ended and the loose stone and driftwood began. To the left, two
piers jutted out into the lake. The closer was old and broken into
three sections; the other, new-looking one had a white-and-red
lighthouse at its end.

Sophie was not much older than I was, I guessed, ten years or
so, but I found myself deferring to her in a way that had once been
second nature to me. Beneath her hat she wore her grey hair in a
ponytail, which fell down her back between her shoulder blades.
She seemed aged beyond her years, and after a few minutes I began
to suspect her skin was partially translucent. I had noticed the

absence of colour immediately, but now it seemed much more than that. Despite the wide-brimmed hat, I could see a lone vein, blue and bulging, on the right side of her forehead. A network of fibrous red membranes spread out beneath her eyes and cheekbones. It occurred to me then that this woman was ill and, instead of playing the gardener or partial host, should be resting in bed, if not a hospital.

"You live over there," she said, pointing with a mixed degree of pleasure and strain. "New York is over there, a good distance now, mind you, and to the east some. But it's there. You would know we lived there for many years. Did Anton tell you that?"

"Yes," I said. "Your husband told me."

She nodded, distracted, it seemed, by the work still at hand.

"This is all really marvellous," I said.

She was bending over a rosebush. I watched her hold out her hand, shaking slightly, and wait for a ladybug to crawl up onto her index finger. Once aboard, it crawled over her skin in its blind, stupid searching, then she raised her hand to her mouth and blew it into the air. "You can't imagine the things that make their home here," she said. "There's all sorts of life."

We continued along a path parallel to the lakeshore till we reached an arbour at the bottom of the property. Its wood frame was lightly stained—cedar, I guessed, wildly—and draped in a flowering riot of, as she explained, pointing, iris and meadow rue and New England asters. Underneath was a small statue, a cheap Greek plagiarism of a naked boy tilting a canister of water over a fish's mouth.

As I was led along its southern edge, I was struck by the size and complexity of the garden. Animal shapes were cut into the plants and trees, like in the print I'd noticed in the old professor's office. But many of these had overgrown their edges. I could still gather from the rough outlines what they were meant to represent. Foxes

with large tails and open-winged birds and what looked like leaping schools of fish. Sophie kneeled slowly and plucked some
weeds, and we started up again along the path.

"It never ends, though," she said, stuffing the cluster of leaves
into a pants pocket. "I'm afraid at this age it's a losing battle, my
dear."

The tall grass and beach sand and rocks were to our right, and a
large piece of driftwood, nearly an entire tree, brought in by some
storm.

Her husband found us there and delivered three glasses of
lemonade, which we drank as we mutely admired the sailboats
pulling their white hulls through the dark water.

After Böll excused himself, just after one o'clock that afternoon—
to tend to some pressing concern, he said—Sophie led me downtown at her snail's pace to show me around. By now I was
convinced that she was quite ill, though of course I was in no position to ask about her condition. Her body seemed to be slipping
away from her. Physically, I could tell she was straining, even walking as slowly as this. But when she asked if I would like anything
special for supper, or if there were certain things I couldn't eat, and
I told her I hadn't planned on staying, she smiled radiantly and
said, "Well, then, we'll just have to get something good enough to
change your mind."

The town was quite small, easily small enough that I would
stand out. I wondered for a moment what nicknames I might have
been given if I'd grown up here. Everyone I saw that afternoon was
white.

There were two banks I counted on our brief walk, some
tourist shops, a few dozen family businesses, stationery and the
like, and a small café called Swiss Canadian Bakery. In one store's

window were hung a dozen or so dream catchers, two dark cherry-wood canoe paddles and a family of Indian dolls. We were trailing a grocery cart behind us, the two-wheeled kind lined with a blue sackcloth to prevent smaller items from slipping through the mesh. People in summer shorts and cotton dresses and sandals crisscrossed the nearly carless street, licking at ice cream cones from behind sunglasses. Only occasionally did I feel a pair of eyes following me, head slowly rotating with my progress as I walked alongside this odd woman, who surely was familiar here.

Of course I knew what it felt like to stick out in a crowd, to be different, but I hadn't been stared at since my girlhood. It was my skin, obviously, though these people might not have known what it was that attracted their curiosity. They couldn't recognize, in the shimmering light that reflected off these shop windows, that other-worldly sheen on my grafted skin. There was only the hint of scarring left, barely noticeable, but I was never sure what impact it had on people.

Nor did it help that the town was as white as it was, as aggressively uniform and, it seemed, of a single mind. This was something I remembered from my first years away from home, the destructive self-consciousness that followed me around before I was able to teach myself to close my eyes to it. Before I knew what sort of person preyed on the hopeful and vulnerable girl I used to be.

"Actually, I was planning to speak with your husband about this—the reason I came. I liked those films he showed me. But in fact I'd like to ask him some questions, and I didn't get the chance. He just disappeared after you showed me your work in the garden."

"He likes to keep busy. Usually he doesn't trust people like you," she said. She was to be admired for her honesty, anyway. I gave her that. "He's afraid of getting his words twisted. I'd consider this quite an honour."

I gave her my promise not to twist his words.

"You must put his mind at ease, dear. He worries about the future. He thinks about the way the world is going. Oh no, he'd never say as much. You don't expect that from his type of man, being a scientist, all progress and onwards and upwards and so forth. That's how they think, you know. But he is so very *ethical*. That's not a word we hear very often these days. Are you married, dear?"

I shook my head.

"Well, a woman will know, regardless. Most men aren't hard to figure out, not when they want something of you." She paused and touched my shoulder, to lead me into a fruit-and-vegetable store. "My husband is not typical in that way. He does not give secrets away very easily."

It was cooler inside, a garden of fresh produce, but I was no happier with the progress I was making here. I waited for her to select what she needed, careful not to distract her attention for fear that this shopping expedition would drag out even longer. I had come a long way, and was becoming increasingly agitated. This was time wasted. I couldn't deny her sweet interest and honesty and the importance and sense of mystery her husband still seemed to hold for her. But, though admirable, that was not the reason I'd come. She seemed the type of woman who might take in stray dogs or pass her days mending a bird's broken wing. What I wanted was to get the man himself, then be gone. I'd taken vacation time from work and, when this work was done, had plans to meet up with two friends, translators from the UN, who'd flown on ahead of me to a small fishing village in Washington State, near Port Angeles, where we would stay at a small cabin overlooking the Pacific.

She introduced me to the cashier, who offered her hand across the counter. "A friend of my husband," Sophie explained, and I tried to smile.

2

I bought my first movie camera in 1966, at the age of twenty-eight, and thus set upon a journey, without any conscious intent, that turned out to be a life-long and defining passion. The camera was the type families were buying in those days for the purposes of documenting moments of domestic bliss, birthdays, anniversaries, vacations, that sort of thing. Home movies broadcast on a wobbly screen you propped up in your living room. I would guess that most families have a reel or two tucked away in the attic or basement, unbending to the will of time, moving portraits of distant childhood antics and Grand Canyon landscapes as seen through buggy car windshields.

Of course I had no family to film. But very quickly I felt the power this new device brought to me. I enrolled in a film course and began making embarrassing and extremely inexpert short documentaries: clouds drifting past the Empire State Building, subway platforms filling and emptying, people talking over coffee. It was, I think, the necessary stage in which a woman of artistic inclination must indulge in the early years, and which everyone else must endure, before any artifact of value is produced. What held me was a fascination with the energy of my world of exile. The sheer force and weight of New York held me in its grip. I documented the city as it was revealed to me, raw and without comment, and believed that through its documentation I achieved a simple and fundamental truth. I look back fondly now on these naïve sentiments, more suggestive of optimism than ability. It was a period of greedy and needful self-expression, the entirely artless result of which I have not viewed in nearly thirty years. But I recollect those times now with a nostalgic sense of pride and warmth for a young woman whose sense of adventure and fascination for the world had not been diminished, despite her circumstances. That, to me, is remarkable. All the more so because that young woman does not exist anymore.

I grew up in New York and learned its language. I worked odd jobs while studying at the UN School, and was rewarded for my hard work with a post in the UN's translation department. I was in no rush to leave this position—though, when the opportunity to concentrate on my work in film was presented to me, I could not turn it down. This, again, was an expression of that optimistic nature I had no right or reason to possess. A short documentary of mine had been accepted by a number of competitions and won some recognition. Though it was not a great amount by any stretch, with that exposure came enough money to develop two other projects I'd been putting off for a number of years. I walked away from my translating. The two subsequent projects were completed within a year, and those, too, helped to gain me something of a reputation. I was not yet forty. People made much of the fact that I was young, and my voice something of an oddity. Within three years of that first round of competitions I was known to a small group of filmmakers and artists. I began to receive invitations to sit on the juries of those very same festivals.

In 1983 I decided to retrace my journey from Japan to New York, and on to Los Angeles, where I'd been obliged to appear on a television program. In tracking down the show's principals, I found Dean Hollands, the host, living in a pink villa outside Pasadena. I got him talking. Wearing dark sunglasses, he floated in a chair in his swimming pool and talked about the golden age of television—it was an idea dear to his heart. TV isn't what it used to be, he said.

I'm not sure I suffered from the sense of isolation immigrants are supposedly prone to; maybe I did. At any rate, such a life is easier in a place like New York, where you are surrounded by people from all origins, each of them, like you, an oddity most anywhere else. My isolation was of a different key, played on an entirely different instrument. My hard mask of skin, healed now but still dead to all sensation, never let me forget who I was. On the outside I was different from the woman I knew myself to be, most certainly and clearly different from everyone I saw on a daily basis. If you passed me on the street, you wouldn't have looked twice. No, it was what the bomb had done to the inside that marked me for good. Those surgeons had accomplished their task. Of the twenty-five girls they worked on, my case was one of the most successful. My face wasn't perfect and never would be—you could see the scars up close, over coffee, while eating your pastry—but a glance told nothing of what I wore inside.

I knew I was different. Everything I had lived through made me so. To the world I was not the person I knew myself to be, the girl behind the eyes. Long ago I had given up waiting for the moment my new face would again resemble who I really was. Then, one day, something strange happened that forced yet another change in my life. It was the day I approached the professor at the university to ask for an interview for my documentary. I knew that somehow this otherness that I suffered from, that defined me, also connected us. As I listened to his words I saw he was as distinct and as lost to the world as I had always been. Something about him drew me into his story, despite the role he had played in my life, and when he asked if I would like to visit him and his wife in Canada, I saw an opportunity to discover something about myself.

I did get a chance to interview Böll later that day, after Sophie and I returned from our shopping expedition. I had just resolved to leave for the hotel when he came out into the back garden and invited me to set up the camera down at the arbour.

He sat with his back to the water. I arranged the camera so the lake's horizon was the entire background, and told him not to look into the lens or move his head too much. "Talk directly to me," I said, "just like a normal conversation." I assured him it would be edited for brevity and precision only, and never as a form of manipulation. Then I started, with what I thought would be the obvious question.

"I saw you in New York, during the celebration of the anniversary of the bomb dropped on Hiroshima, just three weeks ago. That was not the first time you attended one of these memorials."

"No."

"Why do you bother?"

"This is my history, too," he said. "Because we have all lived through this. You get to a point in your life when the temptation to look back is greater than the temptation to look forward."

"Do you feel connected to that date, August 6?"

"I do."

"Why?"

"Because there are still some among us who can admit to themselves that we did what needed to be done. I am one of those people. Although there was a price to be paid, and we knew it, we were able to complete our work. I'm not saying it was for the betterment of humanity. No, that is obvious. That is a luxurious position to be in. None of us thought to claim such high ground. To save lives, yes. It was to finish the war, to finish the work others had started. That was our aim, and we achieved that aim."

"You said there was a price to be paid?"

"The price people like you are asking me to admit to. You are waiting to see evidence of a troubled conscience. In anyone connected. In anyone who brought the war to an end, believing, as only we could, that we were serving a greater cause. Lives were saved. You can't forget that. You might think yourself a principled woman. I will respect that. I will give you your due. But I am also a man of principle. Do not sit in judgment over me. That—to answer your question—is why I attend those memorials. Because I was part of this history, and we have paid, too. I have paid. My principles have paid, and, like you, I do not want my part in this glossed over."

"Is there more here than right and wrong?"

"That is precisely what I'm saying. With the bomb, ideas of right and wrong ceased to exist. To be a principled human being doesn't mean you pay lip service to right and wrong. That's too easy. Children think like that. I do not have scars on my face. I do not deny the pain caused that day, and every day after that. For the rest of your life. Everyone's life who was there. I am not an animal. No one in their right mind would say any different. But this is what I know. I know the world requires a certain payment from us all, pain and suffering, hunger, destitution, solitude, for the freedoms we enjoy. We have all paid. Or will. It is not right or wrong to have used the bomb. But it was necessary."

"But you did see the aftermath?"

"You saw those film reels. I was there, yes, some weeks after. I remember it clearly."

"How did it affect you? What did you think when you saw what you'd helped do? What your involvement led to."

"I thought, 'That is the end of it, thank God. There will be no more fighting. And, the Russians will not dare after they see this.' Many of us had lobbied for a demonstration on an unpopulated area. With Japanese officials present. That did not happen. We failed. Then we thought, Well, if not, it will be used on a military target. It was not. I deeply regret that. That is something else. That was a political decision, one I did not support. Understand, yes. I understood why it had to be used. What I thought those days was, 'Thank God it's over.'"

"You had saved lives?"

"We had saved lives, yes."

"Why did you start filming there?"

There was a pause.

"I thought it would be a good way to communicate with Sophie. Like a talking letter, only with pictures. I missed my wife. Filming myself doing things there, or not there but places I wanted her to see me in, might put her mind at ease. I think I made one— I can't even remember—before I got there. Then I stopped when we got to Japan. There was too much work to do."

"What sort of work?"

"With the Manhattan District," he said. "We carried out preliminary radiation readings. To determine contamination, whether it was safe for the rest of the groups to come in and start work. Testing."

"You started filming the city. You forgot about your film-letters?"

"It was no longer appropriate. I filmed things there. You saw them. There are more, in the shed. I'll show you them if you like. Things, some people I met."

"Was it your way of showing respect?" I asked.

"I don't understand."

"Showing the human side of what you'd done. Your group was there for different reasons from that. You were there as a scientific observer. Am I correct in saying that?"

"Not respect. Maybe horror. Maybe curiosity. I wouldn't call that respect."

"An interest in the human side of things. Maybe document what had happened so others would know?"

"You can see it that way," he said. "I don't know what the reasons were. You'll have to accept that. I don't think I was thinking too clearly. I was a very young man then."

"But you said you were glad it was over. 'Thank God the war was over,' you said. You could go back to your wife. You were, what, in your late twenties? There was still time left to have a normal life. You wanted to get it behind you."

"I'm not forgetting that."

"You helped end the war."

"I did."

"But you weren't thinking straight. Why weren't you thinking straight?"

"I was looking at a lot of destruction. You know what I was looking at."

"But not from your eyes. I don't know what your eyes saw."

"You're asking about a clean conscience. No. I did not have a clean conscience. The war was over. Relief, yes. That part I was glad for. But that does not mean—"

"—that you felt good about yourself?"

"I did not feel good about myself. What I felt is not important." *Anton's Humanization*

"I would like to make this about what you saw, and how what you saw made you feel. It is, therefore, about you, Professor Böll."

"You do not feel elation at the conclusion of a war. You do not feel pleasure. I felt tired. I just remember feeling tired. My heart was tired."

There was another pause. "Can we stop here?" he said.

"Yes."

"We can start again later, if you like. If there is more you'd like to ask."

I got him talking again. This time on the flagstone patio just outside the sliding glass doors that led to the garden. The camera was set up as it had been earlier, a few feet from his face. It took him in from the waist up, and got some of the garden in behind him.

"Tell me why you left Germany when you did."

"I was scared."

"Was there a single reason or event that prompted you?"

"No one held a gun to my head, if that's what you mean. There were reasons to go. There were also reasons to stay. I didn't fully understand at the time. As a researcher I was treated well at first. That was my main concern. I had access to most facilities that were available to those in my field of physics. Then I began arguing with Walther Bothe."

"He forced you out?"

"Not in so many words, no. But I was ready to leave after that. I knew I could never do my work there. Their minds were cloudy. Their calculations did not make sense. History knows this. This is why the Americans beat them."

"That's why you left? Because you could pursue your work better? Not because you disagreed with the reason the war was being fought?"

"Scientifically, I knew I could not make the advances that would be possible to make in America. We knew that was the place that attracted the best minds. That's where the international community was going. Fermi was already there. Szilard was there. Bohr was there. Klaus Fuchs. I was one of the last to arrive. They all left fascism. I did not leave fascism as much as leave a place that could not accommodate my work. Yes."

"Is that because you didn't know what was happening in Germany? At what point in the war was this?"

"Early spring 1940. It is true. I was very sheltered at that time. We did not have access to the outside world to any great extent."

"You were not aware of the larger picture?"

"The larger picture as painted by my peers. It was favourable, naturally, and benign. Our victories were merely advances through the ranks of the disorganized Poles and their herds of cattle."

"You did not understand what sort of apparatus you were aiding?"

"That is correct."

"As late as 1940 you didn't know anything about the Nazis? Are you saying you had been sealed off from the truth of the place you were living in?"

"You find that hard to believe?"

"I find that hard to believe. I find that statement incredible. I have interviewed dozens of men who came out of similar circumstances. You are the first to suggest this."

"I was not living in the world. I could have been anywhere. I was living in my head then. I had shut myself off. Anywhere, under any conditions. I am not proud of this. But this is the nature of concentration, or discipline."

"I don't accept that. I can't accept what you're saying to me. It's a cop-out. You absolve yourself of all responsibility."

"Ask yourself that same question, then," he said.

I stared at him blankly.

"Ask yourself why the Japanese fought as well as they did. Why there was virtually no domestic opposition to that country's war effort."

"That is very different," I said.

"Tell me, then, or tell your camera, why it is so different."

After a longer pause, I said, "They were lied to. The *gunbatsu*, the military cliques. They were the ones who deceived us. We knew no better. It was a population of ignorance."

"I am asking why we participate in unjust wars. Is it simply propaganda and ignorance? Or because we willingly accept those lies? Why didn't the people of Japan rise against their Emperor when he proclaimed that Korea, then Manchuria, then America should be claimed in his name? *The Hundred Million, Bright and Strong.* Do you remember these slogans? *Light of Asia. Extinguish America and Britain and Make a Bright New Map!*"

"I was a child," I said.

"*Burn All, Kill All, Steal All.* This is what the Emperor of Japan ordered for Asia."

"I was a child."

"But you had parents?"

"Yes," I said.

"Was your father a pacifist or a soldier?"

"He was not in the war."

"I see. He rejected the lies?"

"He was unwell. He was tormented because of it."

"As a noncombatant? Are you saying he wanted to fight and was not permitted, on the grounds that he might've hindered the Emperor's cause, not helped it?"

"He was unwell. He suffered from polio. He wanted to enter the war but was unable. That is what he had been conditioned to believe. It was a question of honour for a man like him."

Another long pause followed, during which I wondered how I could break away from this line of questioning. But he spoke first.

"So you see," he said, "it is easy to say you were lied to. We were all lied to. In one way or another. Finally the door opened and I went through it. Within a month after I crossed over, the Spanish border was sealed. I was one of the last intellectuals to get out." He stopped and waited a moment—sizing me up, I thought. "Would you like to stop now?"

"No, no, go on."

"Then I met Sophie. Here, in Canada. Three months after that I was in Chicago, working with Enrico Fermi, then Los Alamos. I was the only one in Germany as far along as Fermi was. We both understood that the answer to the problem of finding a pile moderator was graphite. Walther Bothe thought heavy water was the better substance to go critical. That was their fatal mistake."

"Tell me about your work there, in Chicago and New Mexico."

"It was very particular. Technical concerns. In Chicago we were designing the plutonium-producing piles. These were small, tedious experiments that required months of preparation. We knew, the purer the graphite, the greater amount of energy we could generate. The problem of impurities, whether of nitrogen, hydrogen or boron, this problem had to be solved first."

"Did you witness the test at Alamogordo?"

"I was there."

"What do you remember of that day?"

"Everything. I remember the cold air that morning. It smelled of coconut oil."

"Coconut oil?"

"That was the flavour of the suntan lotion we had been provided."

"What was the purpose of giving you suntan lotion?"

"We thought it would guard against the radiation. That tells you what we knew. I remember feeling great anticipation. You cannot imagine how many thousands of hours had gone into research and tests, how many years had been invested up to this point. Years of research, development, even decades. We all knew—I did, anyway—that this moment would last. It was a defining moment. I watched from a bunker ten thousand yards from ground zero. That split second when the sky lit up, the light reflecting off the San Cristo mountains, I felt great elation. A tremendous light flooded my soul."

"You did not feel fear?"

"I did not. The fear would come later. At that instant only elation."

"Later?"

"Moments later. When the sound and then the heat came, it was like someone suddenly throwing open a furnace door. Then I felt it. Yes. Of course."

"'Destroyer of worlds'? Where, right then, was Oppenheimer?"

"I did not hear him say that. They say he said that. I don't doubt it. He was a very poetic man in some ways. I do not doubt he said that, or thought that. But I did not hear this. My heart was pounding too deeply. There were upwards of twenty people in that bunker."

"What did you do next?"

"We waited until it was safe to go out to the site and begin an analysis."

"And that night?"

"That night we were silent. We had done what no men had done before. We were awed. We had solved the oldest riddle known to man. We had found the key that unlocked the greatest source of energy our universe has to offer. It was no less grand than this, and we understood that."

"Do you think that any of you, at the time, had concerns? For how it might be used, I mean."

"Some of us, I believe, were still hoping against hope that it might be used against a military target. But I knew better. At that time they were fire-bombing Tokyo day and night. In terms of numbers, the fire-bombing was worse. We were burning people in the thousands. By then civilian targets were acceptable, even preferable. The point was to break a nation's spirit. It was realistic to assume this policy would not be changed because of a new bomb. I knew Truman understood the potential of this new weapon to do exactly that. In that way he was not original. We'd been going after civilians since Guernica, in Spain, during their war. If it ever had been, once upon a time, war was no longer conducted with any goal other than beating the other side into a pulp. I just wanted it to end. The fire-bombing alone was killing thousands every day."

"For you, having the bomb did not require a new kind of thinking? That a long-standing policy of targeting civilians should not have been challenged?"

"It should have been. In a perfect world. But we had long since left a perfect world far behind. It would not be changed. They knew a civilian target would be more effective. It would get the mission completed more quickly."

"The mission of ending the war."

"I am speaking realistically, considering the numbers. Hirohito would not have come under the same degree of pressure had the bomb been used on a shipyard. It's that simple. I am not talking about justice, and certainly not about the pain you have suffered. Expediency won the war, not justice. It is a terrible thing, but, historically, this cannot be denied."

The glass door slid open then. "May I?" Sophie said.

"Yes. Come save our poor guest. She already thinks I'm a monster."

"Oh, I'm sure she thinks nothing of the kind," she said.

I didn't say anything.

3

I drove up to the highway, just over the railroad tracks, and headed west on the freeway in the direction of the grim cluster of hotels roughly halfway between Port Elizabeth and Toronto. I had decided on the Journey's End on my way to meet Böll, for the mere fact that it had been the first hotel I saw, its vacancy sign lit up and flashing. After checking in, I rode the elevator up to the fifth floor, found my room and closed the door behind me. Then I called the airport to change my reservation. The person at the other end of the line asked if I had an alternative departure time, to which I responded that I did not. Things were shifting too quickly under my feet. I didn't know it yet in so many words, but I had already lost the sense of control I had brought with me. I deferred to curiosity and, for the first time in my life, rising emotion.

After that I picked up messages from my machine at home, one of which was my two friends calling from out west to say they'd never seen anything so beautiful, get out here quick.

Outside, the warm August night was busied and bruised by the sound of what I imagined to be businessmen and lovers and vacationing families, their cars and minds pounding toward home or a

few extra miles to the next likely hotel. The window accounted for
most of that south-facing wall. From here I saw a desolate stretch
of road cutting through what once must've been a beautiful landscape. The lake lay out there in the dark somewhere to the south. I
imagined a scattering of communities along its shoreline, and the
freeway that linked them like a single black thread, and the thousands and thousands of lives being lived out to their natural and
sometimes unnatural ends. It was a flat country, at least seen from
the fifth floor, and in the distance to the right I could see the glow
of Toronto. I guessed the small pocket of lights shining in the
southeast corner of the window belonged to Port Elizabeth, where
I'd just come from, though I had no way of telling, and that the
dark edge where those lights ceased was the shore of the lake, and
that somewhere in this cluster of lights the old man was nursing
his dying wife.

I closed the curtains and stepped across the room to get my
video camera, which I'd placed on the small table by the door,
under a mirror with dark wood trim. I wanted to look over what I
had shot that afternoon, but when I glanced up and saw myself, I
realized this was the first time I'd looked into my own eyes since
leaving New York. There had been no mirrors anywhere in the
house I had just come from. None whatsoever. I was sure of it now,
and wondered how that could be, since I'd visited the main-floor
bathroom twice, yet somehow that strange omission hadn't registered until now. I stood there entranced, as if this were the first
time I'd seen my own reflection. Though what I saw did not
resemble what I knew was truly there. I did not see a childless
woman, tired and increasingly confused, the memory of scar tissue
shining like a waxing moon in the unforgiving neon bursts of light
that hotel-dwellers are often forced to endure. Instead I saw a
young girl peering out from behind a dark flap of curtain at a
world I would soon be forced to step into.

• • •

As the program began back in May 1955, I had yet to understand what was expected of me, or to grasp fully that I'd be front and centre at its conclusion, my image transmitted through the magic of television to the hungry eyes of the entire nation. Before the broadcast began, Takako and I had seen the host, Dean Hollands, talking with a stage director who with his large hands would cue me when the end of the show approached. But that strange world of television seemed more one of circuses and prancing horses, of sudden clouds of smoke and quick exits. It was more the world of my grandfather's fairy tales than anything real I'd known or imagined on my own.

I remembered clutching my stomach with a free hand to calm the monster that seemed suddenly to have grown inside me, trapped there and pulling at my guts as I waited for the cameras to turn on me. An anxiety I'd never felt was gathering there, growing harsher. Cameramen wheeled their large contraptions over the smooth polished floor, rotating the big lenses from face to face, retreating, then insisting again like probing one-eyed giants. I felt nauseated, but this discomfort was not the physical sort of pain I was used to. I had been assured it was a tremendous privilege to be invited on the program, and that this appearance would aid our cause. But it was also a dream I had lost control of and could not stop. Partially hidden, I waited for the ON AIR lights to flash as I'd been told they would. I imagined tonight's guests, myself among them, blown to countless pieces and spread thin across the land. I closed my good eye and saw a rain of limbs and disembodied ghost faces leaping between transmitters and relay towers, over desert flats and sharp mountains. I feared the countless peering eyes that would bear witness to my shame. I feared the pity and disgust these bright lights would find in the hard mask of scar tissue that obscured my real face, and their power to mock the girl they had made of me.

Reverend Yasaka sat at centre stage. He waited impatiently, his dull, rounded fingernails picking nervously at the armrests of his chair, perhaps preparing himself for what he was about to be subjected to. I surveyed the audience from behind the curtain. I had been told the whole country would be out there watching this modern wonder, as recent and rejuvenating as it was terrifying. I'd been told this was a program not to be missed on Sunday nights here in America. The whole nation waited all week for its favourite host to smile into the camera and speak his famous introduction.

But tonight he would be talking about us, the scarred orphans of Japan. We were his backdrop, and he would be out there along with Yasaka and the other guests.

In a moment the stage was cleared of all those who had been milling about, the large cameras took their positions and steadied themselves and Dean Hollands buttoned his suit jacket. I did not understand a word of what was to come, though I could follow what was going on by watching the reverend's face and body—his reactions, I mean—and the sound effects and music and the images that appeared on a large screen behind the two men; however, years later, upon reviewing a tape of that broadcast in preparation for the documentary I would later film chronicling my journey to America, I was finally able to fully understand what had been said that evening.

Applause signs were lit. Hollands smiled broadly to receive the audience's imminent applause, and a man standing beside one of the big cameras counted down on his watch, retracting each finger until he was left with a single index finger, which he pointed like a pistol at the man at centre stage.

"Good evening, ladies and gentlemen," Hollands said, bowing graciously, "and welcome to *This Life in Focus*." His voice fluttered down over the heads of the audience from speakers placed throughout the studio. "Tonight, we will meet a man whose life was changed forever by the most devastating power known to mankind."

He turned to his guest and asked him his name.

"Reverend Tanabe Yasaka," his guest said, then leaned back stiffly in his chair. It looked to me like he was attempting to assume a relaxed air, but he was not successful. Already I saw the anxiety spreading over his face, the desire to stand up and walk out, though he could not, because he had brought us here in order to help fund our stay.

"First tell us about yourself, Reverend Yasaka."

"I am a minister, from Japan. My city is Hiroshima."

I felt a wave of excitement and apprehension roll through the audience then, as if they could sense where this was going. "My city" could mean only one thing to them. Then Hollands asked Yasaka where he was on August 6, 1945, at eight-fifteen in the morning, and when he began to explain that he'd been on the outskirts of town on some errand or other, a mechanical sound began, distant at first, difficult to identify. It seemed to emerge from a photograph of the sun rising up over a blue horizon that had suddenly appeared on a screen behind where the two men sat, and when the host spoke again it was clear that this was the sound of a large airplane. As the sound grew louder, the monster inside me grew with it. I held myself and listened to this mysterious language.

"Now we are approaching Hiroshima," he said, "and in a short moment we will be given to understand something of the nature of the power and the terror that our kind guest, Reverend Yasaka, witnessed firsthand on that fateful day, August 6, 1945." He turned to Yasaka again. "As we near our target, Reverend, we shift our focus back to you. Tell us when you first came to the United States."

By now it was clear from the reverend's voice that he no longer possessed the confidence he had tried to instil in us for this appearance. I pressed down on my stomach harder with the increasing noise of the approaching airplane, whose distinct sounds I knew so well.

"In nineteen thirty-one," he said.

"And what was the purpose of that first visit?"

He told Hollands that he'd studied theology for ten years at Emory University before returning to Japan.

"And, before we contacted you, had you ever seen or heard of *This Life in Focus*?"

"Not until I arrived in New York," he said.

Hollands nodded with an expression of interest, or unrehearsed surprise, and the sound of the plane began to fade, my anxiety subsiding with it.

The picture of the sun and horizon was replaced by dozens of smaller photographs of people from the reverend's life. "These faces you see behind us, ladies and gentlemen, belong to some of the many people who have crossed paths with the man who sits before us on life's uncertain journey, and during our show we will meet as many of them as we can. But first, a word from tonight's sponsor."

When the OFF AIR sign lit up to the left and right of the audience, the reverend rolled his head in a circle above his shoulders and shook out his arms as if to cast off a tingling sensation at the tips of his fingers. He squeezed his eyes and fists shut. Still watching him, I withdrew from the waistband of my dress a piece of paper with the written statement they'd prepared for me, whose pronunciation the reverend had helped me with earlier in the day. He opened his eyes then and turned his head, and saw me, and our eyes met. He tried to smile. He shrugged his shoulders as if to say, Don't worry, it wasn't as bad up here as I thought it would be, when your turn comes everything will be all right.

Men with tool belts and wires slung over their shoulders crossed the studio floor. Then, before I knew it, a voice called "ten seconds" and the technicians cleared out and the studio clock flashed and the show was live again, the green light on Camera 1 lit up, and the same sun appeared, now more full and bright to indicate the broadening of daylight. No horizon was visible. The roar of the plane was there again, only closer now, and Hollands welcomed his audience back and began to speak while the four studio cameras were ridden over the polished stage floor like mechanical horses.

"It is a beautiful morning in Hiroshima," he said, "like so many August mornings before today. Fathers are getting ready for work. Mothers are preparing breakfast for the children. And as the bright sun spreads its renewing powers over this city, suddenly the sound of an air-raid siren cries out. Then another, and another." The wail of a distant siren rang out in the studio now, and, though muted, it still sent a chill up my spine. Then, offstage, a voice, microphoned and focussed, rose above it.

"About this time I was making last calculations, double-checking everything. There was a lot of back and forth between Captain Tibbets and myself." As the voice began, a light glowed out from behind a screen and a man's silhouette appeared to the left of Hollands and Yasaka, who seemed to flinch under his blue Western-style suit. "We were at thirty-one thousand feet. I was waiting for the Aioi Bridge to appear between the crosshairs of my bomb sight. We'd trained for months. That was where we wanted it to go."

The voice and the light behind the screen faded as Hollands turned to Yasaka. "This is the moment your life suffers its dramatic shift, in this moment of ravaging fury. This is the moment we all know about, when a man faces certain death, but that few among us have ever experienced. When a whole life flashes before your eyes. And now the question must be asked, sir." As he paused, attempting to build the suspense, an angelic music lifted over the crowd, and with it people from the reverend's past commenced filing out one by one from backstage. "Did you," Hollands said, "see your life in focus?" And suddenly the applause began. The first of the reverend's friends, from the Theology Department at Emory University, stepped out opposite me at stage left, arms open, face lit up and grinning, pleased, it seemed, to be part of this incredible moment.

Behind the screen the light rose again, followed by the voice. "It was a beautiful morning. Visibility was clear. I could see the city, and there was no mistaking it. When I made visual contact with the target I knew what to do. In many ways it was a routine drop. Clockwork." The light faded from the man's silhouette and Hollands continued.

"And so the bomb plunges downward toward your city, Reverend, and as the air-raid siren insists, by now you know something is gravely wrong. This is not one of the many drills you have come to move through automatically. This is real. Your threatened life takes on even greater focus. All these people you know and love continue to flash through your mind. . . ."

And out they came, the television embodiment of the reverend's longing to return to the safety of his mother's arms. Three decades limped and walked and swaggered past his eyes in the time it took to cross the stage. Members of his family appeared, weary after their trans-Pacific flight and awed by the quantity of hot lights and glowing spectators—all this attention paid to a man they'd always known. Such an odd people, they must have thought, these Americans, making this man one of their own, celebrating his loss so strangely. The cameras swung from face to face as his friends and family appeared—a schoolteacher, an uncle, his best friend from Emory—but always returned to the reverend, whose expression was a mixture of confusion and terror now and, in one case, joy, when his wife emerged from backstage, all the way from home.

The greater the surprise, the more deeply the cameras seemed to probe.

Then the silhouetted voice resumed: "We were still dropping to pick up speed when the detonation occurred. It lit the sky up. It was already full daylight, but the sky lit up all over again, and slowly this magnificent cloud rose."

Maybe those familiar with the show might have known that nothing was impossible here, that such an individual would be dug up from the past. Of course, it hadn't occurred to me when I saw the nice-looking man in uniform pacing back there before the show, rubbing his hands together. Maybe no one out there watching that night knew who it would turn out to be. Of all the people connected with the bomb, who do you choose? Einstein, maybe. Fermi or Oppenheimer? Men who hadn't set foot in Europe or the Far East since the beginning of the war. But there were forty million potential customers of Hazel Bishop cosmetics and Prell shampoo out there, and the producers would give it all they had.

Then Hollands again. "Rare indeed is the case when one man gets to meet the person who has directly influenced his fate, Reverend Yasaka. That man, whose life has so directly and profoundly touched your own, is here tonight in order to help us put a face to the hand of fate, and a face to the unprecedented power unleashed that day. Ladies and gentlemen, let me introduce Major Thomas Ferebee, United States Air Force, the man who released the first atomic bomb over Japan."

He stepped out from behind the curtain amid thunderous applause, grinning, and walked stiffly across the stage floor and embraced Tanabe Yasaka with long, nervous arms. I saw the pained smile fall away from the reverend's face and the sweat form on his forehead. He returned the embrace, and as he did so, arms only half raised, half there, it looked as though he was going to be sick. I knew how hard the reverend had worked the last ten years of his life, trying to repair the damage that had been done. Working with people like me. He had lived through the war. He had seen things. But he was not ready for this. From where I stood that much was clear. He struggled to maintain his composure. He may have endeavoured to remember the reason all this was happening, in order to keep himself upright, resolute, determined to raise money for the expenses we would accumulate while in America.

He turned in my direction just as a hand touched my shoulder to pull me back from where I had been watching. This man led me behind the thin curtain Ferebee had just emerged from. Takako was already waiting for me, and I climbed up onto the stool and assumed the position they'd shown me. On the broad flap of my dress I flattened out the piece of paper. My mouth was dry. I held my hands in tight fists to stop them from shaking.

Hollands nodded in appreciation and motioned with his hands for quiet, and when the audience finally fell still, he began to explain what was to come next. There were two girls here from Japan, he said, and they would remain partially hidden—in an attempt to prevent any embarrassment they might feel on account of their facial injuries, and also (left unsaid, but clear enough) because the people watching on their television sets back home might find it distasteful, even repugnant, if their living rooms suddenly filled with the sight of our mutilated faces.

Immediately a hot light placed directly behind us threw our shadows against the screen, and the stage director, standing just out of camera range, pointed to me now with his finger-gun. I hesitated a moment, searching for moisture on my tongue. My mouth was too dry for me to speak. The words I held in front of me looked back at me blankly. I believed the silence I had perfected would serve me now. This was my only opportunity to save myself. I would not let them harm me anymore. But the monster I had been struggling to keep inside me, pinned against my rib cage, rose up again. I sat perfectly still, then straightened my back. The sheet of paper shook in my hand. I attempted to clear my voice. I would not cry. I would not speak.

"Thank you for bringing us here to America," I said. "We are happy for your kindness. Thank you."

The Parting Gift

Sophie walked upstairs and attached herself to the machine, then lay down on the bed in her work clothes. She pressed the tips of her fingers into the flesh above her kidney and proceeded to massage gently. She no longer watched the blood leave her arm on its cleansing journey through the machine. Now the dialysis too had been consumed by routine and ritual. She simply closed her eyes and tried to sleep.

As that spring and summer had progressed, her mid-day naps had grown longer, her breaks more frequent, the aching in her joints deeper and more persistent. All these things she knew to expect. She had long since become expert in the art of monitoring her body's symptoms, the mounting severity of which was recorded continuously in her head. At the start of the new year she had noticed the renewed progress of the disease over her arms and chest. The old white skin, long ago scarred by the first siege of lesions, erupted again in red bloom. Not since Stony Lake had those discoid rashes surfaced—but suddenly they were here again. She had studied their advance in all the mirrors of the house, and was convinced Anton hadn't noticed this morbid practice, her terrified glances stolen out of the corner of her eye.

At first the disappearance of the small mirror in the front hall scarcely registered in her distracted mind. Merely a slight rearrangement of furnishings, easily passed over. Then another mirror went missing, this one in the guest room, where she sometimes sat for the view to the lake, and a third and a fourth. She knew what was happening by the third.

A week before Emiko arrived Sophie retired to the bedroom one afternoon and found the mirror above the dressing table covered in a white sheet. She had said nothing about any of the others, realizing this was her husband's clumsy way of keeping her mind off the disease's advance, and of taking on the smallest part of her suffering. She would bear the pain, there was no changing that, but he would limit her exposure. He did not want her to be reminded of her condition. At least he would bear in solitude the spectre of her encroaching death.

But she had been strangely moved by his gesture. What else, after all, could he do for her? The disease must run its course. That had been made clear to her years ago in New York. Lupus was a long-suffering, inevitable splitting and falling away of the skin. She had lived with it for over a decade in this advanced form, and now the kidneys were going. This had been the true subject of Anton's last talk to his students, the one about the mysterious bond that held him to his wife, and she to him—full of implied responsibility and regret, he understood now. He and his wife had been told what to expect, that there was only so much time left. Still in Brooklyn, they had come to the conclusion over a period of three months that the time remaining would be hers. He could not deny her the choice of where to live out her last years. "A piece of land," she'd said. "All I want is a piece of land."

"To grow things?"

"That's all I ask. It can be anywhere, away from here. Yes, maybe to grow things. Do you remember a promise you made to me when we were young?"

A smile came to his lips then.

"A promise you made to me after the conference in Pugwash, about where we'd live one day. Somewhere on water, we said."

He shook his head, a touch of disbelief and admiration that she should remember this from so long ago. "I imagine you're holding me to that promise?"

"We could go back there," she said.

She recalled that now, lying in bed watching the ceiling while Anton talked to the Japanese woman downstairs, no doubt about her, the sick wife. But she could not sleep today. Through the soft humming of the machine at her bedside she listened to their footsteps and wondered about this Emiko. Why, for example, she had not changed her name upon arriving to America—wasn't that common? To Emma, maybe, or Amanda, whatever its translation might be. Forty years was a long time to hang on to a name that would always mark you as an outsider, one that would stump people and be quickly forgotten or confused.

But maybe that was a good thing, she considered. She herself had been forced to leave something behind when she came here. She had been required, like her Hungarian neighbours, to reach into the dark past and bring up into the light the ghosting memories and the half-remembered *Yiskadel v'yiskadash sh'may rabbah*, chanted now, near the end of her life, with an unsure child-like pronunciation. To surrender so much at such an early age, when so little besides loss and upheaval seemed definite, had established an absence in her life that remained to this day. The rituals of a distant past were observed with the earnest hope that something might be reborn within her; but too often they served also to remind her that the absence she sought to dispel would always exist in her. The past could never be fully reclaimed, unlike a lost baby bracelet recovered from some dusty attic. Such attempts came at a high price and rarely produced the desired effects. Better to seize hold of it in the first place, she thought now, even if it was not a matter of choice. Even if the one robbing you of your childhood, or your faith, has a gun pointed between your eyes. She feared she'd made those concessions too swiftly. She had accepted her fate. Wasn't that it? When she received word from the Red Cross in Manhattan that her people had not been located, she'd decided that a return to Austria would prove too difficult. She tried to be strong. She had ignored the urgings of the young Italian. "Go find your people," he'd said. "Come with me. We will find our families." She'd explained that strength came from looking forward, not back. "You must accept your lot," she'd told him. "You cannot expect to find a thing back there."

That's when he'd left her, after three years of begging her to accompany him. She could not. She would not leave her husband.

"You have no husband. He is a jailer. You stay with that man, what will you have? You deny who you are. Your history. You will be alone all your life with a man like that."

Anton pushed open the bedroom door and asked in a quiet voice how she was feeling.

"Come in," she said. He sat on the bed and took her hand.

"What shall we do? Shall I send her away?"

"No."

He looked at the white sheet over the mirror.

"It doesn't trouble me to have someone around. It gives you something to do. She'll keep you busy. And you need to talk with her."

"She's staying," he said, "at one of those hotels just off the highway."

She closed her eyes.

"Probably she's more comfortable there."

Later that day Emiko sat on a rock at the water's edge, watching the sailboats. Anton came down from the house and told her that his wife was feeling better, and that she should stay. There was no need to leave.

"What's happening to her?"

"She has lupus. She needs a kidney transplant, which she'll never agree to. She's been on dialysis three years. Three times a week. We've known this for years. That makes it a little easier."

"Why does she want me to stay? For you?"

He considered before answering. "Yes."

"She believes you need to talk to me. That I'll provide you with some sort of peace of mind?"

"Something like that."

"That's not why I'm here. I have no interest in reconciling with you."

"She believes you might be the person," he said, "to do just that."

"She's free to believe whatever she chooses to. I will not tell her any different."

"You are that magic person she's been waiting for me to meet."

"To absolve you?"

He nodded.

"Do you believe you need absolution?" she said.

"That is what my wife believes."

After supper the next day, while Sophie rested from her latest bout of fatigue, Emiko accompanied Anton on his customary walk up Spruce Street, across Lakeshore Road, then over to Palmer Avenue, where Jackson's Hill lay quiet and green under a mid-evening summer sky.

"You never experienced anything like this, I suspect, before you came over?"

"Small-town life? Peaceful evenings?"

"The things you do in a small town. In wintertime kids play here."

"I've never tobogganed, no, if you're talking about a normal childhood. . . ."

Bats were beginning to appear in the air above their heads, darting in and out, snatching the flies swarming in the thick summer dusk. They continued on in the direction of the railroad tracks that cut across the north end of town; sometimes, late at night, he explained, when everything was still, you could hear the freight trains all the way down at the house.

When she asked if they'd ever had children he did not revert to the old excuses. Still walking, he simply shook his head.

"Because of Sophie's illness?"

"Back then they said such patients should not bear children. They were wrong, it turns out. But that was the thinking back then. It wasn't a very well-understood disease."

"I don't think I was meant to have any," she said. "I've accepted that. Some people just aren't meant to."

"Why do you say that?"

"Because I have no way of turning back the clock."

"You never married?"

"I was never able to understand boys, men, whatever. I always expected them to be like my grandfather, I think. It wasn't until too late that I figured out I was comparing them to a seventy-year-old man. He was my only point of reference. The ten or fifteen years you're supposed to spend figuring out that stuff about boys and girls were taken away from me. I spent most of the time in hospitals, then in America, more hospitals, and being a foreigner. I'm not sure I would've been the dating type, anyway."

He drew Sophie's bath as he usually did, after she awoke from her nap. He made sure the water was only just warm enough. After years of observing Sophie's reaction as she lowered herself into the tub, he knew the temperature that best eased the aching in her joints, usually only a few degrees above room temperature. He also knew the correct amount of bath oil to add, to counter the chronic dryness of her skin. When the water was ready he came for her and helped her out of bed and down the hall and slid the robe off her shoulders and hung it on the door. He held her elbow as she stepped in and lowered herself into the bath. There was not much talking, only the sound of her bottom squeaking audibly against the rubber mat and the soft swirl of water against the sides of the tub and her body. She had never been one for daily baths until the aching joints had become a problem. It was all very un-European and indulgent, she thought, but found the warm water helped ease the pain. Often Anton stayed, soaping her back or sitting still, watching, on the closed toilet seat. Sometimes he would tell anecdotes, even jokes, to distract her from the old scars and the occasional new rash that cast a shadow over her skin as if clouds were drifting over their heads.

He lowered his hand and brought up a palmful of water, opened his fingers and let it trickle down her back. He traced a finger over her left shoulder, creating as he did small loops and circles over her skin. He knew to avoid the new rashes, which had just surfaced the day before and were painful to the touch. There was not much unaffected skin left on her back. Her face was still fine, though, clear and unblemished, distinctly handsome, if you discounted the signs of age and stress that accompanied the pain she dealt with on a daily basis.

"More aspirin?" he said.

She touched his hand, which rested on her left shoulder now, and squeezed. No, the touch said. Just quiet.

Gently and unrushed, he continued casting water over her. This silence might last the duration of the bath, or through to next morning. He was used to it, and knew it was her effort to stabilize something in herself, to find a centre point so as to regain a momentarily lost balance, or simply to deal with the debilitating exhaustion.

Later, when the water began to cool, he opened the hot-water tap and brought the tub back to the correct temperature. It was a long and shared ritual, whose duties, when required, were at once unspoken and immediately understood.

When she was finished she pulled the plug and stood. Anton draped the towel over her, and while she patted herself dry he removed the corticosteroid cream from the medicine cabinet, not mirrorless, and opened the jar. It had a clean medicinal smell, not entirely unpleasant; something he was used to, anyway. She sat

down again, facing inwards on the edge of the draining tub, to dry
her still-aching feet as Anton spread the cream over her back and
arms. She turned when he asked her to, and he applied the cream
to the large rash that had recently spread over and under her right
breast. He lifted its unhealthy thinness with his left hand and with
his right massaged the white cream until it disappeared into the
skin.

"Where is the girl?" she said.

"She's not such a girl anymore."

"It's hard to think of her any other way." She did not say, *Like a
child. Of an age our own might have been.*

"She's gone back to her hotel," he said. "Would you like her to
leave?"

"Are you done saying what you have to say to her?"

"She's the one with questions." He raised the second breast,
looking to see if the rash had migrated across her body. He found
nothing. "You're fine here," he said, then replaced the lid on the jar.

That night there commenced a gradual fading, and when she
awoke she knew immediately what this was. She was filled with an
amazed and bewildered calm as she watched it rise within her and
remembered the warm winds and deep hollow sounds that echoed
up from the ship's hold as she waited there, alone in her single bed,
in the Havana harbour. That was where her life had veered off
track, she thought. Yes. Maybe a life can be reduced down to its
first mistake, an initial weakness, not the cause but the point at
which matters of death were made real and inevitable. Her own
death was at hand, and it was not as she had expected. That distant
memory of frostbite in the Caribbean came back and seized her as
the coma crept forward, sending through her body a chill that
reached deep within her kidneys. It was not the sensation of comfort she had always hoped for, but instead a deep, freezing ache

that unsettled her soul. It was physical, and so much more. In the panic as she slipped wordlessly closer, deeper and deeper, she endured the terrifying thought that, yes, this was it, and that whatever work in this life was as yet unfinished would always remain half formed. Nothing would follow her but the cold feet of her own death, a mourning husband, a stand of weeds, a patch of disturbed earth. Isn't that something, she thought. All those years, pointing to now. Nothing.

She remembered her father's quiet patience, the sound of his working tools and the thick old earth-wood smells she had loved as a child, sitting in the square of light that entered through the window above the shop door. Watching the women haul their carts up the street to market, babies in strollers, old men with hands folded behind curving backs. Occasionally at lunchtime the three of them would climb the five flights of stairs to the top of the building—up past Feldman's Insurance Agents and Reinholt's Printers & Co. and the two other small businesses housed there— and make a picnic on the gently sloping roof. From here the view to the Danube was unobstructed. In the distance beyond, mountains rose to the summer-blue skies. As a girl Sophie would imagine the foreign lands across those mountains, all the wonderful secrets to be discovered when, one day, she became old enough to strike out on her own. And she remembered all the things she would never return to, despite the man she had loved once, Stefano Danella, who'd offered her the chance to return with him and seek out their families. This view of the mountains and the uncertain fates of her parents she now saw in her mind's eye. He had offered this to her; but she had been afraid of the burnt heart of Europe. The likelihood of what awaited her had terrified her. She would go later, she'd always told herself. Not with this beautiful young man. She would find the right time to leave.

But that moment never came.

Now she gestured for her husband. She touched his shoulder

and he awoke, at once alert. She was staring at him, her eyes wide, wild. She grimaced, a little smile stretched to distortion. A slight moan split her throat. With what strength she had left she threw her arm towards him and he sat up immediately. But he would not help. This was not her asking, *Please, Anton, please bring me back.* She wanted him awake and to be with her. Only that. He would be her last person in this life. As she had wanted, as she had expected, as she had explained.

He touched her sweating forehead. Her breathing now was troubled, erratic. He knew this was a conversation with death. *No, you will not. Yes, please come.* A dance he knew she had prepared for. He knew, too, that he should not interfere, should not do as he'd done on previous occasions, which was to rush to make the phone call that would bring an ambulance to deliver her from this death watch. This was his last duty to her. The final promise he had made to her.

He sat forward, his mind running white. He touched her cheek with his lips and held his mouth close, waiting for her to leave him. Eyes closed, unable to look now. He cried into her skin and into the darkness that was quickly replacing the fading light that had been her face and suddenly, like the escape of some binding secret held within us the entire length of our lives, he felt a slight, then brutal, shift. A change in the air. And slowly it became known to him that he was alone in this room. This empty house. He peered into the absence that had established itself before him. Suffocating in this absolute solitude, this fearful silence. He removed his mouth from her face wet, where his tears had run, and picked up her left hand and cupped it, cooling, between his. The delicate fingers possessed the strangeness of an artifact just dug from some stone field, so dead was it. The impossibility of this being his wife rose up in him, a defiant howl of ignorance, of mistaken fates. This was not the end of their life together. He waited beside her, sitting as the warmth drained from her fingertips, until the last touch of light stored deep within her was gone.

He endured tea and condolences at his kitchen table the next morning after Sophie was taken away. He had told Bela and Eva after making the necessary calls, and then Emiko arrived and sat with them and drank her tea without speaking. When the teapot was finally empty he thanked the three at the table, saying he needed time alone.

He walked slowly through that unremarkable town, not thinking where or why, or who he had become. His mind was numb. He needed simply to move. For over an hour he sat on a bench in a small park whose name he could not recall, though he must've sat here scores of times, and watched two young men with the Parks and Recreation Department busy at work digging up the earth. He recognized one, he thought, but at first could not tell from where. They worked beside a wheelbarrow of black-eyed Susans which they reached into rhythmically, taking up fistfuls of the flowers and dropping them into shallow holes in the soil. Unbidden, words of an old song returned to him then, for no reason he could have known, about cutting down the forests in the parks of Berlin, *Im Grünewald / im Grünewald / ist Holzaktion,* and in the silence of his head the tune played without regard for his confusion and misery.

The bright line of flowers lengthened on the other side of the path as the words floated by. The wheelbarrow was slowly emptied. He measured the young men's progress, straining his ear against the music to catch a snippet of their conversation. But their work took them farther and farther from where he sat. He watched them wipe the sweat from their brows and unbend their backs. He admired the delicacy and swiftness with which they planted and covered the roots of the flowers they handled. They planted and

covered and reached forward and removed fistful after fistful of
the perennials and dropped one after another into a long line of
waiting holes and edged farther away from him on their knees, one
rising occasionally to keep the wheelbarrow even with them, then
sinking back to his knees into the soft expectant soil. He had
observed Sophie at such work as this countless times, and had
thought nothing of it. And now the work of strangers was as close
to her as he was ever likely to get again.

What could he say about her now? She had tended her garden
like weather massaging the land? Is this what he had learned from
her illness, from her life? Sentimental metaphors, an interest in
strangers. He straightened up against the back of the bench and
pulled his feet under him.

The days he had spent under the chestnut trees that lined the
Ohlauerstraße in Tübingen returned to him then, waiting for the
fruit to fall and burst onto the pavements below. The anticipation
fluttering about in the air. That's what trees meant to him. Suddenly they were there. It was not a question of planting and tending but merely of harvesting. How full those days had been, despite
his father's stern gaze upon his life, when he and the other neighbourhood boys fanned out over those streets with bags slung over
their shoulders, collecting the nuts for their school games, and
possessed of the hope that everything was possible, that they
would not be condemned to relive their fathers' horror.

Then he remembered who the taller of these two men working
across from him was. This was the son of the carpenter who'd
rebuilt their home shortly after they came here, already fifteen
years ago. He was a man now, perhaps in his early thirties. His
tanned face was rich with health, still ignorant of his own flirtation
with the inevitable.

Emiko

When I called my friends out west to say I'd be detained a few days more, I got the machine in the cabin, which was helpful, I admit, because I didn't know what else to say. Just that I was detained, there was important work for me still to do, that the scheduling was beyond my control. Purposely, I raised the tone of my voice a notch to lend it a level of excitement that might make my decision to stay on seem natural, perhaps fortuitous. I didn't want to alarm them, though by then I'd decided that the uncertainty with which I walked through this old man's life was more profoundly unbalancing than anything I'd experienced in years.

The first morning in the old house, I awoke in a room I didn't recognize. Only after a confused moment did the set of old pictures and strange mementos on the walls merge to form a vision of the long journey that had delivered me here. Having come in search of an interview, not so different from the many others I'd pursued over the last half-dozen years—though always in New York—I now found myself, inexplicably, on the verge of assisting at the funeral of a woman whom I didn't know and couldn't rightly pretend to care about. The professor had asked for help, and it had not been in my power to say no. I lay still, trying to determine precisely which forces had drawn me in.

As the room filled slowly with light, I saw over my head a large poster of a castle of some description—an upside-down palace I couldn't identify from this position, blinking with sleep, head turned back on the pillow. There were photographs everywhere, of the sort that any family might possess and, for reasons of a crooked smile or squinting, never display in more lived-in areas of the house. I noticed an antique snapshot of a child, perhaps ten years old, standing on a beach and puffing out his chest; he stood beside a sand castle whose tallest tower reached just past his knee.

Under the window overlooking the garden was a small writing desk, on top of which sat a decorative candle, a coffee cup filled with pens and a model of an airplane I had learned to identify, by the age of six, at thirty thousand feet. Seeing it now, in daylight, sparked memories of days my brother and I had spent playing in the river, back in another time. I looked beyond the desk to the lake, running up against the rear of the property. Only then did I dress myself and push the bedroom door open.

The hall lamp was still lit, glowing dimly now in the morning light. Anton had turned it on last night as I'd prepared for bed, saying I might not know where I was if I woke up before dawn and needed to use the toilet. I switched it off and closed the bathroom door behind me; here, in the medicine cabinet, I saw the collection of prescription creams similar to those I had used years before.

Downstairs, in the kitchen, I poured myself some juice and buttered a heavy slab of bread left out on a plate by the toaster, then stood at the counter eating as I looked out the window. It was just after seven.

What lay before me was a long day of telephone calls to the hospital and funeral home, to family and friends, as yet unmentioned and possibly nonexistent. This step-by-step organizing, I realized now, was the centripetal force I'd felt, without being aware of it, almost from the moment of my arrival. I was resolved now to break its hold. I would tell the old man that I would help in any way I could, once he came downstairs. That was the least I could do. He was an old man, without much support, I'd guessed by now, except perhaps from his neighbours. But I would not attend the funeral of a virtual stranger. Not if I'd been unable to attend my own grandfather's while I was getting my face put back together in America. Though, as soon as these thoughts formed, I considered the shameful truth of the matter: At least it wasn't me. At least it is not someone I love. My dead about to be buried. It was a selfish thought, and perfectly natural, I thought, given who this man was—or, rather, what he represented. No, I decided, these few extra days here would give me time to collect myself before I went west.

I slid the screen door open and stepped onto the back patio. A slight tang shifted off the lake—old seaweed, maybe, or decomposing driftwood and dead fish. Whatever its nature, the smell wafted up through the garden and filled the air with a sense of disintegration and decay, or perhaps a rising tide of pollution. This was one of the Great Lakes after all, I thought, and hardly pristine. I considered this possibility as I walked the length of the beach to the broken cement pier I'd seen my first afternoon here. On the section farthest out in the water, a gull and two ducks, each on a single leg, stood balancing themselves. A hundred yards distant, the pier with that lighthouse was positioned where the river drained its muddy belly into the lake.

I'd tried to keep connected to the real world over the past three days, calling my machine back home from the hotel room, at first. Now, after taking over the guest room on the second floor, I walked up to a phone booth in town to call. I didn't want to use his telephone, and didn't mind having this excuse to get away from the house, and from the anxious feelings that had descended over me.

Most of that day we spent seeing to the arrangements, which were more involved than I would've suspected. Funny, I thought, how many deaths you can live through without once attending a funeral.

I called up a few associates in New York, too, whom I'd told about this interview. I was making good progress, I told them.

The day before the service we talked through most of the night. I wasn't sure if he opened himself to me, or simply to a shadowed and unknown face sitting across from him. Maybe just to himself. He told stories of Sophie and the war and their life together, and about the letters he used to send her from Japan, his voice rarely above a whisper. He'd fall silent and peer at one of those strange spiralling shapes that inhabited the near dark: a fish, a fox, a frog. Removed as they were from their natural context, they unsettled me as surely as partly formed dreams pushed suddenly into the waking world. He would resume speaking, his head lowered, and stop suddenly, sometimes in the middle of a thought, and raise his eyes to stare, for what seemed like five or ten minutes of uncomfortable silence, at one of those freak shapes over my shoulder.

"I remember when she made that, that one there." I followed his pointed finger and saw a deer emerging from a bush. Then he cast his thoughts farther, it seemed, into the past.

"I had never seen a desert before, of course. I could convince myself of anything in those days. I was a young man capable of whatever he desired. That *is* the definition of an idealist, don't you think? I thought I was doing a good thing. The right thing. I remember being driven through the desert. A driver had been sent to Santa Fe to collect me. The sand was everywhere, such a lovely place after Europe. For half a day I thought I'd found paradise."

He paused.

"But what wouldn't have seemed lovely? Europe was already a graveyard. I was glad to leave it."

Again a searing gaze passed over my shoulder.

"I remember the sight of that horizon. You could almost believe you were at the edge of the world. Nothing out there at all, but still the expectation that you would go searching."

He rubbed his right eye with an open palm and turned toward the lake. "I'm starting to remember things, just now, since yesterday. Things I haven't thought of in forty years. Fifty. All at once, it seems."

I waited.

"The things you remember . . . stupid things," he said. "Never the ones you should remember."

I looked directly into his face. "Is there anything like a God or religion in your life?"

"I don't know."

"Those memorials—aren't they a kind of worship? No matter that it's in a crowd of strangers."

"Is that the reason you go?" he said.

"I go to meet people like you."

Echoes

1

He stood without moving, not a muscle, and listened to the ailing
rabbi as chickadees and starlings churned the sky above. If he'd
known his birds he could have identified them by their sounds as
they ventured out from the tall pines and maples that bordered the
cemetery. It was still early enough that mourning doves could be
heard cooing softly and confidently, set with folded wings as they
observed the small group huddled beneath them. But he did not
notice these birds any more than they knew or cared that the dead
woman had no family other than the husband who had come here
to bury her at the beginning of this beautiful August day. Nor
would they see any children except for the blond-haired girl with
beautiful hands, or friends other than Bela and Eva Szabo; leaving
only the retired carpenter who had helped reshape the Böll home,
and the Japanese woman who seemed to be looking at all this as if
through a lens, not her own two eyes.

The highway passed just north of where this silent group now
stood. The few cars that moved along it disturbed the air only
slightly, heard at a distance of a couple hundred yards of open
field. Off to the left, the Burnt River Valley opened grandly on the
far side of a sudden, brief but dense wall of trees. Often children
slid down its shale-slick incline to where junk tires were scattered
amongst other refuse. But no children played there today.

This cemetery had seen larger, more worshipful crowds. But
Anton Böll noticed none of this. He didn't notice the birds and he
didn't notice the young girl whose name he once had known; and
he did not glimpse the blue light through the wall of trees, or think
about a river running its course or the turning of seasons. He did
not think about birth or rebirth or the absence of children in his

life but only about the end of things. None of this was surprising. He'd had time to prepare himself for this moment. But now that it was here, he did not know what conclusions he was supposed to have drawn. He was not able to conjure the small, comforting notion that his wife had lived fully, and girded herself for death. If ever he had determined such a thing, he was unable to recall any preferred means of committing his beloved to the earth. Was there a right thought to think at a time like this? he wondered. A corner in his mind where he had stored some secret hope, some warm, lasting memory that might sustain the survivor?

He would not have remembered, for example, had he asked himself, why he'd insisted that Emiko stay at the house. It was uncharacteristic, inviting others into a life he had kept, by inclination and training, private. Was it for himself he had requested of her these extra few days, possibly to lessen the burden? Surely Bela and Eva, as his oldest and most reliable friends in this town, and perhaps anywhere, would have made themselves available. But he did not know, because he was unable or unwilling to ask himself. And so, for the time it took to commit his wife's remains, he forgot the will of God's design, if it could be seen in these terms, as on this one occasion he would have preferred it to be. Instead he remembered only his grief and confusion. The moment he had long anticipated was upon him. That was all he knew. The moment they had anticipated together, he was now walking through. He remembered Sophie's words. "When I am gone," she used to say. "When I am gone . . ."

But that possibility had never seemed real. Not with her there, breathing, holding his hand. "Your life will not end when I'm gone," she once told him. "You could even meet someone. Take that as my final blessing."

"Funny woman," he said, smiling and shooing away this offering, or idea, like a plate of unwanted sweets.

What was done was done. There was no urgency today. This

last tribute would be given with as few words and thoughts as possible. As the small semi-circle formed, he looked up and tried to offer a smile of thanks. The rabbi's presence was Eva's suggestion. He was a tall man, uncertain on his feet, because of either old age or some unstated illness which might have clung thickly to the backs of his dark and weary eyes, lowered to the ground now as if anticipating their own descent into blindness. Anton watched, wondering how close he—or each of them here—was to death. That was a privilege of the living, this awareness of your own mortality, even in the midst of grief. Especially then. He knew this from experience. Straightening, he moved through the rest of the ceremony as gracefully as possible. He would give his wife this last noble portrait of the man she had married. Silent in his suffering.

He looked up from the casket to see Emiko standing on his right, seemingly transfixed. She'd suffered her own losses, he knew, and would understand this instinctively. A woman well versed in the intimacy of pain, maybe she was the only one present who truly understood why he had brought her here. She would remember and remind him, if he were to ask.

Perhaps it was fitting that she be in attendance, mourning a woman who had experienced such an oddly shaped rash on the same day, fifty years ago, as she, Emiko, had felt those unnatural scars riot across her body. Perhaps at the same instant. He'd heard stories of such lively coincidence, almost fable-like in their synchronicity and monstrous beauty. But Anton would not relegate such mystic portent to the realm of the impossible, or even of the unlikely, despite the fact that he had bound himself to the reason of science and the reverence of logic.

He lowered his eyes again to the coffin. Yet this notion would not be dislodged: such a deeply felt connection between these two women, one lying lifelessly before him, the other standing here in the best suit of mourning that could be rummaged up in a matter of hours. Was this why Sophie had been so insistent about this woman's interviews, that they be as thorough as possible, as deep as her husband's memory would permit—and that in order to accomplish them the woman should postpone her own plans while she tended to the ramblings of an old man?

Anton accepted Emiko's offer of a drive back to the house. She waited for him while he crossed the parking lot to tell Bela, whom he'd come with, and watched him gently touch his neighbour's shoulder.

He climbed in beside her and stared straight ahead without speaking. She didn't attempt to engage him.

"Thank you," he said.

She manoeuvred the car out into the familiar streets of his town, turning onto Douglas Avenue, then Palmer, past Jackson's Hill and finally onto Spruce Street. The old Victorian homes here were invariably large, shaded under tall oak and birch, children playing on front yards and sidewalks. The breeze that flowed through the open car windows smelt of freshly cut grass.

He didn't receive people after the service, not that there were many to receive. Even if there had been, he would've preferred silence.

Emiko brought a plate of cold-cuts and sliced tomatoes out to the back patio, and set it on the table at which Anton sat watching the lake. Dark clouds were moving in now after a brief sun shower, creating a vivid rainbow over the horizon. He looked to her and managed a smile, but showed no more interest in her, or the food.

The golden light filled the garden's shadows while its figures seemed to come alive, their presence growing in the rain-thickened air. When the heavy rain began then in earnest, he moved indoors and watched from the window as the lake bubbled and peened and popped and the rain steamed the air. A tremendous roar beat down on the flagstones and roof of the house, and the raindrops slapping against the leaves of the trees raised a chorus of tiny drums in his ears.

When the storm finally ended and the returning sun laid its early-evening shadows across the wet lawns, Anton pulled open the sliding doors and walked stiffly into his wife's garden through a thrum of cicadas and sparrows. He'd heard Emiko leave the house through the back door. She was out here. He'd heard the harsh snapping of garden shears.

When Emiko heard the door slide open and shut, she imagined he was coming to thank her for staying on. That would be it; then she could leave. She lowered the shears to her side and waited as he circled the bushes, strolling without hurry. She listened for the slow shuffle of the aged, the imminently infirm. She knew his habitual posture, hands clasped behind his back like a grandfather out for an evening stroll, stopping to pause and test the air.

He stopped on the opposite side of the cypress hedge and watched Emiko spear the wet earth with the opened shears. Together they walked between the line of cherry trees leading down to the edge of the garden, where the shadows had already fastened themselves like silent ravens onto the sculptured ferns, and side by side they settled on one of the turquoise cast-iron benches facing the lake.

After he'd rested, they walked down the shoreline to the pier at the mouth of the Burnt River. Near the edge, he said, "She'd made me promise her. She asked for my help. Sophie wanted me to help her die."

All around them men were casting lines into the coming sunset. With September approaching, the salmon run had begun. The fishermen were scattered loosely along the length of the pier. The one nearest them reached into a sack and produced a small bottle, which he opened on a red-and-white lure held tightly in a clenched fist; it popped and fizzed, and the cap bounced against the pier.

Soon it would be dusk. Perhaps twenty minutes remained before the sun, suspended like a jewel over their right shoulders, initiated its rapid descent, and the nighttime quiet settled over the water. The light breeze was trailing off now, and as far as the eye could see, the surface had already assumed its patient vigil.

Many hours Anton had spent out here with Sophie. He remembered how she'd carry the old rod he'd found for her at a garage sale, clenching it like some heavy garden maul. It was a different sort of fishing from the type he pursued alone farther upriver, a relaxing of the rules they'd implicitly agreed upon. As it had been when he helped her with her plants. More than anything else, it was an excuse to enter the other's life for a small moment, this walk out to the pier at sunset. Fishing was not the point. They'd watch the sunset fire the entire sky, moved by this vast presence, and this shared spectacle seemed to lift the grey ribbon of unease that had brushed against them for so long.

"I helped her die," he said again. "Can you understand that? She had nothing left. I knew what the doctors would have done. I could've saved her. But she didn't want that."

He wanted to hear Emiko say, *Yes, in such a case . . . There are limits to the suffering we should endure. When responsibility falls to the living to help those who can no longer . . .*

But instead: "I'm sorry." Only that.

So this was the mystery, Emiko thought. Here was a man guilty of helping his wife end her suffering. A terrible thing, yes, that blood on your hands. But how many were forced unnaturally to make such a choice? How common was such suffering, the necessary end to a cancerous or crippled or simply old, wasting existence?

The lake rose and fell in broad, shallow sheets, gently and unrushed, like echoes from a distant and unheard shuddering of the earth deep below. *This cannot turn out well,* he thought. *Let this go.*

Anton turned away.

"But if she asked you to help her," she said suddenly, as if she'd been thinking this through these last silent minutes, "that's some consolation. She asked you. She knew what was coming."

"Yes," he said. "It was like that."

"If she asked, she was ready. So that was your last gift to her. You can be comforted to know that."

They watched the thinning of light against the darkening wall of sky. The lake blushed and turned a fiery orange that cast a purple-and-gold halo around the men standing by the lighthouse. Both hands in his pockets, with the fingers of his right Anton massaged a single packet of sugar that remained there.

Walking back up, he stopped in the middle of a path and said the names of plants, touching each as he spoke. Yarpon holly. Blue-bell. Dianthus. He had learned these from his wife. Creeping ivy. Forsythia.

"I remember something remarkable from that time, though," he said. "Suddenly the cornflowers and gladiolas came up while I was there. In the city. After two weeks or so. Morning glories and lilies. Colours bursting up." He leaned forward to smell a flower cradled in his hand. "Only the day before, Hiroshima had been charcoal. Nothing left. I saw it. But such beauty came so suddenly. We were all taken aback. The whole team noticed it. It was quite unheard of, for flowers. To grow there."

He turned then, and raised his hand to touch her face. She stopped herself from stepping away. His open palm rested there.

She felt an unusual electricity, a warmth on his hand that moved into her face and into the bones of her mouth. She took his hand in her own and placed it more squarely there, where the scar had been repaired. He offered no resistance, and his fingers tingled as she guided them over her skin as if introducing herself to a newly blinded man. She felt the warmth coming through his touch, the slightly sticky night-sweat, the small dead points on her skin near the left eye. She raised his other hand to her opposite cheek.

"What you've done," she said, "can you feel it?"

He dropped his hand to his side and nodded. "I know what I have done. I remember when you were still a young girl . . . when Bertrand Russell spoke out that first time. The news from the Bikini Atoll."

He paused.

"You know who Edward Teller was? Let me tell you something. He was pushed out of the H-bomb program after leading it for three years, but obviously he wanted to know if all his work had been successful. He had no way of knowing at the time. He wasn't allowed to attend the tests out in the South Pacific, because he'd been blackballed. By now he was at Stanford. So he went to the seismology building that day and listened to the echoes. This was the only way he could tell whether it had worked. He sat down there in some basement, watching the seismograph. He knew within a minute or two. He saw the little bounce. He knew that was it." He lifted his eyebrows expectantly. "A message from the other side of the world."

She moved backwards, only slightly.

"You were already a young woman then. I was watching that night. The night you thanked America for what they'd done for you."

"You saw that on television?" she said.

"No. There. In the studio." He concentrated his voice, attempting absolute focus. He wanted her to see that he was not a threat.

"And then . . . there you were at my lecture, three, whatever it was, three weeks ago. It was like you were waiting for me. Like you'd come looking, after all that time. Holding out your hand to me. I thought of Teller then. Sitting in that little basement, waiting for news."

He reached out his hand again. This time she stopped him.

"When you survive a war, comfort is enough for some, I think. Sophie might have been thankful to me for taking her away from the camp I found her in. Grateful, but not in love. She always knew that, and it haunted her. She knew that long before I knew. She knew me for who I was, and accepted me. But I was unable to help myself. She is not to blame. She waited for me to get on with my life. She waited and waited. We were tired. Already as young people we were tired."

"Do you regret helping her the way you did?" she said. "Is that what you're saying?"

"I did what I could for her."

"You helped her. She asked for your help."

"Yes."

"But some things you push away," she said. "You blame yourself for other things instead."

He shook his head dismissively. "I do not blame myself for anything. Old age is built on a foundation of regret, not blame."

"Tell me what happened to her family," Emiko asked.

"They died. I'm not sure."

"*You're not sure?* She never found out? Never went back?"

"She thought it best to look forward," he said. "As we all did in those days."

"Did you ever know your wife, Professor?"

"That is a ridiculous question."

"Did you ever think about what *she* lost in the war? Not just what you had become, but what she'd lost?"

"She was a strong woman. She had no need to look backwards. I knew my wife. Do not presume to speak to me about my wife."

Neither moved, each waiting for the other to declare this meeting over with and finished.

"She would be very strong," Emiko said, "to stay with you."

At that he only smiled.

It was long past midnight now, the shapes solid and black in the garden beyond the stone pathway. She sat under the arbour, the lake still and glassy under a ringed moon.

The door slid open and he stepped out onto the patio with the old projector from his office, and a white bedsheet, maybe pulled down from that mirror, she thought. He set the heavy load on the picnic table and draped the sheet between two cypress branches. Then he ran an extension cord through the sliding doors.

She watched curiously, not speaking.

In a moment he produced a small wooden box full of old reels. The white sheet moved slowly, rippled by night air, in anticipation of full stillness.

Neither spoke as he prepared for what was about to happen. She waited stiffly, wondering what strange relics he was about to reveal. Might there be something new, then? Did this man dole out his memories in increments?

When he switched on the projector a funnel of light directed a square—slightly tilted to the left and off-centre—onto the sheet strung between the branches. It didn't take long for her to see that he'd used that camera for more than he'd admitted to.

There were outtakes from as late as the seventies, by the look of the cars in the city pieces. He'd continued shooting long after he got back. Long after the end of the war, and his tour with the Manhattan District. He'd carried this obsession forward through the decades.

A protest scene in Central Park. The mayors of Hiroshima and New York City, old men in hats shaking hands. Late sixties, maybe.

Then moving backwards and forwards in no particular order.

Some minutes of the bombed city, and half a dozen men from the Joint Commission and three from the Manhattan District, himself the fourth—a very young man with jet-black hair swished back in the fashion of the day, standing, staring blankly. For the first time it occurred to her that he'd been a good-looking man. The lips were large, expressive. He smoked like a movie star.

Then, somehow inserted into the film, there was a still of the twelve men who'd delivered the bomb to its destination. They wore eager grins, standing before the nose of their Flying Fortress. Playfully elbowing one another in the gut. *Let's go get 'em.*

Then back in New York, early seventies again.

He was changing reels quickly now, a practised hand.

The Daughters of Trinity stood at the Sixty-Sixth Street entrance of the park with cardboard bombs cutting through their hearts and mushroom clouds sprouting like daisies from their heads.

An unsmiling group of NYU drama students conducting mock trials of American war criminals, the names of the accused written in blood on a wall-sized backdrop suspended between two Japanese cherry trees. Two mounted cops pulled up their horses and looked on uneasily while the guilty verdict was passed in the pretend Oppenheimer trial, then trotted them snortingly through the crowd, the mighty haunches rippling with power.

Activists hung blood-spattered Macy's mannequins from lampposts faster than anyone could cut them down.

In accordance with the day, the sun shone atom-packed on this particular memorial, whenever it was, maybe a distant twenty years, maybe more, heat radiating through layers of skin. It was a day of white wooden crosses stuck into the ground and children piddling behind bushes. The camera followed the crowds, jumping, cutting in and out, looking for the shocking, the scandalous, the scarred.

She imagined him behind that camera, holding his eyes wide open.

A skywriter wove *Hiroshima Mon Amour* over the Hudson River in red dust. Streaming out from the plane's tail, shifting over the sheet between the cypress branches with the slow drift of New York wind, the letters became distorted with a few good gusts into the demented bloody-edged script from a house of horrors. Then the wind took them away.

The sound of the projector clicked and sputtered. Bugs collected in the funnel of light.

He'd been witness to some of the best guerrilla theatre the city had ever offered, it looked like. He'd got it all down, the perverse festival of guilt, the lascivious grief she detested the most. You almost didn't have the right to show up for something like that if you didn't know exactly what it was all about, which no one did who did not wear that day on his skin.

The lens walked through a spectacle of long hair, bell bottoms, flowered shirts. It wasn't hard to tell when this might have been, but you might have wondered where all these people came from, the interpreters and delegates and scientists and shame-ridden victims among throngs of the curious and the bored-looking. Maybe they were trying to absorb some of that free pain, heighten the passions, enliven themselves by rubbing up against those who really knew how to suffer. Maybe that's what Anton was doing there. Maybe he got off on this somehow, and needed it to keep himself alive.

All the sins enacted beneath the wide arch of the sky since the beginning of time were here pinched down into a single week's reckoning. A day filled with speeches and miracle forgiveness and relived nightmares. A week's worth of talks and mayoral proclamations and television crews boiled down to a couple of five-minute reels. This was the day Central Park filled with mothball-scented blankets and beach towels and PortoSan line-ups, of feeling magnanimous because here you were soaking up this remorseful feel-good atmosphere in spite of all the inconveniences.

Never again, they said. She could hear their chant, though the film was mute. *Never again*.

Then a crowd scene came up again and the lens wandered roughly for a moment, gaining ground, before, surprisingly, it stopped on her. Emiko saw herself, twenty, twenty-five years younger, standing in that long-dispersed riot of people. The camera focussed on her standing there, her hair much longer, fewer wrinkles gathered around that map of shiny skin on the left side of her face. And for a moment she was surprised, almost delighted, by this coincidence, this random luck.

The camera moved closer. She saw herself blink and notice, not him, but the camera itself. She stepped away then—whether in embarrassment or irritation, she couldn't now tell—into a large group of people, but the camera trailing after her was no mistake. She could tell that from here, suddenly, and her feeling of curious delight spoiled. This had been neither a coincidence nor a random act.

She turned to him, the question on her tongue.

He smiled and nodded. "Yes."

The images continued in front of them. The light fell over their faces. Sophie standing proudly beside a topiary scene, in some English garden, of a fox hunt. Then a younger Emiko appeared, again and again: different memorials, different clothing, different hair.

"But I found you," she said.

"I let this happen. I waited for you. I knew you would find me one day. I saw you there, always waiting, so for years and years I waited for you to come and to tell me who you were."

She was silent, shocked, trying to comprehend this. He'd been playing with her, she saw, all along. She had let herself get sucked into this old man's strange fascination, but still did not know why. The nervous fright that had seized her body years before, during the television show, threatened now to return, its monstrous, hulking frame bearing down upon her. She placed an open hand against her stomach.

How long had he waited for her? She had seen decades up there, decades of being spied on, documented, displayed like the insides of a lab rat.

"I don't know what this means," she said. "Stay there." She raised her hand and held it between them.

"It means our lives are connected in ways you could never dream of."

"I want to know why you followed me."

"When you finally came to me this summer, I knew then you were ready to hear what I have to say. I'd seen you in Los Angeles. I was in that audience, one of the guests, the people scheduled to appear. But finally I refused. I panicked. But I did stay to watch what happened. I saw you behind that screen. I'd always known I would tell you what I knew. But not then, not at that moment, because I wasn't able. No, I decided to wait as long as I had to."

She was afraid to provoke his desperation. These were the cryptic workings of an unbalanced mind, she thought, edging away. The density of the bushes between where she stood and the street meant that she would have to pass through the house in order to leave quickly.

"To tell me what?"

"That you were there because of me."

"I know that."

"No, no." He smiled. "You don't know." He rose from his chair and slipped another reel onto the projector arm. In a moment Emiko's old house came up, its destroyed front, the tossed trees and bushes and smashed windows.

"What is this?"

The hand that held the camera, jolting from side to side, walked in the front door. It jumped awkwardly as it was taken down from the shoulder and placed somewhere—the kitchen counter, she thought, yes—then was picked up again and focussed on her grandfather standing rigidly at attention. He bowed to the man holding the camera, straightened up and waited, unsmiling, in front of a low table set with bowls of rice as the camera was propped up once more. Anton, still youthful and handsome, that same big head of hair but dark, walked into view and shook the old man's hand and bowed. After they sat down, Emiko's grandfather began to pray—she knew his every gesture, the touch and smell of his skin as it would have been, as it had been, almost rising to her nose—and when he finished he held out the bowl to his guest and slowly, without speaking, they started to eat.

Suddenly the sheet went white and the tail-end of the film was flapping against the projector. They faced each other under the glow.

"I went back. For your grandfather's sake. I gave him hope, in the last years of his life, that you might lead a normal life. It was his wish. I would have walked away. I never would've put your name down on that list without his blessing. It was your grandfather's will. After seeing your brother die, after watching helplessly, he needed—he *deserved*—the opportunity."

Emiko stared at him from her chair. "*Put my name down?*"

"I'd helped him at the hospital where you and your brother were being treated. That is how I came to know him. He could not bear his grandson's suffering. He was a man of medicine, yet could do nothing. No one could. We each had enough English to communicate. He did not want the same to happen to you. For you there was still hope." He removed a reel from the wooden box and slipped it on the projector. In a moment an adolescent Emiko, speaking into the camera in Japanese, addressed the camera directly.

My name is Emiko Amai. My age is fifteen. I would like to go to America for surgery. My grandfather also wants me to go to America. I know this will be very difficult and I am prepared to be strong. I think life can be better for us when our faces are restored.

Off-screen, to her right, an American voice: *How many months did you spend in the hospital after the bombing?*

A Japanese voice translated this for her.

Fourteen months and seven days. She looked at the voice off-screen.

Look at the camera, please.

She turned her head back.

Do you know these procedures will mean more time in the hospital? There will be more operations.

Yes.

Some of these operations will be painful.

Yes.

You are willing to undergo these painful operations?

Yes.

Have you ever been outside of Hiroshima?

No.

What do you think you will miss the most if you go to America?

My grandfather.

Anything else?

No.

Are you afraid of what might happen to you there?

She hesitated, shielding her face from the camera, then turned back: *No.*

What do you want to be when you grow up?

I don't know.

Think hard, Emiko. Anything. What dreams do you have?

I have no dreams.

We all have dreams.

My dream is to wake up. Silently she stared into the camera. Then a chair off-screen scraped against the floor, followed by a nervous cough.

Thank you, Emiko.

She stood and left her seat.

The screen went blank. Then a scarred girl, whom Emiko didn't recognize, appeared, and was taking her place when Anton switched off the machine.

"Do you see?" he said. "I brought you here. I gave you your face back."

"No. Bernard Simon. The other surgeons."

"They made your face, yes. It was their hands, their skill. But you were there because of my intervention. I got you in the program. You would not have been considered otherwise. Thousands of girls prayed for such a chance."

"My grandfather took me to the doctors as soon as the Hiroshima papers announced the program. It was on the radio. Everyone knew. He asked me if I wanted to try these new techniques."

"He asked you this afterwards, after I contacted him. After I assured him that this was possible. Your grandfather wanted every chance to be given you. I went in 1954 as an observer of the program, nine years after my work there with the Manhattan District. I saw your grandfather again. I sought him out because I remembered him so well, and you. I told him about what the doctors could do. That I could find you a place among them. The other girls. You were not simply chosen. I picked you. You were there because of me, Emiko. I put you there. I gave you this new life. Who you are is because of me."

"That was you? With the camera?"

"These were made for evaluation purposes. For you, a formality. I had already seen to it that you were accepted. Yes, that was me."

Her head shifted slightly. Fear rode up her arms and spine, the danger of surprise. "Why?"

"Because I remembered you, Emiko. I saw you there, in your bed. Soon I knew you were your grandfather's only surviving relative. I had worked with him. I felt I knew him. It was one thing I could do. He was the only man I always remembered. I could not forget him."

There was a pause. The last of the moon descended into the lake. The air turned from black to blue. She sat silently, held within its cool grip.

"He was the only person I knew there. When I heard about the team of surgeons, and the interviews to decide on the best candidates, I went thinking of you. I'd met one of the surgeons at a conference at the New School. He was interested in radiation burns, so he obliged me. There were thousands of eligible girls. For them you were as good as any. They didn't care who. You were all the same for their purposes. But they told me your scars could be repaired, and I told your grandfather. He was thankful. He knew it was your only chance at a new life."

"Who are you?" she said. *"Who are you to do that?"*

The accusation came with a violence he had not anticipated. "But this was done *for* you. This was giving back what had been taken from you. As much as possible."

"What gave you the right?"

"It was not anyone's right. It was a gift. As I said, I wouldn't have continued without your grandfather's approval. Without *your* approval, in the end. You consented. You were not pushed."

"But I knew nothing of this. I never had any idea my life would be given over to your need to reconcile yourself with what you'd done."

"This was my opportunity to give something back. So much had been taken from you. I needed to help any way I could. Only a small gesture, a moment of grace. You would deny me that? You would have been left back there, don't you see? Your life would be different. You would be horribly scarred. Still that little girl. Forever that little girl."

"You kidnapped my life," she said.

"This was your freedom. You don't understand what I did for you."

"But it wasn't for me. You did this for yourself."

"You were given a second chance, while thousands of others weren't. What does it matter, my motivation? I gave you that chance."

She was silent.

"You're right. I gave both of us something. Yes. But is a father selfish when he gives his daughter a gift? Because he enjoys the smile on her face? There is pleasure in giving. Of course. I felt that."

"But you *created* all this! You manipulated me. I had no choice. No understanding."

"I gave you freedom, Emiko."

"This is *your* life," she said.

He shook his head.

"You robbed me of the last precious thing I had." She stared at him. "You went back to Japan to ease your conscience. To help one of thousands. Helping *one* doesn't erase the memory of the thousands you didn't."

"No," he said. "But it is one person."

"That person didn't want your help!"

"I am telling you the truth. It is a certain truth, naturally. I thought you would want to know the hand that has directed your fate. I wanted you to stop wondering. That is my gift to you."

2

Anton had often imagined the twelve men leaning as one body into the long gentle roll that brought the plane into position over the harbour, far above the seven finger-shaped tributaries of the Ota River. This, the unintended hint that might have alerted those below whose curiosity compelled them to look up from their morning newspaper, their innocent games. He often imagined their will to abstraction, seven miles overhead, its overwhelming power, and its necessity for such an endeavour. Just as his own will to abstraction had been overpowering, living as he had been, almost happily, on the dry moonscapes of the New Mexico desert. When you are possessed of a driving need to live in the theoretical world, he'd discovered, a desert is just the place. Removed entirely from reality, so that everything there was imagined. Everything but the sun and parched earth. Anything was possible there. If need be, you might even create your own universe.

But what had they seen that day? Until then, nothing but blue ocean and more blue ocean. Perhaps a trawler trailing its wake of fattened gulls—or just the sun hanging over the horizon? Then the occasional whitecap thrown up by a touch of wind miles below. Would you see signs of yourself, of loved ones and places you missed? What about Ferebee, nervously running through the tasks at hand, but in a small corner of his head looking forward to the bottle of Coors that awaited after debriefing, ice-cold, so cold it would bring a pleasant ache to the teeth? His pack of Chesterfields sitting beside the ring of condensation on the table, maybe a game of Ping-Pong in the rec room. Feet up, mind off. What was so unusual about this?

Did they realize what they were getting into? Did they understand the nature of the cabal of murderers they'd signed on with?

He'd had his own mental getaways. Like picnicking in the Frijoles Mountains, and the soft imaginings of his young wife. He recognized this need to avoid thinking about it, to think about something else. Concentrate on the promise of home. For Ferebee it may have been the red Chevy pickup that had been up on blocks for as long as he could remember, a weeping willow out back with a yellow rope-swing tied to its boldest limb. Maybe the easy assurance of a woman—his mother, or his first sweetheart—moving silently through a shaded kitchen.

All those promises, like Sophie, writing letters at the kitchen table back home in Brooklyn. Knowing only vaguely where he'd disappeared to, and what disappointments lay ahead. Given the haunting realities of the theories they spun down there, she, too, had become merely a theory by then. The theory of ease, of grace, of getting out of here.

Anton could only guess what Ferebee and the others had been thinking. He hadn't had the stomach to ask, the day they'd met at that doctor's office in Tokyo. Though he knew who he was. But maybe it was this. Maybe bombardier Major Thomas Ferebee had convinced himself he was flying through the deep-blue skies of America. Yet another test. Another smooth ride through friendly grids and vectors and latitudes and seconds, unshadowed by the approach of history. Just another test run. There was no other way of getting up enough courage to drop a bomb like that. Absolutely not.

He heard a dozen men's electronic transmissions fill the plane's hollow body, heard its shiny hull vibrating with information as surely as if he were up there himself, not standing here in the dark on a summer night at the end of his life. Altitude and wind speed, colourful language, mostly and almost always spoken in the short-hand Southern drawl he'd grown familiar with during his time down in New Mexico. He heard those voices spiral along radio wires into swollen eardrums, ricocheting off helmets and oxygen canisters and shining wrist-watches and the glass-faced altimeter. They were in constant communication as they flew headlong into a new age that only a handful of people knew anything about. But Ferebee should have been able to guess. His thumb ready, eyes peeled.

He could testify to the fact that there was more talking up there than at any family reunion, all preparation and confirmation, check and double-check and triple-check, because there was no margin for error, no time for a moment's silence, no time to feel the slickness under your thigh or the building pressure on your bladder. Too much information was required if this was to go off smoothly. One false degree either way and that Chevy would stay up on blocks for eternity, so just get on with it.

There was a certain art in being open to the big picture. That's the view Anton had. That's what had kept him going all this time. Maybe those men knew that all along, which was how they'd been able to do what needed to be done. Theoretical, clean, of one mind. No single man more culpable than the next, all communicating relevant data to and from the cockpit, and the headset peering over the cross-hairs. And each one harbouring his own version of Sophie, sitting back at home all the while and waiting for the end of the war. Or at least for the next letter.

Ferebee blinked, concentrating, counting forward. He might already have heard about certain precautions, and he wasn't worried too much about the goggles. He'd been told that the men responsible for the on-board cargo had lathered themselves in coconut-flavoured suntan lotion for that first test. Word got around. He'd heard plenty of things, and to the best of his knowledge those guys were still fine. Most of them had been living in the desert for twelve months or more, soaking up God's rays while in the process of perfecting this thing carried down in the bay. Someone just happened to have a tube of the stuff handy, probably, someone who by the mere fact of his mere presence was assumed to know what he was doing. At any rate, nobody seemed to think it odd, according to the story, that you'd be putting on something you could buy at a grocery store to protect yourself from the invisible cancers of the new age. Because they did it and they were all somewhere ten thousand miles away, quite alive, waiting for news, or washing dishes with Mozart playing on the radio.

He wasn't nervous about the eye damage, no, though he would've slipped the goggles on anyway if what he was doing didn't require the naked eye. And there might be time once the drop was made. Numbers flashed in his mind. From thirty thousand eight hundred feet, it would take approximately fifty seconds for it to fall, to find zero. He'd done the calculations dozens of times by then, that deep into the flight. As Böll had done before him out in the desert, in anticipation of that splendid, final moment.

Those twelve men forever up there in his imagination worked in perfect synchronous industry to get that plane over its target. He saw the last three with the protective dark glasses still pulled up onto their foreheads. Like Alpine skiers standing at a canteen between runs.

There was work yet to do that required the light of day, strangely enough, after four hours of flight in darkness. Because they'd been training for this moment for months and nothing was going to stop them. Not even now, fifty years on.

He knew Tibbets probably could've flown that jalopy in total darkness, and that Beser could have just turned up the shimmer of his radar screen to full. Ferebee, though, required the soft touch of the human eye. The success or failure of this great leap forward would be decided in the cord of nerves that ran between the eyeball and the brain of a twenty-four-year-old boy, waiting for the cross-hairs of his bomb sight to overlay the T-shaped Aioi Bridge.

As for the rest of the crew, he could only imagine them waiting anxiously for the main event to kick in, for the flash of blinding light to streak across their faces. The pounding of the engines and the electronic chatter expanding in the head; vibrations rumbling up through the body of the aircraft, its very walls humming.

Part of the protocol insisted on by the head of the Health Physics Department—who had no idea about the coconut oil—dictated that those dark glasses must separate these men from the history they were about to make. The glasses would help tone down the early-morning fire-storms somewhat, dimming the realization. They'd been designed to keep the shocking glare from the men's eyes. But what none of them knew yet at eight-eleven that morning, really understood at the deepest gut-level of certainty, was the meaning of the silhouette their presence cast on the ground below.

The heart and lungs of these dozen men were pushed down into their intestines when the plane jumped some ten feet with the sudden release of the nine-thousand-pound bomb. Anton saw the man whose face was downturned over the scope, like a boy on a roller-coaster ride, close his eyes for a split second, wondering why he'd got himself into this. Cramped, his guts sloshed about, he forgot what the attraction had been. Holding his bladder for almost an hour now. Where's the fun in this? But when he saw the bomb fall away like a great dinosaur egg, his sense of purpose returned. He knew how powerful this thing was said to be. But he'd trained himself not to contemplate it. Remember the big picture, he thought. That will to abstraction. Win the war.

The device wobbled a second—the imagination suspending in the air one last hope of ending it right here, a cancellation of plans, the forward momentum of the plane pulling it along as if it were a balloon on a string—then, the hope breaking, began its rapid descent towards the waking city. Automatically he mouthed "Bomb away." Even though the sudden lurch of the airplane was unmistakable, the young major said it, because that was part of his job. The aircraft banked a hard hundred and fifty-five degrees right and began a steep dive to get up her speed so as to torque them out of here, because a B-29 needed more time to clear the area than you need to reach up and snap down your welder's goggles. Fifty seconds or so, he knew, meant only five miles between It and Them, and the concussive shock was going to be out of this world.

The plane pulled away from the old man's imagination and then, like a cloud scudding across the sky, entered the memory of the girl who had been playing down there on the mud bank of that river, who later, lying in the guest room, could still taste the sickness in her mouth, recalling the instant she felt the push of fire against her body, the sucking for air. She saw Mitsuo's smooth, unburned skin, and quickly the poisoned face of her grandfather was branded into her dead brother's back and she sat up and began scratching violently at her own burning skin.

Before full light came that morning, Anton fell into a dream. In his dream he raised himself on his right arm and cocked his head and listened to a sound come to him through the half-light of his open bedroom window. He waited for the sound to come again, fighting the exhaustion that pushed down on his chest, buckling his elbow and shoulder. He had no idea what time it was, or to what day that time might belong. He could not see the face of the old bedside clock from his position. Somehow it had been moved during the night, or by the dream he was inside. He didn't remember coming in from the garden and changing into the grey-and-white-striped pyjamas he wore, loose, like flowing veils, and sliding stiffly into bed. He looked at the back of the clock, at its exposed levers and windings, and his eyes burnt. He scratched a temple with a sharp, curling fingernail and blinked with surprise.

The doorbell rang.

When he brought his finger away from his temple he saw a dab of blood, which he cleaned brusquely against his sleeve.

In his dream he pulled away the light sheet and swung himself around and up. His warm feet meeting the cool oak floor, he shuffled to the closet, where he donned a tattered robe. Only when he switched on the overhead light did he see the ghostly trail of sweaty footprints left on the floor. He felt as though he'd been wrapped in a damp blanket all night. The bloody cuff of his sleeve, even the material on his chest and back, was heavy and cool with perspiration.

The bell rang again, two hollow waves of sound that resonated through the empty house.

He followed the stairs down to the foyer and stood quietly, beside the coat rack, behind the front door. The floorboards beneath the blue-and-red mat creaked underfoot as he inched back the curtain to the right of the brass doorknob and saw the police cruiser in the driveway, its lights out; the car was black, strangely hearse-like. He opened the door and nodded to the lady officer, who was dressed in military gear, gas-mask, khakis, boots.

Anton Böll?

Yes, he said.

She handed him a plastic bottle, a size that fit into his palm.

You will come with me.

Her heavy leather boots filled the quiet between them.

The woman's face—what he could see of it—wore an expression of authority and kindness. Yet there was also an unease in her manner, in the way she held herself and gestured for him to follow her. It was still early. His judgment was off. Opposite the house the three powerful oak trees he'd always wished were on his property stood in darkness, undeclared against a charcoal sky. At this early hour, immensely tired, he was aware only of something peculiar here—something unwelcome and beckoning.

Come with you? he asked.

. . . the room, yes, the officer was saying.

She took him by the shoulder, led him upstairs to the bedroom and turned back the white sheet on the bed. Though the corpse he saw was scarred and burnt, he recognized it as his wife's. Where it was not charred black, along the body's right side, a mass of open sores, red and oozing, bubbled as if possessed of a life of their own. The woman in the military garb pointed at the plastic bottle in his hand, which he raised in the air above the corpse of his burnt wife, then squeezed slowly and watched as the oil dripped over her body.

He awoke, frightened. Stock still, he breathed through his mouth. A dampness had accumulated under his body, chilling the sheets and mattress. The room filled with the light of dawn, and through the open window he could hear lake sounds rising up from the bottom of the garden and the rustling of poplar leaves. He waited for a breeze that might lift away the smell of coconuts and burnt flesh that had followed him from sleep. He got out of bed then and stepped across the hall and quietly opened the guest-room door. Emiko was there, asleep. He moved inside and stood over her bed. He took the framed picture down from the wall and read the words inscribed in the bottom right corner.

Stefano—Pescara, 1927.

Emiko

I cannot say why I awoke with the dream of twelve men in my head. While not wholly new to me, it was not one I dreamed often. Others, such as the one in which I watched the darkly gloved hand pressed over my brother's face, were far more common; in fact, that dream in particular could be said to have shaped my life. But now that I understood that the hand had actually belonged to someone, was *real* in a sense, that dream seemed to recede from my mind. What returned to me instead that morning was the slow, glistening approach of silver on the last day of my first life.

I rubbed the sleep from my eyes and watched the light erase the shadows and the grey trim lining the guest room. The coming day filled this space as calmly, as surely, as that airplane had loomed ever larger in the sky years before. It was then, lying in bed, that I decided Böll's intervention could be as he'd claimed: an act both generous and selfish, not one more than the other. This was the nature of his character, and perhaps even a larger truth regarding the history I'd been forced to witness.

But I would never really understand. Clearly, I'd never see things as he did, or as he wanted me to. Some facts, I decided, and most lives must remain mysterious and unsolvable. Intentions were forever obscure. But who could look at me now and see more than a burned child fully grown, held hostage in another world? Who could see beyond the history I have survived, and factor into that the loves and terrors and banalities of normal experience?

You will never know a life as well as you remember it. The remembering is easy. This is what I decided that morning. In recalling your past there is precious little knowledge, which remains our most difficult quarry. In memory there are simply shapes that appear before the eyes of who you are now, and who you might've been, the shapes as incomplete and changeable as the times. But they are all we have. I would truly never know who I'd been before being brought here. Sure, certain memories of myself would remain; but they suggested another person's life to me now, not my own. Yet somehow I was not saddened by this thought. Now that the girl I'd been was released from me, I felt unburdened by her pains and solitude, and by my need to remain that girl. At once the stern and brutalized face with which I'd confronted the world was no longer capable of representing me. I was someone else now. My history was no longer my own.

I got up then and from the window looked down over the garden. Even though certain corners and recesses of the property were still shaded, its maze seemed less crowded and confusing at this angle than when standing within, surrounded by its lush patterns. I studied the walkways and tributary paths, maybe half of them at least partly visible. The slate of those smaller paths, scattered like tiny pools throughout the property, reflected sunlight up to my window like mirrors. Though I was able to see the overall design more clearly, as well as the larger movement and directions it suggested, the detail Sophie had busied herself with for years was difficult to detect. I saw few traces of the animals she'd created. The creeping ivy and holly resembled less the long neck of a giraffe and running legs of a fox than a meandering, jumbled mess of forest. The riot of fish that had been partially completed before the last onset of illness looked more like a pile of dried sea grass rolled up from the lake.

On one occasion he'd spoken to me of walking sleepless through this garden maze, eyes closing and opening in hopes that he would find something before him that seemed new, unplanned and unforeseen, a clue, perhaps, to the mystery that surrounded him. But he was not a man well equipped for mystery. Not of this sort, I thought. He was a man of science, a man blind to the possibilities that lurked beyond the scope of his learning.

At that moment he emerged from the shed carrying a pair of

shears and stepped onto the main path that led down to the water. For some reason the fairy tale about the beautiful Moon Princess came to my mind, and the lesson it might have taught me as a girl. Something about beauty and mystery and the unexpected. The tale of a young child who cannot live long in this world. Maybe I'd just been meant to see more than he had been able to. Maybe his lot in life had been that of a blind, unknowing cog. As I watched him start down the slope, something in his movement reminded me of the *kyodatsu,* the condition of despair and exhaustion that possessed my people after the war. With the loss of his wife, and the knowledge of who he had become, Anton Böll seemed to me that day diminished, a man overwhelmed by his own sense of defeat.

He continued along with what seemed a kind of inertia, under a perfect blue sky—and again a different morning sky came to me, and the white plume of smoke trailing it. Briefly I pictured myself stepping up from the sand and mud of the Ota River like one of Sophie's fish rising up from evolutionary waters. Those twelve men up there, I wondered, would they ever land, ever deliver me safely from their terror?

Then he stopped, leaned toward a single flower and lowered his nose. Watching him breathe it in, I leaned out the window, resting both hands on the sill. The air off the lake and garden was warm, fresh; and the scent he may have tasted drifted just then, up to my face—alive, clean-smelling, touched by mint. He'd started back down when, suddenly, he stepped off the path and was gone.

Once more, I wondered why his wife had opened her home to me in what she must have known were her last hours. I wondered if we, the two women of his life, had for all these years been bound to the world by the same ignorance, somehow embodied by or focussed through the same man. But as I considered this I resisted the urge to make such favourable connections between myself and a woman I knew next to nothing about. I had little desire to view

my life as anything but painfully and coincidentally connected to
his, and none whatsoever to help him. I would never give him that
pleasure.

But maybe the answers to all his questions concerning Sophie
were evident enough. Maybe her patience had outlived her, because
she'd waited too long for him to discover what she had left out
there for him. Not once had he seen anything that served to illumi-
nate her heart, according to what he'd told me those dark late
nights after her death. But maybe there was something out there
that connected him to her still, without his even knowing. Those
shapes, those desperate poses. I wondered what she'd tried to tell
him with them, and if there were still a pulse, a heartbeat, within
them that he and I might ever be able to feel.

I waited a minute, straining to hear, but there was only the
morning birdsong. I wondered if I shouldn't walk down and seek
him out among his wife's flowers. Perhaps to ask him more questions, or to confess that I could never understand what he'd done,
and therefore not free him from the impossible burden of explana-
tion. But from up here the view over the lake was so clear and
undisturbed and brightly lit in the morning sun that the world
briefly seemed blessed with a peace and restfulness I could not
account for.

I had thought of the ocean on various occasions as I looked at
the water from my window those days after Sophie's death, or
from out on the stone pier. I was grateful to have these mornings
here to myself, and for the time they allowed me to get myself
together and tell him I was leaving. Somehow I now was free of the
quiet desperation that had held me for so long, having learned of
my grandfather's great secret, and witnessed the death of a woman
I now felt I should've known. I needed this respite, especially on
this last morning. When I saw the ocean in the lake before me, I
was not pretending I was somewhere else. The feeling just came to
me, with all its pleasing associations, and I breathed in the tremen-

dous sense of possibility I always felt when faced by great distances such as the one I was now looking into.

I waited for him to step back up on the path, but apparently he'd found something to occupy himself with behind that bank of shrub and bush and flower. I didn't feel like waiting any longer to tell him, so I put on the dress I'd taken from Sophie's closet three days before and walked down to the water. I didn't see him, and didn't make a point of searching him out; he could've returned to the house by some side path, or carried on farther down the shore. Instead I turned my attention to the lake and let its light breeze lift the hair off my shoulders like an invisible hand. I moved down to the rocky beach and watched boats piloted by morning sailors and, I imagined, young sons, as yet unaware of the world's demands on them, of its need for sacrifice and suffering; and, maybe, by adventurous lovers exhausted from the night they'd shared, now drowsy and alive with a connection and purpose that for me had long since passed into memory.

The beach was as wide as a narrow road, rocky and lined by small strips of coarse, dark sand like the markings of a fish. Kicking off the slippers I'd borrowed, also from Sophie's closet, I walked out into the water until it was up to my knees. I don't know why I did this. It wasn't a particularly inviting stretch of beach for bathing or swimming, and the water was much colder than I would've guessed. Its cool touch quickly stripped me of the lazy warmth I had carried from my bed, and there I stood, peaceful and slightly chilled, facing open water. Just after dawn I had heard him moving downstairs, as he'd done every morning I was there. I knew his shuffling footsteps practically in my sleep by now, and the slow, nervous energy they contained. I heard the glass door slide heavily on its rail, and his footsteps on the hard stone walkways of the garden. He moved out there among his wife's creations with a dreary, obsessive and unsettling melancholy, despite the beauty of the asters and dianthus and hostas blooming along the pathways, of the sweet iris hanging from the latticed arbour. I'd watched him secretly my first night here, and since then felt disinclined to intrude again. I had left him alone to play the guessing game of unresolved meanings, of memories of Japan and of picnics in the desert, and to look for explanations he should've known would never come, for absolution that would never be extended. Instead I had lain awake feeling the gathering dawn warm the air, and gazing at the gently silhouetted baby's breath and cosmos that crept up the window frame.

Standing there facing the lake, I found in the silence the strength to enjoy the beauty of this place one last morning. I'd walked the length of the beach and felt the sand and pebbles wedging themselves between my toes, but I had never gone in. Now the water rose to my thighs, and I was able to walk some distance out, thirty or forty feet, before the bottom began to drop beneath me. At this point I stopped, unwilling to immerse myself fully, and looked back to the shore. From here the house, almost entirely hidden by its flurry of bush and leaf, was just a tiny speck. Off to the left I saw the stone pier with its red-and-white lighthouse, and farther on the bell tower of a church needling above Port Elizabeth itself.

Then I spotted something in the array of bright flowers and dark, surrounding green. As if it were drawn by my own hand, I saw the ears and twisted mouth of my grandfather's face. That funny grin I'd mud-painted by the river. I held my gaze steadily, afraid it would disappear into the bush as easily and suddenly as it had emerged. After the initial surprise—it was almost certainly there, I thought—I considered that the most likely source of this face was my own hopeful perception, nothing more than what I'd wanted to see, and my need to make sense of the history that had been brought to me. This, combined with the powerful alchemy of resignation and a peculiar interaction of summer light and overgrown leaf. But what I thought I'd seen was suddenly gone again.

So it was only that, I thought: just a rare bending of light, a coincidence of angles and distance.

Many times as a child I had seen in the cracks in the ceiling above my bed certain stories and figures no one else could ever make out. Up there I'd seen a future displayed before me that never came true. Not even Mitsuo, whom I'd coaxed countless times into staring up at that same bedroom ceiling with me, ever recognized what I was pointing out to him: all those lovely creatures and existing adventures figured into the designs like rays of light streaming out of an enchanted bamboo grove.

So this illusion, too, was gone. And all that remained was this day, this garden, this life.

ACKNOWLEDGEMENTS

I wish to thank Liz Calder for her early faith; Phyllis Bruce for her profound wisdom and insight, and the tireless attention that helped bring this book to life; Gary Fisketjon for his particular and wonderful magic; and Special Agent Bukowski for always speaking clearly into her shoe phone. I would also like to acknowledge the financial support of the Canada Council, the Ontario Arts Council and the Toronto Arts Council, as well as thank the K. M. Hunter Foundation for the honour of its Literature Prize. Of the many sources consulted for background historical detail, I found Katherine Davison's Moon Magic: Stories from Asia *especially helpful. Appreciation also to "el peregrino," Bob Ward; to John and Franc, for reasons they will never know; and to Antoine. And to Andrea, finally and foremost, who lived through all of this and so much more during the years it took to write this book— my deepest gratitude and love.*

A NOTE ON THE TYPE

This book was set in Minion, a typeface produced by the Adobe Corporation specifically for the Macintosh personal computer, and released in 1990. Designed by Robert Slimbach, Minion combines the classic characteristics of old-style faces with the full complement of weights required for modern typesetting.

COMPOSED BY
NK Graphics,
Keene, New Hampshire

PRINTED AND BOUND BY
R.R. Donnelley & Sons Company,
Harrisonburg, Virginia

DESIGNED BY
Iris Weinstein

P.S.

Ideas, interviews & features

*

About the author

About the book

Read on

Author Biography

DENNIS BOCK was born in Oakville, Ontario. He grew up with German parents; his mother spent many hours weaving and his father was a carpenter. He attended the University of Western Ontario and took one year off during that time to live in Spain, where he tried to write. After graduating with an honours degree in English and Philosophy, Bock spent five years teaching English and writing in Madrid. It was there that he began his collection of connected stories, *Olympia,* a semi-autobiographical work about a German-Canadian family. *Olympia,* which was published in 1998, won the Canadian Authors Association Jubilee Award, the Danuta Gleed Award for best first collection of stories by a Canadian author and the British Betty Trask Award for best first book of fiction by an author under 35. *The Ash Garden* is his first novel. It was named a *Globe* 100 Best Book of the Year and won the Japan-Canada Award. It was also a finalist for the IMPAC Dublin Literary Award, the Amazon.com/*Books in Canada* First Novel Award, the Kiriyama Pacific Rim Prize and the Commonwealth Writers' Prize for Best Book (Caribbean and Canada region). Dennis Bock moved back to Canada in 1994. He lives with his family in Guelph, Ontario. ❧

An Interview
with Dennis Bock

What sort of reading and historical research did you undertake before starting *The Ash Garden*? How do you, as a writer, manage to balance a story of such historical sweep with the lives of three individuals?

The characters in *The Ash Garden* are fictional. Someone once told me that this novel wears its history lightly. I was pleased to hear that because this is not an historical novel. It has its historical setting, its real events, but no one in the book—besides the peripheral figures like Oppenheimer and Reverend Tanimoto—is real. Only the bomb is real.

That being said, I sifted though dozens of books to help build the historical background of the novel—not the facts so much as the colour, the feel, the tone. Research helps carry the plotting, and certain historical realities and details help to focus the narrative. You can't deliver a character to Los Alamos without reading about the place and time, and it's often the detail you're not looking for that stays with you and ends up in the book—stuff that comes out of nowhere, that surprises you, like the messages on the billboards they had set up to inspire the workers there; or the fact that the core group of scientists, the people who ▶

> ❝ It's often the detail you're not looking for that stays with you and ends up in the book. ❞

3

An Interview with Dennis Bock (*continued*)

witnessed the first explosion at Alamogordo, wore suntan lotion, thinking this was going to help protect them from radiation sickness. You find a detail like that and you know it's going in the book. And not just as an aside. It becomes a crucial metaphor for the innocence of those times, of just how new this science was—even for the brilliant minds behind its creation.

The sections on the aftermath of Hiroshima are among the most powerful parts of the novel. How difficult were they to write? Did you draw on eyewitness accounts?

The Hiroshima sections were not more difficult to write than any other section. In a way they were easier because there can be only one emotion you're hoping to inspire in your reader when you write about something like that. Emotionally there can be little subtlety. A city dies. What else can you feel? You write for the pit of the stomach. There are few, if any, nuances available.

Anton is a fascinating character because we expect him to struggle with guilt but he seems not to. Why were you drawn to such a character—why does moral complexity appeal to you as a writer?

> You write for the pit of the stomach.

4

As a reader I've always been drawn to "Big Question" books that might introduce certain questions to the reader's mind but do not claim to provide answers to those questions. I love a good mystery, but not in the conventional sense of that word: the mystery of right behaviour, moral choice, responsible action. I'm put off by novels that pretend to answer the questions they raise. There can't be answers—not sincere or meaningful answers—to the questions of moral action raised in a great book. A serious writer, in my mind, attempts to expose the flipside to any commonly held belief. It's a shell game of sorts, with each shell containing, or seemingly so, the seed of truth. Point to it with anything resembling conviction or certainty and you will be proven wrong.

That being said, a novel isn't a game. It doesn't try to cause the reader to stumble, but in resisting an easy answer regarding a character's choices the reader might find himself in the confusing position of simultaneously loving and hating a character, his choices, his beliefs. For me a novel is at its best when it brings contradiction to the surface of a character's life and when those contradictions and confusions are highlighted by virtue of a dramatic conflict between characters. In exposing those contradictions by the right positioning of character, setting and drama, you approach the heart of what it is to be human. There is in ▶

> **❝** For me a novel is at its best when it brings contradiction to the surface of a character's life. **❞**

An Interview with Dennis Bock (*continued*)

this world, instead of the simple black and white universe of poorly imagined fiction, an infinite variety of greys.

***The Ash Garden* opens and ends with water imagery. Why did you choose to use this structure?**

As a writer I am a firm believer in the seren-dipity of accident and chance. Some things just happen. Some images occur. They insist. They reoccur. Suddenly you have a motif on your hands. Then you look at what you've got laid out before you and you ask, Could I use this? Can I turn this into something signifi-cant, meaningful, even powerful? There's a lot of alchemy that happens right in front of you as you write. I believe that an artist must possess an inner sense of aesthetic balance, just as a musician has an "ear" for his music that will help him deal with the accidental nature of creating art. That's why I create so many drafts when I write; then, when I feel the time is right, I start sifting. Yes, the novel begins and ends with water imagery. What is the significance of the water imagery? Water can signify birth, of course, and there is, at the start of the novel, a most horrifying birth. An ogre is born, and so too is a new age. At the end of the novel we witness a second birth, a re-birth, and the beginning of a new life.

> **"** I am a firm believer in the serendipity of accident and chance. **"**

The Second World War was in many ways the first "media" war. Film, radio and, later, television—the ways in which non-participants experience war—seem important in this novel. Can you talk about this aspect of the story?

There was a time, long ago, when only soldiers fought wars. Wars happened out there somewhere, over the hill, well away from mothers and babies. Not so now. For forty years now, wars fought on the other side of the planet have arrived in our living rooms with a horrifying and depressing regularity. We are all, in a sense, casualties. We all know what a war zone looks like. We all know the shape of a child's mangled body. My three central characters are non-combatants yet their lives are fundamentally changed by war, as each of our own lives has been. Here is the sad reality of the modern media-flush world. What power do we have to strike out, to free ourselves from history? Who is immune? The reality is that very few indeed are immune to the fallout of war. Global conflict is the sad central fact of the twentieth century. All of us are not so directly affected by the bomb as are these three central characters; yet it is not so difficult to see in them the sea change of an entire generation. ✍

" Global conflict is the sad central fact of the twentieth century. "

The Facts Behind the Fiction

The Manhattan Project was the code name for the development of an atomic bomb in the United States during the Second World War. At that time, rumours were circulating that Germany and Japan were in the preliminary stages of developing the atomic bomb, and the Americans began to rush their project in order to be the first to complete the task. Under extreme secrecy, top scientists, including Robert Oppenheimer and Enrico Fermi, gathered to carry out this mission. Under the direction of General Leslie R. Groves, the team performed the first nuclear test on July 16, 1945, in New Mexico. There were two more detonations: the first over Hiroshima, Japan, on August 6, 1945, and the second on August 9, 1945, over Nagasaki.

At the end of 1945, approximately 140,000 people died in Hiroshima as a result of the bomb, a number equaling almost half of the city's population. Much of the city burned to the ground due to the intense heat from the bomb (5000°F at ground level). Those within a few kilometres of the detonation suffered from varying degrees of skin burns and most died instantly or within the following days. Air pressure from the enormous blast caused the collapse of buildings and houses, crushing many people who were inside them.

Many others died immediately from radiation. Survivors suffered long-term effects, including loss of hair, internal organ malfunctions, leukemia, cancerous tumors and high infant mortality rates.

Those who did survive—and who continued to suffer with terrible burns—included a group of women called "The Hiroshima Maidens." These single, young females were brought to the US to receive plastic surgery for their burned faces and stayed with local Quakers before and after their procedures.

While there had always been opposition to nuclear weapons, the events in Hiroshima and the press "The Hiroshima Maidens" received opened the eyes of thousands around the world to the devastation these weapons caused. Bertrand Russell, a renowned philosopher and mathematician, was one of the leaders in the cause to "Ban the Bomb" after the Second World War. He formed the Campaign for Nuclear Disarmament (CND) in 1958 with Reverend Canon John Collins. Russell went on to become an advocate for causes such as women's rights and the peace movement. ✒

Recommended Reading

Embracing Defeat
John W. Dower
(W.W. Norton & Company)

The Hiroshima Maidens
Rodney Barker
(Viking)

Hirohito and the Making of Modern Japan
Herbert P. Bix
(HarperCollins)

Hiroshima
John Hersey
(Knopf)

*The Enola Gay: The B-29 That Dropped the
     First Atomic Bomb*
Norman Polmar
(Potomac Books)

*Hiroshima: Why America Dropped the Atomic
     Bomb*
Ronald Takaki
(Little Brown)

*The Nuclear Axis: Germany, Japan and The
     Atom Bomb Race 1939–1945*
Philip Henshall
(Sutton Publishing)

*American Prometheus: The Triumph and
        Tragedy of J. Robert Oppenheimer*
Kai Bird & Martin J. Sherwin
(Knopf)

Hiroshima in History and Memory
Michael J. Hogan
(Cambridge University Press)

*Picturing the Bomb: Photographs from the
        Secret World of the Manhattan Project*
Rachel Fermi & Esther Samra
(Harry N. Abrams)

Hiroshima Notes
Kenzaburo Oe
(Marion Boyars Publishers)

*Children of the Atomic Bomb: An American
        Physician's Memoir of Nagasaki,
        Hiroshima, and the Marshall Islands*
James N. Yamazaki & Louis B. Fleming
(Duke University Press)

*Ban the Bomb: A History of SANE, the
        Committee for a Sane Nuclear Policy*
Milton S. Katz
(Greenwood Press)

Web Detective

**www.atomicmuseum.com/tour/
manhattanproject.cfm**
A historical tour of the atomic museum,
including photos of the people and places
involved in the Manhattan project.

www.pcf.city.hiroshima.jp/top_e.html
The official homepage of the Hiroshima
Peace Memorial Museum.

www.humanities.mcmaster.ca/~bertrand/
Biographical information on Bertrand Russell.

www.pugwash.org
Homepage for the Conferences on Science
and World Affairs.

**http://library.thinkquest.org/17940/texts/
timeline/manhattan.html**
Information on the Manhattan project with
quotes from the scientists involved.

www.theenolagay.com
A site devoted to the Enola Gay bomber and
the events surrounding the atomic bombing
of Hiroshima.

**www.biography.ms/Atomic_bombings_of_
Hiroshima_and_Nagasaki.html**
Detailed source of information on the
bombings.

www.enola-gay.org
Homepage for the Committee for a National
Discussion of Nuclear History and Current
Policy.

www.rerf.or.jp
Homepage for the Radiation Effects Research
Foundation, which focuses on studying the
health effects of radiation in the survivors of
Hiroshima and Nagasaki.

Also by Dennis Bock
An Excerpt from *Olympia* (1998):

We are all subdued from the night drive home from the lake, where we have been for the last day and a half, sorting out details with the police. I've had my tie in my pocket since the accident. I take it out and lay it on the wood mantel above the fireplace, beside the photograph I haven't seen in years.

Nobody has said anything since we got in the car three hours ago. The crickets are in full force outside, excited by the thin chemical smell of swimming pools and expensive artificial fertilizers. Silently, my mother carries my sister up to her bedroom, careful not to wake her. On the way home, I massaged Ruby's feet while she slept. I knew her new shoes had broken the skin, though she hadn't complained or said anything the whole time. Only the stove light in the kitchen is on. The refrigerator is humming softly, like a dirge. Outside in the back garden my father's watering the sunflowers, though they're already covered in night dew and fast asleep.

From the mantel I take down the photograph of a group of twenty-two girls. It's been hidden for years behind the giant redwood pine cones my aunt Marian brought when she came from California to visit, and the large dusty candles shaped like eagles. In the picture my grandmother sits in the front row cross-legged and smiling, showing off her dimples and good health. This is her seamstress class, 1927, back in the black-and-white days of uniforms and vocational schools. On the back names and ages are written with little slashes through the middle of the sevens, European style. "Seventeen" is scrawled beside Lottie, my grandmother's name.

I examine each face, imagine the course each life has taken since this photograph was made. I want to believe my grandmother's smiling because they've been let out early that day. And because they're excited. I let my imagination slide backwards. Only a few have ever had their photograph taken. The camera still something exotic, in the same class as the zebra, which all of them have seen but never ridden. They've all looked at photographs in magazines, seen wedding photos, fashion prints, pictures of the war.

There are four girls out of the twenty-two who seem to be taking this picture business very seriously. Two sisters, Louise and Greta Schriebmann, who no one likes to associate with because of their suspiciously dark hair. Last year in history class we studied anti-Semitism in Europe, Germany particularly. We watched films of the liberation of Jews from the camps. The sisters are intense and determined, their eyebrows lowered slightly, teeth clenched. They're standing in the back row—only two ▶

Also by Dennis Bock (*continued*)

rows—so you can't see below their waists. Maybe they're holding hands.

Erika is the third girl. The girl with the long pointy nose. I can see the whole length of her body because she's standing at one end of the group, to the photographer's right. She doesn't want to smile in case the principal of the school asks for a copy of the photograph, which he will undoubtedly do. Since 1921 these class photos have been displayed under glass in the lobby of the college. Erika was gravely impressed the first time she saw them and hopes to affect future generations of students in the same way.

The fourth girl looks more sad than stern. This is Silke, my grandmother's childhood friend. On the back of the photograph, drawn beside her name in a youthful flowing hand, there is a heart pierced by an arrow.

—From "The Wedding"

Praise for *Olympia*

"Bock's evocative writing signifies the emergence of a strong voice likely to go the distance."
—*Maclean's*

"This is a fine, fine book. . . . Bock's sentences and stories are as edgy and vernacularly North American as Cheever's. His sensibility is as sensitive to the fierce winds and unquiet waters of suburbia as Updike's. . . . *Olympia* is world-class."   —*Ottawa Citizen*

"*Olympia* tells of one family's struggle to come to terms with its place in history. At once intimate and far-reaching, Bock's understated and unusual handling of a difficult subject is a significant achievement."
—*Literary Review*

"With decided skill, Bock juxtaposes a family's small triumphs against its crushing, often heartbreaking defeats."
—*The London Free Press*

"[*Olympia*] is weighty, full of the detritus of history and studded with tragedy. But almost all these stories deal with a family, and Bock leaves room for laughter."
—*The Vancouver Sun*